A Banner
EXTENDS

THE AMATTA VALLEY CHRONICLES
BOOK 2

S.C. DUCOMMUN

A BANNER EXTENDS
Copyright © 2025 by S.C. Ducommun

ISBN: 978-1-4866-2677-9
eBook ISBN: 978-1-4866-2678-6

Word Alive Press
119 De Baets Street Winnipeg, MB R2J 3R9
www.wordalivepress.ca

WORD ALIVE
—P R E S S—

Cataloguing in Publication information can be obtained from Library and Archives Canada.

For Scott and Staci

— Prologue —

JUST OUT OF REACH

An uncomfortably warm breeze blew down on the knot of soldiers and horses that ringed the cloaked figure and the man kneeling in obvious fear in front of him. Dark eyes stared out from the depths of the raised hood in utter silence, and then turned away from the pathetic fool on his knees to gaze up the slope of the pass.

Gerig, High Commander of the First Legions, frowned thoughtfully. The hunters he had sent should have returned by now. It was not that hard to run down one lone woman.

He turned his gaze back over the heads of the soldiers as if he could see the long lines of the advancing army making its lumbering way through the mountains to the south. It would take almost three more weeks to arrive. It shouldn't be an issue. The majority of the fools in the valley beyond would not know he was even coming until troops and wagons were pouring down out of the pass like a flood. Then it would be far too late to fight. Far too late to run—unless they weren't completely fooled by this presumed trade treaty. Of course, every plan had its risks, and no plan survived entirely intact after contact with the enemy.

The sound of snarling shifted his eyes to the black lupine forms held by the chains of their handlers off to one side of the ring of soldiers. These and the ones that had been sent after the woman numbered little better than a score. A gift from the Master, they were single-minded killing machines with all the subtlety of a thrown rock. He had sent an equal number ahead into the valley under the cover of the last new moon—a little offering to foreshadow what was coming. But to his disappointment, they had not had the desired effect.

Gerig's hand clenched, and the letter he held crumpled further. He looked back down at the man in front of him. The wretch flinched as if struck. He had reason to flinch. The rest of his companions had already been dispatched and tossed over the cliff. There was no need for any further pretense at this point, and senseless cruelty pleased the Master greatly. But perhaps this one thought he'd escape the fate of his friends.

"What do you know of these five children spreading rumours about us?" Gerig laced his tone with both command and threat, speaking softly.

The man shuddered and bobbed his head. "Only that they are saying you're bringing an army." His voice sounded on the verge of panicked tears. "They're saying the Valley is going to be destroyed when you arrive."

"Destroyed." The murmur that emerged from the darkness of the hood sounded almost amused. "Where do you think they got this rumour from? One of your stinking trader friends talking over a mug?"

"What?" The man sounded shocked and affronted. He briefly forgot his situation entirely. "No, never! The Oath is unbroken by all who take it!" He stopped suddenly in realization of his precarious position. When he continued, it was in a contrite tone. "The rumour is that a Maylak of the Living God told them."

The doomed man's mouth snapped shut at the sound of a snarl. His eyes darted up to the hooded man towering over him and then toward the mass of dark hounds to his right. He wasn't sure where the snarl had come from, but he wasn't anywhere near certain it had been the beasts. He looked nervously at the hand that held the letter from the Lady. Was it shaking?

As for the hooded Gerig, he stood completely still. A black primal fog of hatred seemed to pulse through him and his vision clouded. The Master rarely ever shook the Bond in this way, and he wondered if he was about to lose all control. Slowly the hatred flowed back like a great wave ebbing from the shore of his consciousness. Behind it a deep rage boiled. Out of it rolled impressions: almost a sense of outrage that some rule had been broken. Some deep sense that the Enemy had cheated. Cheated them of their plan. Cheated them of their surprise. But also a sense of expectation. The Master was not truly surprised, just frustrated. Certainty suddenly flooded through him. The plan was adjustable.

"Release the remaining hounds," he commanded. "They have rabbits to hunt."

He looked back up into the top of the pass. The others had not returned, would not return. But there was a sense of grim satisfaction in the Master's constant presence. The five youths were close—too close to escape.

Five faces flashed through his thoughts. Young faces that he hated but had never met. Five targets for the hunt. Suddenly a sixth face appeared out of the boil. The thoughts of the Master seemed almost troubled; uncertainty surrounded this face. Gerig considered the young man. Not much older than the youths. Why should this man trouble the thoughts of one such as the Master?

Pain suddenly racked his head. That kind of thinking was not allowed.

"Six then," he murmured. "We will run down all six."

He looked back at the commander of his guard. The big man's eyes were everywhere, and yet always ready on Gerig. He gave the man a nod and the soldier immediately barked orders. They would be ready to ride in minutes. The trade wagons would be sent back to the advancing army with the handlers of the dark hounds. The beasts would not be coming back. The kneeling man was dispatched immediately, and his body was already being dragged to the cliff to join his friends below. The commander stood observing the efficient results of his instructions and waited on Gerig's further orders.

"Stow all uniforms and markings." Adjustments to the plan unfolded in Gerig's mind. "All clothing fitting a merchant guard, weapons to suit. We've got at least two weeks of mischief to sow. Send word for the vanguard to increase their advance."

"They will make little better time unless I send a rider with spare horses," the commander pointed out. "These wagons will take over a week to meet them."

"Delicately." Gerig's murmur raised the commander's eyebrow. He shook his head to dismiss the question. "Every move we make now must be made with delicate precision. Our Enemy has raised up a standard against us. The last thing we need to do is move too aggressively or rashly and cause him to extend some banner of protection that we cannot penetrate."

The commander looked uncertain and even a little skeptical. Gerig knew he only saw with the eyes of a military leader. Troop counts, weapons and strategies aimed at armies of men. He knew what lay physically ahead of them and he did not understand how the Enemy could possibly oppose the Sacheth. He looked almost ready to voice that doubt, but he quickly schooled himself to stone cold acceptance. The man was the commander of the guard and leader of the army for a reason. When he spoke, it was of practical matters.

"Are you sure I shouldn't keep back a few handlers? We may not want that many of the dark dogs running around us when we get there." He paused and gauged his leader's reaction to being questioned.

"There will be no hounds left to be underfoot." Gerig looked at the commander in amusement as the man actually showed his surprise and shock. "Ahead of us is no simple enemy, but *the* Enemy. The Master's dark hounds are being sacrificed on a game board you cannot even begin to comprehend. Thus far you've understood your place on it; see to it you do not misstep or misspeak. The Master would be displeased to have to replace any of his pieces at this point."

The big man nodded. He had earned this position. He knew when to question and when to obey.

THE AMATTA VALLEY

Headwaters of the Great River

Gella Lake

Shaar Pass

Cardaya

Bato

N

Katthic

The Crossroads

Pethe

Meletsa

Koreb Pass

Koreb Gorge

The Amatta Valley

Compiled by

Master Mc Scott

Chief Cartographer to the King

Compiled From Oral Myth and Legend

—— 1 ——

A VERY BAD DREAM

It's all a dream, David told himself for the hundredth time as he sat by the fire. *You will wake up and… then what? Never mind.* He shook his head. *The goal is to wake up.*

The man named Simon busied himself making sure the young man's horses were securely picketed. The fire and the campsite at the edge of the avalanche track made it apparent that he had been there for a while. It was obvious that he had witnessed David's sudden arrival, and he kept looking over to the fire as if to assure himself that David had not simply disappeared the same way he had appeared.

Appeared. David shook his head again as the events of the last hour unfolded in his mind. There had been the desperate ride along the highway. The howl of the dark wolves growing more distinct as Nebaya clung desperately to his waist. The poor kid, Ra'ah, whiter than the snow of the high mountains as he held on to the other horse.

They had suddenly come upon Anatellia and her two other friends under the avalanche shelter. It was then he realized they no longer had the luxury of outrunning the dark bounding nightmares. Fear for his sister and her four friends filled him, driving his thoughts into a state of chaos. And then a great flash of light and everything was gone. Everything, that is, except the two horses and himself.

And it really was everything. He felt the panic rising again as he looked back out over the valley. It should have been farmland on this side of the river from Meletsa to Kathik, where the river made its great bend. But all he saw were trees—a great unbroken forest of trees. No farmland, no highway, no avalanche shelter, and no Meletsa at the end of the valley. The mountains were the same, the valley had the same shape, but every other familiar thing was gone.

He returned his attention to the fire as the panic made his head swim. He gave it a shake, and the feeling retreated downward to form a knot in his gut.

This had to be a dream, but what kind of nightmare lasted this long? He tried to remember more before the flash. Maybe this was what death was like? Had the wolves actually killed him and he simply hadn't carried the memory into death? Why did the afterlife include the horses and not Anatellia, Nebaya, and the others? And who was Simon?

He looked over to the older man, only to see that he was being studied back intently. The cloak that Simon wore was far from new, but extremely well made. Beneath it, the man wore armour of leather and fine chain. Every movement demonstrated the familiarity of a lifetime of wearing it. No one in David's world wore armour like that. No one he knew even owned armour. Myriad questions flashed suddenly across Simon's face, mirroring what David assumed was his own expression. The man then seemed to make a decision about David and silently came over with a carved bowl and spoon.

The smell of the stew that had been cooking over the fire suddenly wafted up to erase all questions from David's mind and he realized he was famished. He silently took the bowl Simon offered and held it out as his host ladled a generous portion into it. Then the other man filled his own bowl and sat down across the fire. Without a word, they ate.

David found his courage to speak at the bottom of the bowl. "Am I dead?"

"Dead?" Simon's eyebrow rose in surprise and he looked around the valley thoughtfully before returning his gaze to David. "I honestly cannot say. The way you appeared might suggest you're a spirit, but you're solid enough now that you're here and eating my stew."

"Yeah, about here…" David looked nervously over his shoulder at the valley now draped in the setting sun. "Where, exactly, *is* here?"

Surprised amusement crossed Simon's face. "You don't know where you are? You've been staring around you like a man who returns home to find it burned to the ground." He paused to study the younger man and then shrugged. "But as for us, the people I am a part of, we call this valley the Amatta."

"But that's impossible," David murmured, and then in a wellspring of emotion he gestured out across the valley. "I mean, this isn't the Amatta I know. Where is the highway? Where are all of the farms?" He pointed violently down the valley to the pass rising in the distance. "Meletsa is gone! Next thing you'll tell me you've never heard of the great city of Kathik!"

At that name Simon went white as snow. He regarded David in silence for a long time as the young man stared back at him, fighting the rise of panic once again. Finally he held up a hand as David made to speak again.

"I know that name." His face regained a little colour as his shock passed. "But know, David, that in the time you find yourself the city you speak of is still but a grand idea with very little form."

"In the time I find myself?" David repeated incredulously. "Are you saying I've somehow been sent back in time?"

"Tell me, do you believe in the Living God?"

The question caught David by surprise. His thoughts suddenly scattered like the sparks of the fire and he found himself speechless. Did he believe? Anatellia believed in a way he didn't. So did Nebaya. But *did* he? Something deep inside him stirred.

"Up until a couple of days ago He was more of an idea," David admitted ruefully after a long silence. "But after my long-lost sister showed up with a story of Maylaks and dire warnings of destruction, and after being chased by those damnable black wolves, I'm now thinking He's a lot more real."

"Oh, He's very real," Simon chuckled softly. "But maybe we'll start, if you're willing, with you telling me about your Amatta Valley."

"Well, you fed me; a story is the least I owe you," David sighed. "Do you have anything to drink?"

Simon smiled and handed him a skin. He greedily took a drink and was saddened to taste water. But honestly, what did he expect in the valley where everything else had disappeared? He silently added wine and ale to the list of the day's losses. With a sigh he stared down the

3

valley that he had already traveled twice that day and started describing the valley he knew.

David found a patient and experienced listener in Simon. The sun sank behind the mountains and he talked long into the deepening night about the Amatta that he knew: the four villages, the city of Kathik, the scores of pubs and common rooms, and the many different kinds of people to be found everywhere. For his part, Simon asked questions only when he wanted David to describe something in deeper detail. He seemed obsessed with the people and the way they served the Living God. He was equally fascinated by David's description of trade outside of the Valley and the trade guilds. He voiced surprise that they had ever started trade, and David confirmed that for centuries there had been no trade at all. Then he just nodded and let David continue.

Finally, as the moon rose waxing overhead, he went into the story of Anatellia and the events of the last days. Simon stopped interrupting entirely and listened with rapt attention until David absently mentioned the Sacheth. At that name he jerked and raised his hand for David to stop.

"Did you say 'Sacheth'?" he asked anxiously.

"Yes, they are apparently the people Mother has made a deal with." David was suspicious that Simon had chosen to interrupt at that particular point. "Anatellia is convinced they are connected somehow with the doom that the Living God is warning everyone about."

"They most certainly would be." Simon sighed and rubbed his forehead.

"You know of them?" David didn't bother to hide his surprise. "I mean, way back here, whenever this is?"

"I think it's my turn to tell my story, David." Simon smiled sadly. "I am now convinced beyond doubt that you are here by a miracle of the Living God. I'm also convinced that you are from our future, or at least you are a vision of that future that I hope desperately to change."

David looked at the other man in silence for a long time. His head swam with chaotic thoughts spurred on by the other man's declaration that he had somehow gone back into the valley's past. Try as he might, however, he couldn't deny the evidence. So much was gone that marked this valley as his, but it still had the bones of his valley. The surrounding peaks still looked the same. Even the shape of the river as it cut an opening between the trees in the distance had seemed familiar. He realized Simon was waiting for his attention, and he nodded for him to continue.

"I am part of a large company of refugees. Many years ago we were part of a great alliance of God-fearing nations far to the south of here." Simon's eyes grew distant and he paused. "The details aren't entirely important, but for one reason or another each of those nations, one by one, seemed to forget whom they served. They allowed the cold coat of religion to replace the true worship of the Living God, and they embraced ritual over relationship with Him.

"Many have speculated that this was what our enemies had been waiting for. An alliance of nations who called themselves the Sacheth"— he nodded to David—"rose up and fell on us one by one. These people hated the Living God and mocked religion openly. They were on a campaign of annihilation, and one by one the nations of the Living God fell to them."

The fire settled suddenly in a plume of sparks and Simon paused to tend it and add more fuel. The smell of pine forest and smoke drifted around David as he waited patiently for the other man to continue. With a sigh, Simon set down the stick he had used to tend the flame.

"I could say much about those dark days." He shook his head sadly. "Everyone was given the same choice: renounce the 'religion' of the Living God or be put to slavery and the sword. Because of the cold hearts of many, they chose to openly renounce their God. Others refused and were put through unimaginable tortures before being executed or sold into slavery.

"In the midst of this slaughter, as nation upon nation fell, a message of hope came to a small group of those still faithful in their service to the Living God. 'Gather up the remnant,' the message said. 'Gather up all that still place their hope in the Living God and flee northward into the mountains. Flee into the heart of the mountains until we come upon the very Mountain of the Living God.'

"So that is what we did. We gathered up the remnant who would join us and we headed north. Constantly fleeing before the armies of the Sacheth, we finally made our way to the feet of the mountains that bordered the northernmost of our lands. By then the Sacheth had heard of our flight and sent a great army to intercept us before we could disappear through the high passes and out of their grasp.

"In desperation, it was decided that an army of volunteers would stay behind and hold the first pass. It was hoped that the main group of us, which included many women and children, could disappear into the vastness of the northern mountains and out of Sacheth reach. With our army would be many who possessed knowledge of stone and mining, and the final hope was that they could somehow bring down portions of the grand peaks on either side of the pass and block the Sacheth from moving through it with any great numbers.

"For the volunteers it would be a final stand. Everyone knew and accepted that. In a decision that to this day we all suspect was our leadership's plan, the entirety of the elder generations volunteered. We protested, of course. These were our mothers and fathers, even our grandparents. We argued vehemently, but they stood firm.

"And their logic was simple. The knowledge and wisdom they possessed would continue with us. The road ahead through the mountains was long and brutal and they would not risk slowing us. And in this final act they could stand, full and hale in their strength, against the enemy that had taken everything from them except those that they now chose to protect.

"The roles of leadership were passed to the younger generation. I myself received the responsibility of Chief Archiver. It has been my responsibility to care for those texts and histories that were saved, as well as record the history of the Journey itself."

Simon went quiet; the memories flooding across his face were uncomfortable to watch, and spoke of personal guilt and loss. David took the time to go over the story in his own thoughts. He had a very rudimentary understanding of the origins of the valley's forefathers. Nothing he remembered contradicted Simon's story but now he wished that he had paid better attention to those parts of his lessons. His mother hadn't cared much for the valley's origin legends and therefore didn't stress that part of her children's education. Something stuck out as odd in Simon's story, though.

"So all of your elders stayed behind to protect the rest of you?" he asked incredulously. "It was an army of elderly people?"

"I am considered one of the oldest of the remnant," Simon admitted with a sad smile, "and I have only seen thirty-five summers. Everyone older than myself stood rank upon rank at the top of that slope, over half of us chosen to stay behind so that the other half might survive.

"You could not understand what we faced that day, in that first pass," Simon pushed on as he watched David's incredulous expression. "The Sacheth were like locusts swarming up the arms of the valley toward the pass. They recognized us as the last of the Faithful, and they were determined to annihilate every last one of us. To slow them enough for anyone to escape required no small force. And there was hope we could seal the pass behind us, but that required time to prepare and execute. And that time had to be bought with blood."

"So obviously they succeeded?" David noted quietly.

"Oh yes," Simon nodded and took another drink from the skin. He stared for a long time across the valley

"A few of us hung back at the far side of the summit, climbing the ridge to look down on the glorious army of our elders drawn up to face the Sacheth. You see, we were versed well enough in warfare. We knew that to be peaceful, it was necessary to know war. We had not gone quietly or gently to defeat, although I will not bother relating any of the earlier battles fought with the Sacheth. The army of our fathers and mothers stood at the top of that pass and vowed that this battle would be the one above all others that scarred and blunted the will of the Sacheth.

"Even as they met and repulsed wave upon wave of enemy infantry, those that were skilled with stone and mining were working on the summit sides. The Living God had given us one true hope in this pass that was chosen for that final battle. Jagged stone spires stood high on the slopes, and the evidence of their weak support already lay across the floor of the pass in many places. With enough time, the miners were convinced they could bring down wholesale the sides of the pass and render it useless to the Sacheth, basically shutting the door to the northern mountains behind the fleeing remnant.

"We watched until the light of the setting sun made it impossible to see what was happening. Our army, driven almost mad with the desperation that comes from knowing there could be no retreat or surrender, made the Sacheth pay for every foot of ground. The Elder Army, as we now refer to them, were slowly and inexorably being pushed through the summit of the pass. At some point the command was given to fire the forests downslope, and wave upon wave of arrows like fireflies in the deepening night flew out of sight into the narrow, wooded valley on the other side of the pass.

"Now we knew then that the end was very near, so we stumbled our way down to where our horses waited. The fire wouldn't stop the Sacheth, but it would create many small fires that they would have to contend with or risk a greater fire pushing up into the pass behind their army. The fire arrows were the final signal to the miners and sappers on the mountain slopes that they had better finish fast and bring down the spires or all would be lost.

"The sound of battle carried down the length of the pass far into the night, and the glow of fires burning down on the far side of the pass dimly illuminated the horror of what was transpiring there. We all held hope that a remnant of the army might escape under the cover of darkness as the spires came down. But as the front line of the battle was pushing toward us and snakes of torchlight poured up from the far slopes, we started to despair. In horror we realized that there were torches making their way up the summit slopes toward the spires as well. The Sacheth had deduced our primary plan and were moving to secure the valley behind the front lines of the battle.

"I don't know how long we stood there watching everything seem to fall apart. The only thing I can remember thinking was how were we going to save anyone from the Sacheth if they were allowed to follow us so closely into the mountains? They were relentless and they would easily ride down the slower-moving remnant camp. I have never had a moment of such total despair held at bay with only a single candle of hope: the hope that the Living God would not forsake us utterly.

"And then suddenly the entire valley lit up from one end to the other and we were knocked back by a blast of sound and air unlike anything I have felt before or since. In that light we saw the last of the Elder Amy strung out across the narrowest part of the pass, just an archer's long shot from where we waited. It was obvious in that moment that they had finally been overwhelmed. I looked away from the line of battle and saw the bloom of fire and stone at the base of one of the spires at the far end of the valley. I had never before seen the kind of mining fire that miners used until that night, but I will never forget its effect as long as I live. Looking back, we realized that this had been part of the plan the entire time. And looking back, we also realized they had never really planned on coming out of that valley.

"The first flash became a rolling ball of quickly dying flame and smoke, but the rumble of the explosion was replaced by a deeper rumble as thousands of tons of rock spire collapsed down the mountainside. Then another blinding series of explosions followed in rapid succession along both sides of the narrow valley, and sudden darkness rolled over us as a great wall of wind and stone dust all but blew us over. The rumbling became a roar and continued in the blackness. The air was suddenly full of thick dust and chaos. In fear, we fled stumbling down the other side of the pass—stumbling after the sounds of our panicked horses, as we feared the destruction the miners and sappers had unleashed would overtake us.

"We huddled in fear at the base of the pass, listening for the sound of any pursuit but hearing nothing but the wind in the trees and the slowly receding crack of broken stone from far above. In time the stars appeared above us through a dusty, smoky haze. We were loath to abandon our rear guard until morning. Our morbid curiosity mingled with wild hope that some of the Elder Army had survived the cataclysm unleashed in the pass above. With that hope also came the fear that some of the Sacheth had survived, and we took turns trying to sleep while the rest watched.

"Dawn found us all staring up at the pass, looking for any movement at all. Finally we drew lots, and I won the privilege of going back up the pass to report what I could of the night's chaos.

"The entire trip was a nightmare of jumping at shadows and sneaking from one piece of cover to another. When I finally came in sight of the summit, I was faced with the reality of what the miners and Elder Army had done. Starting only a hundred strides into the valley was a great wave of destruction that rose at least one hundred feet above the original road. The shattered spires had filled the narrow pass and made the valley a nightmare of splintered stone. A cascade of stone came down very near to where I hid, and I quickly realized that even if someone were to try and climb over the pass they would face a nightmare of shifting stones under foot and the very real possibility of rocks from above. The plan had worked: the pass was shut to the Sacheth.

"I brought the news back to the others and we all rode hard down the valley to catch up with the caravan of the Remnant. That was the last we ever saw of the Sacheth hordes. After five years of wandering the mountains, passing through kingdoms and wilderness alike, we finally arrived at this valley. But that is a different and longer story."

"I have never heard either story before," David confessed after a long silence. "At least not in any detail worth comparing. I can't begin to understand what that must have been like to live through."

"I also left out a lot," Simon admitted. "I thought you ought to know a little of what I know of the Sacheth. And to be honest, I wanted to test your knowledge of your own forefathers. Does anything I told you sound like what you were taught?"

"Only in a very general sense," David replied. "And I'm still hoping this is all a very bad dream—no offense."

"Oh, I'm not offended." Simon dismissed the idea with a wave. "I've been wondering this entire time if I'm having another vision. But let me tell you how we got here specifically and why I think you're here now. Would you like more stew?"

"Please," David said. "I've never in my life heard of such a thing as traveling through time, but it's made me hungry."

"I've heard of visions that show the future," Simon said as he refilled David's bowl. "I suppose a vision that shows the past is not that different. But this *seems* different, doesn't it? Now where was I? Right, how we got here.

"I won't bore you with all the details of the five-year journey to get here, in this valley. I've chronicled the entire thing if you want to read it. That is, if you stick around long enough. It was full of hardships and surprises and more than a few disappointments. We were a skilled people and traded much with the kingdoms and lands that we passed through on the way. We lost more than a few friends to the weariness of the journey, although not to death as you may suspect, but to the promise of finally calling somewhere home again. And when we made that final march through the pass over there, we beheld this valley. Then a strange hope and contentment overcame us.

"The valley was so appealing that we decided to stop early although it was still summer. And here we set up our winter village. It's actually up-river from here, where the river makes a great bend and there are open meadows created by the spring floods. We've built on this side of the valley, above the floodplain. It's a beautiful village that everyone is referring to as..."

"Kathik," David interrupted softly as he stared at his stew. "You've called the village Kathik, the home of the True and Faithful."

"Yes," Simon nodded, "Kathik."

There was silence between them for several breaths as Simon regarded the man across the fire. David simply stared into the flames in a daze. This dream was nothing he could have, well, dreamed up. Everything was so real around him. The smoke from the fire stung his eyes; the night breeze moved the trees with the sound of rushing water and filled his nose with pine forest. The soup tasted both familiar and exotic. A feeling stirred deep in his breast, like a sense of pressure or a deep voice echoing through a canyon. He looked back over the fire at the man regarding him with a mixture of wonder and pity and nodded for him to continue.

"Once we decided we would set up for the winter, we sent a small group back over the pass that we named the Koreb. Their mission was to secure more provisions. They also were instructed to secure seed grain and other farming supplies. To pay for these things we sent much of our armour and weapons, although many like myself would not part with theirs.

"You see, David, many of the Remnant believe that this valley is our intended destination." The sudden shift in tense made David perk up. "Many of my fellow leaders and a great many of the people believe the Mountain of the Living God is figurative. They believe the prophecies and all of the leading of His Spirit have led us to this valley, the Amatta Valley. It will be here that we build the Kingdom of the Living God. And from everything you have told me, that is exactly what we will do. What we did.

"And yet there is a group of us that are uneasy. We do not believe we are intended to get comfortable and stay here. For us, the Mountain is close, but it's up there." He pointed up the valley where the Shaar Pass lay many days distant. "It's been a year since we arrived, however, and we have explored the entire valley and beyond. We have sent parties a week beyond the Shaar Pass, which is several days ride north of here." He paused and chuckled. "But then, you probably know that. And in all of our exploring we have discovered beautiful wilderness and forest and mountains, but nothing that could fairly be called the Mountain of the Living God."

"It's somewhere on the north side of the Shaar," David mused.

"What?" Simon stopped suddenly and fixed him with a penetrating gaze.

"If my sister Anatellia was telling the truth, then there is a path and a pass up into the valley where the Mountain of the Living God stands. It rises steeply out of the north slopes of the Shaar and it is well hidden, because my brothers and I looked for it off and on for years. We finally gave it up to being a fever dream. But given the events of the last couple of days..." David simply shrugged. "Well, that is where it would be."

The fire once again settled in a shower of sparks and Simon tended it as he had before. But his eyes darted from the fire to David and back again several times. Finally, he seemed to come to a decision.

"I haven't told you why I'm here, David." Simon looked at him in wonder. "I mean, why I'm camped beside this open avalanche track halfway between the Koreb and the village." He paused briefly to readjust a stray log. "You see, I came here to pray and make a decision. Do I abandon my role as Archiver and lead a remnant of the Remnant onward, possibly to be lost forever in the mountains that lay beyond? Or do I stay and admit what the majority are already saying, that this is where we were meant to stay?

"Earlier I was deeply grieved and in prayer, begging the Living God for a sign—any sign. And as I was praying there was a great flash as of lighting. In the ringing of my ears I swear I caught the sound of gentle laughter and a sudden wave of peace struck me. I looked up in wonder, and blinking away the blindness of the flash, I saw a strange young man with two horses in the clearing. And the rest you know. But what you don't know is that you are the answer to my prayer."

"Well then, I'm sorry." David gave the man a small crooked smile.

"Sorry?" Simon laughed. "Why are you sorry?"

"Because of all the people caught in that flash, I am the least useful to you. The five others should have been sent here. They could fix your mess with ease. They're the ones out wandering the forests of the valley following the Call and seeking messages from the Living God. I'm just the spoiled youngest son of a rich Kathik family. I know nothing of the Living God. Why would He send me, of all people?"

"I do not know much, even after what you have told me," Simon said with a soft laugh. "But He chose you and not the others you mentioned. And he delights in each of us, David. One thing is clear to me: you are more than your demeaning inner voice tells you that you are. Much more. You are the Living God's choice for this moment."

"But if I'm here to change history," David mused, completely spent of any other argument, "then we know I've already failed, because I know what has happened."

"There seems to be a lot that Amatta has forgotten in the span between now and your time, David," Simon admitted. "And our thoughts spin trying to understand the world and the Living God. Just as you don't understand who you are to Him, you do not understand what you are about to do to your history and my future."

"My head hurts." David rubbed his brow and a wave of exhaustion rolled over him. "Whatever the morning brings, I think I need sleep now."

"That is wisdom," Simon agreed. "I look forward to the morning and our journey back to Kathik. My fellow elders will not know what to make of you."

2

A VISITOR IN THE NIGHT

David awoke in the dead stillness of the night to a soft nicker of horses. He looked over to where Simon had set up his bedroll near the fire, but the man's soft breathing and the rise and fall of the blanket in the light of the moon revealed he still slept. The soft nicker came again; he debated waking his new companion up and then second-guessed himself. Carefully he sat up and looked around.

The fire had burned down and the final vestiges of red coals huddled in the carefully dug pit, fighting for the last of life. He peered through the trees to the meadow clearing where Simon had picketed the horses and saw a figure moving among them. The horses showed no signs of fear in the presence of whoever walked there, even showing familiarity and affection. David's mind raced.

He quickly and quietly put his boots on and tied them. With the extra care of a youngest brother, he slipped away from the campsite and toward the figure stirring among his horses. Thoughts raced through his mind concerning who this figure could be, but only a select group of people he knew could elicit an affectionate reaction from both horses. He still moved as stealthily as he could and reached out in the moonlight, preparing to grab the shoulder of this person who was talking softly to either themself or the horses. Suddenly the figure turned and regarded him with eyes that were like deep wells of moonlight.

"I've been waiting for you, David." The man's voice moved through him like water through grass, pushing his thoughts down with a flood of peace.

David took a step back and looked at the man before him. He was adorned head to foot in a riding cloak of dull silver-gray. The fabric seemed to ignore the moonlight and gave off its own muted light as he moved. The man's face and hands revealed features that were both plain and yet oddly striking. Skin that had spent time in the sun, wrinkles that spoke of both seriousness and laughter.

But it was the man's eyes that spoke to him at first of welled moonlight and locked him in their gaze. He felt suddenly broken open and laid bare, his soul a book to be read. David tried to look away in embarrassment and no small amount of shame, but the man's eyes drew his back and refused to let him look away again. Time froze as every hidden secret, every shameful lie, every selfish act came to the surface of David's thoughts. It was like when he watched gold and silver being melted by the goldsmiths, how the dross rose to the surface to be scraped away. Recognition also flooded him. Realization made his legs give out and he fell to his knees before the man who refused to release his gaze.

"Who am I, Lord, that You have waited for me?" He wept tears, unable to stop them even if he wanted to.

"David"—his name washed over him, the flood of that voice washing away all of the shame and embarrassment like the dross—"I have watched over you all of your life. I have seen your heart, your longing."

David shook his head. "But I have served only myself all of my life. I have been selfish. I have ignored Your calling, pushed it aside and used lies to help me ignore it. I am not worthy of You."

Then the man did something that David did not expect: He laughed fully and loudly. The laughter seemed to make everything brighter. The dew on the grass gave off ten thousand shards of moonlight at the sound. David, rather than feeling mocked, felt the merriment of the laughter hit him in the face like a cold shower. He blinked through his tears in wonder, without words.

"I didn't say you have been a great listener, child." The man put his hands on David's shoulders and lifted him to his feet. "But your heart, that is a heart after my own heart. And you can make up for the lack of obedience now."

"Am I really here?" David finally found words in the form of the question. "Did you really bring me back to the valley's founding?"

"I did," the man said.

"Am I to change the valley's history, then?" David asked in awe.

"No, child," the man chuckled softly. "That is Simon's role, if it is anyone's. And that future is written, for the most part."

"Then why am I here?" David asked as a faint flicker of despair marred the presence he bathed in.

The man seemed to suddenly grow brighter and his presence gained a weight that made the young man shake. "David, no matter when you think you are, this is your now. I have brought you here for a purpose. Your purpose. The Calling on your life, you would say. But you still have a choice to make. I have plucked you out of obscurity and set you in a unique time and place. And in this place you have the power to rise up and be a force of good for my Kingdom, or to bring everything to nothing, setting up your own kingdom in place of mine."

"I would never do that, Lord," David started to protest.

"In my presence there is peace, but in the coming days you will not always be in my presence. You will come to a place of decision, a crossroads of two choices that everyone must come to. Choose to serve the Living God, surrender your own plans, ideas and way of doing things." Here he held out one hand, palm up, representing a wealth of possibilities. Then he lifted the other hand, palm out and away from them both. "Or choose to serve yourself. The possibilities of who you can be on your own. When the time comes, I believe you will see clearly which is the better choice.

"But for now, collect your bedroll." The man turned to the horses. "We have a place to be before sunrise."

David nodded blankly. He was quite overwhelmed by what he was experiencing and by who he knew the man was without understanding how he knew. He wandered back to Simon's camp in the moonlight and stared silently at the still-slumbering man beside the fire. He rolled up his bedroll and gathered his few belongings. As an afterthought, he added wood to the struggling coals. Then he returned to the horses to the sound of flame greedily taking to the new fuel.

The horses were already saddled and waiting when he got back. His brain twisted a bit at the thought of the man in the cloak saddling horses, or doing anything menial. He was already mounted atop Storm and he reached down to hand David the reins of his own horse. The cloak slid away from his wrist in the moonlight, revealing a scar from some old wound. How peculiar that this man would bear scars.

He mounted silently and they rode into the forest toward where Kathik was and would be. The cloaked man rode ahead of him, finding a trail that David could not see. It almost seemed like the forest parted for him. Even under the boughs of dense forest the light of the moon still seemed to illuminate everything, or else it was the man who illuminated everything. Finally, as David's questions and curiosity were about to overcome his silence, they came into a clearing with a merry campfire burning and food roasting on a spit.

David looked around for the campsite's host but it was empty except for them. There was a place set aside for the horses and fresh grass placed in a makeshift manger. The cloaked man dismounted with surprising grace and invited David to do likewise.

"Whose camp is this?" David asked in confusion.

"Ours," the man said simply.

The eastern sky had started to lighten as they had ridden and David looked out across the valley to realize that he was now high on the western slopes. Looking down he could see the smoke of a settlement far below them and the great loop of the familiar Valley River as it created the fertile arch that would become the jewel of farming in his day.

"We're north of Kathik," David murmured. "But how? We only rode a very short time."

"I know paths no man can find," the man said quietly.

"Who are you, Lord?" David finally burst out. "To my head you are like the Living God manifest."

"I am," the man declared quietly, but with a force that made David quail. "When you see me, you see the Living God and no one can see the Living God but through me."

"I do not understand," David replied.

"Much knowledge was lost when the remnant fled. Much more has become muddled. I am the Ransom for many. I am the Gatekeeper to the Kingdom. I am the Good Shepherd."

The man took the reins from him. For the first time, David noticed a stream that flowed from a rock and into a small pool to one side of the camp. The man let the horses drink from the pool before securing them by the manger. He then came back and offered David a spot beside the fire. The smell of the cooking food suddenly filled his nostrils, and he sat hurriedly.

"Whoever set up this camp went to some effort to catch us fish," David noted.

"It was I." The man smiled to himself as he took a skewer of fish and handed it to David. "I have a particular fondness for fish."

"Do you have a name, Lord?" David asked sheepishly as he tore off pieces of fish to eat. "I mean, you listed off titles, and I am very comfortable calling you Lord. More comfortable than I understand."

"I have many names, because names are but titles men use to identify something. And I am many, many things." The man stopped and ate a piece of fish, appearing to contemplate thoughts that David couldn't fathom. "I am fond of a name that in your language would be pronounced Joshua."

"May I call you Joshua?" David asked, slightly incredulously.

"Yes!" The man named Joshua laughed heartily and slapped David on the shoulder. "You may call me Joshua, David. If another name is required, I promise you will know. Is that agreeable?"

"Quite, Lord Joshua." David nodded quietly, still unsure how to take the man with the inner light and eyes that knew every part of him.

— 3 —

THE FORESHADOW OF CHOICE

They ate the fish in silence. It was the best fish that David had ever tasted, and even though his mind flitted back and forth with questions, he was content to eat. Finally the fish was gone, and Joshua returned his penetrating gaze to David.

"The moon rises full tomorrow night, David," he said matter-of-factly. "When it does, I want you to lead the remnant of the people to my Mountain. You know enough from Anatellia's story to find the trail. That trail will then lead you to the Valley of Death. It earned its name by claiming the faithless and unwelcome. Once you pass through that valley you will find the pass into *my* valley and the Mountain of the Living God, upon which has been built the City of the Faithful.

"Understand also that no one may pass through the Valley of Death who does not put their faith in the Living God and their trust in the Good Shepherd. You must make that clear to them all, David. It would be better for them to stay behind than to enter that valley with unbelief.

"Before you can lead them to my Mountain, you must also face your own choice," he continued gravely. "There is one who will come to test you. He is a master of the test. I want you to know that in this he has been forbidden to lie to you outright. You will know immediately if he does. But he is also a master of manipulation and half-truths."

"What will he try to make me do?" David asked in dread curiosity.

"He will try to make you choose yourself. That would be his greatest victory."

"I don't understand." David shook his head.

"You will," Joshua assured him. "And one more thing, you may not enter Kathik—the village is off limits to you."

David nodded without understanding. "So I can go anywhere else?"

"There is a path through the trees by the pond." Joshua pointed. "That path will lead you down the slope to the valley floor. You will come to a clearing and a junction between the path you are on and a path worn by the remnant of the remnant. Take the left path and you will come to their clearing where they have set up a camp away from the village. There you will find Simon."

"And if I go right?"

"Then you will quickly find yourself in the village, and your choice will be made," Joshua said sadly. "Consider the clearing on the valley floor to be a physical manifestation of the choice before you. Until tomorrow night you may go down the slope and go left to the remnant's clearing. But if at any time you turn down the right path and enter the village, your choice is made."

"Why can't I enter the village?" David pushed.

"There are times when the command is given and that is enough," Joshua's tone had a finality to it that shut tight David's mouth, full as it was of further questions. "I will stay here and look after the horses if you wish to go down and see Simon and the others."

"Why don't I just move down to the remnant's clearing now?" David found his tongue again. "I will make the choice now—I will choose you and the Mountain. I'll lead them through this Valley of Death. Enough talking."

"I love you, David, but the choice cannot be made here, in my presence." Joshua smiled with sadness. "The Living God wants your whole heart. He wants you to choose Him in the darkest places, when you have nothing but your faith and the choice."

"I don't understand," David admitted again.

"You will, David," Joshua assured the young man. "I know your heart better than you do right now. But go, find Simon—he needs some encouragement with his own decision that has been set before him."

4

THE REMNANT'S CLEARING

The trail opened up before him as he passed the pond, and he looked back to assure himself that Joshua was still there. The cloaked man waved farewell, and the sight of him filled David with deep joy.

He turned reluctantly and followed the winding route down to the valley floor. There, as promised, was a clearing amongst the dense forest and a worn path leading right to left across his own. He looked warily to the right, half expecting some evil creature to bear down on him and drag him kicking and screaming to the village. When nothing materialized, he took the left path and sighed with relief as he started for the next clearing.

After ten minutes of brisk walking he could pick up voices ahead of him. There was an argument occurring among a large group of people ahead, and one voice that rose above the din of the others carried clearly. After the trail passed through a thicket, he stepped into a large clearing full of young adults. They all stopped shouting at the man with his back turned to David and stared in wonder at him. The man, realizing he'd lost his audience to something behind him, turned, almost ready for a fight, and then his face split in a broad smile.

"David! My vision returns in the flesh!" Simon rushed forward and grabbed him in a bear hug. "I thought I was going to have to tell your side of the story to these unbelievers all by myself!"

A tall dark man with broad shoulders in the front of the large group stepped forward. "Simon, who is this man?"

Simon pulled David around to stand beside him. "This is the man I told you about. The one who appeared to me on the southern slopes day before last. The one who disappeared like smoke into the wind."

The crowd of young people looked between David and Simon with disbelief written plainly on their faces. David returned the stares with his own. These people seemed to have stepped straight out of a storybook. The people of his time were muted characters compared to this group. Every different physical look imaginable was represented in this crowd. They all wore armour of leather and fine chain. Swords hung at their sides, and bows rested across many shoulders. They looked like a group ready for a fight, and he felt suddenly like their target.

Swords were relegated to fireplace mantles in the Amatta he knew. Passed down from generation to generation or simply sold off for something more useful. There were probably more swords on hips in this clearing than could be found in all of his Amatta.

From the small rise he stood on, he could see a crowd of at least five hundred. This was the remnant of the remnant, he realized. This was the group the Living God wanted him to lead to the Mountain, through the Valley of Death. He felt suddenly ill-equipped and unprepared. He looked helplessly at Simon and realized the man had asked him a question.

"What?" he asked.

"What happened to you?" Simon repeated. "I woke up and you were gone, horses and all. Not even tracks to follow. I thought for sure you'd been a vision after all."

"Maybe I still am," he laughed weakly, unsure where to start and feeling oddly reluctant to talk about Joshua with such a large audience.

"I've never heard of a vision shared by five hundred," Simon laughed, "but no matter how you got here, you are here now. Would you tell the story you told me, about the Amatta Valley you're from and what is happening there?"

"I, uh…" He found the stare of hundreds of almost hostile eyes before him to be a little intimidating. He closed his eyes and pictured Joshua in his mind. The memory filled him with a new strength that he hadn't had access to before. "Yes—I mean, of course I will. What have you told them?"

"Everything I could remember, but I made a bit of a mess, I think." Simon looked extremely apologetic. "I should have written it down before I did anything else, but after you disappeared I felt an urgency to return. But it looks like I'm saved, because you are here. Just start by describing the valley as you know it, and then tell them all the story of your sister and her friends."

David nodded and Simon motioned him to a large rock that placed him well above everyone's head so they could all see and hear him. With a deep breath he began, and everyone stilled. They all stood in silence and listened for the entire time that he talked, their emotions playing out on their faces before him like a choir of disbelieving and shocked people.

He got quite animated in describing the valley as he knew it, talking of the villages and the highways and the great city of Kathik. In describing the city, he felt an odd lump form in his chest, like he was talking a little too much and too long about a forbidden subject. He quickly moved to explaining the events of the last days: of his sister's message from the Living God, and of the Sacheth. There was great murmuring at the mention of the old enemy, but they quickly silenced themselves and let David finish his story with his sudden appearance on the mountainside in front of Simon.

As soon as he finished the questions started. How far into the future was he from? From where had the black wolves come? What did he know of their group? Did they leave the valley or did they stay and settle? Many started debating how long such a build-up of the valley could take. Some asked if he knew their families. He looked helpless as the meeting degraded into a noisy mess.

Finally, Simon stepped up onto the rock with him and waved his hands. The bedlam slowly died down as everyone realized that answers wouldn't be coming until peace was reestablished. Eventually Simon nodded and started ticking answers off his fingers as they came to him.

"From my own conversation with David, I have deduced that he is indeed from a very different and distant Amatta Valley than the one we find ourselves in today. From what he has told me, the valley will exist in peace and prosperity for well over a thousand years. But in the end the Sacheth, who apparently still exist, will still find our valley, and according to the warning that has come through David's own sister, they will destroy this place and everyone in it. Much of what the elders hope to lay as a foundation for the Amatta will either be forgotten or corrupted by David's time. And I do not believe, despite David's appearance here by the hand of the Living God, that we can change anything of this future. Maybe, once the others hear his testimony, we'll be able to convince them to join us. After this meeting David and I will go see the elders in the village.

"I can't go to the village," David interrupted.

"What do you mean you can't go to the village?" Simon demanded in exasperation. "Who made that rule?"

"The Living God," he responded lamely, looking for an explanation of his time with Joshua.

"You admitted two days ago that you didn't know much of anything about the Living God, and suddenly you're talking with the Living God?" Simon looked at him in frustrated wonder.

"He came to me last night," David replied in confusion. Two days ago? What did Simon mean? It was just yesterday. "That's why I disappeared. He told me I have a very important choice to make, and it affects us all. And if I go to the village I make the choice, but not in a good way, if you get my meaning."

"Simon, this is too much," the man from earlier protested loudly. "Who is this man, really?"

"He is exactly who I said he is, Temian," Simon responded testily, never taking his eyes off of David. "But I need to get to the meat of this new development. Leave me with my new friend and we'll have a clearer story when I'm done."

Temian opened his mouth to protest further, but one withering look from Simon sent him wandering off with the others, leaving them with a large open space of privacy.

"I sense far more to your story, David." Simon tapped his finger on the young man's chest. "Now get over your reluctance to share what's happened to you after you were whisked off two nights ago, and get talking."

"It was last night for me. And I woke up to someone walking around the horses. I honestly thought it was my sister, because only my sister gets along with those horses like I do, but it wasn't. It was a man. But not a man. I cannot explain it very well."

"Try, my friend! I think it's important that I understand what you've seen and heard. Something about you has changed."

David looked out at the others milling around the clearing. Could he trust Simon? Would the man think he was crazy? *Was* he actually crazy? He looked back into the concerned eyes of his new friend and came to a decision. If anyone here in this time and place could be trusted, it was Simon. So he quickly began describing everything that had happened since he had gone to sleep the night before.

He found some parts of his conversation with Joshua impossible to articulate. Simon just stood and listened with confusion and wonder playing across his face. Even after David finished with his arrival to the clearing, Simon remained silent.

"Well?" David pressed. "What do you think? Who is Joshua?"

"That name has ancient origins," Simon finally said, and then he continued with a shrug. "As to everything he told you, I cannot say. I have no experience with this kind of thing. Even the holy texts, to my knowledge, don't include an example of this kind of meeting."

David shook his head in frustration. "But there was something about him. Something that made him feel more than just a man. And where did the missing day go for me?"

"I simply cannot say," Simon repeated apologetically. "There are warnings of one who walks around masking himself as a Maylak of light. He is the great liar and an enemy of all who serve the Living God. But from what you have told me, I cannot say this is that man."

"He did say there would be one who would come to test me," David mused. "Maybe that is the one you speak of?"

"Maybe." Simon looked concerned but said no more.

"It would be better if I stayed here," David declared, ignoring what Joshua had told him. "Right here, in this clearing. I've already decided: I'm going with you all to find the Mountain of the Living God. So why go back to Joshua's clearing at all?"

"You mean to try to avoid the choice that this Joshua fellow mentioned?" Simon looked dubious.

"I'm not avoiding the choice," David insisted as he ignored the nagging warning that the choice was not that easy. "I'm *making* the choice. He said I couldn't make it in his presence, but he's not here. I know what I want to do, and I choose to stay here."

"What about your gear? Your horses?"

"Maybe someone could be sent up to get them?" David suggested. "I would just go but time has been a little unpredictable for me. I might wander up there to get the horses and find out it's tomorrow night when I try to come back."

"This is all very peculiar." Simon laughed softly. "But if that is what you want to try, I'll help you. Temian and I will go up the slope to retrieve your things, and maybe meet this Joshua for ourselves. You just have to show us the trail you came down on."

"Sounds like a plan!" David slapped Simon on the shoulder. He felt like he had somehow found a loophole in making his choice. He again pushed down the feeling that it wouldn't be that easy.

———— 5 ————

A Choice Made

Simon hurried off the stone with David in tow. He looked around briefly and then went straight to the man that had protested.

"Temian, I need you to come up the mountain with me to get David's horses."

The man looked David up and down, and his expression showed that he had come to an unflattering conclusion.

"David, this is Temian. A more loyal friend you will never have—once you convince him you're a friend worth having."

David gave a nod as the other man simply stared at him suspiciously. Simon waved to a tall woman nearby, and she came over to join them.

"David, this is Kawani, Temian's sister." He smiled up at the woman and introduced David to her. "David is going to show us the path he took from his camp so your brother and I can get his horses and gear. I need you to be sure he gets back to camp without wandering into the village or something. Keep an extra careful eye on him—he tends to disappear when he's not being watched!"

"No problem, little brother." Kawani laughed and gave David a wink. "He'll not wander off on my watch."

Simon laughed back and led them all out of the clearing. He pushed David into the lead down the narrow path and David uncomfortably made his way back to the clearing where the paths converged. He looked back at the others once, only to see both Temian and Kawani staring back at him, one with even deeper suspicion and the other with open curiosity. Turning back to the path, he wasn't sure which look he was more uncomfortable with.

The path back to the clearing took longer than he remembered, but finally they came into the sunny opening in the trees and he pointed to the path snaking up the slope.

"There it is," he said triumphantly.

Temian strode over and looked up the path. After a long pause he looked back at Simon and shook his head. His sister regarded the path with open surprise.

"That wasn't there when we came to the meeting this morning," she pointed out to the other three.

Simon shook his head as he returned Temian's stare. "No, it certainly wasn't."

"It has the appearance of a worn path, though," Temian muttered, and he gave David a new, more appraising look.

"Score a point for David's story," Simon noted cheerfully. "Obviously we're allowed to go up, so let's gather David's things. Do you want to change your mind and come back up with us?"

David shook his head. Somehow he didn't trust that returning to that camp wouldn't lead to the Choice. Simon nodded and then looked to Kawani.

"Look after my new friend. Don't let him out of your sight, for his own sake."

"He'll be my friend as well by the time you two get back to the clearing," she assured him cheerfully as she positioned herself right beside David.

Simon motioned Temian to lead and the tall man gave one last appraising glare at David before he headed up the trail. David felt a nervous knot forming in his gut but he ignored it and looked off into the forest toward where he knew the village must lay. He froze as his eyes locked on a figure staring back at him among the trees.

Dressed in a riding cloak similar to the one he'd seen the night before, the figure looked very much like Joshua from a distance. So much so that David almost called out to him. But then a few differences struck him. The man's cloak, for starters, failed to shine but rather seemed to throw the light around it in all directions and made it hard to focus on the figure itself. The eyes, seen as points of reflected light from beneath the hood, had an icy hardness to them. David shuddered; he almost caught a hatred in those eyes directed solely toward him.

"You look like you've just seen a ghost!" Kawani's voice was on edge as she turned from the trail her brother had just gone down to see his stricken face.

"What?" He looked at the tall woman briefly and then back to the figure in the forest, but the figure was gone. "It's... it's nothing. I'm seeing things in the shadows."

Kawani followed his gaze into the forest; not seeing what he had, she looked at him in concern. He smiled at her and motioned back down the path toward the remnant's clearing. She regarded him in silent speculation for many seconds before gesturing for him to lead. Ignoring the unasked questions on her face, he glanced one more time back into the now very empty forest before setting a hurried pace back to the safety of the clearing ahead.

All the way back, he tried desperately to congratulate himself on his choice and the smart solution he had found.

Kawani found them some lunch when they got back. Sitting on stumps around a communal fire, she peppered him with questions about himself and his family. At first he thought she was just making small talk. But as she asked about his brothers and their wives, he caught a sly smile crossing her face.

"So, David, youngest son of the silk merchant," she asked coyly, "your brothers are all married. How about you? Is there a lady in David's life?"

"A lady?" He looked down at his bowl in uncharacteristic embarrassment. "No, no lady."

"But there is someone back there you're sweet on, no?"

An image of Nebaya's face flashed through his mind. He felt a sudden pang of loss and longing that confused him. Kawani's question brought up a line of thinking that he hadn't realized he'd been harboring ever since he'd seen her again in that market inn outside of Kathik. He shook himself back out of his thoughts as Kawani called his name.

"Sorry?" He looked up at her apologetically. "What was that?"

"Never mind." She gave him that knowing look that only a woman can give. "It's obvious there is someone. What's her name?"

"Nebaya." Her name tripped out of his mouth.

"Nebaya…" Kawani drew the name out teasingly. "She must be pretty."

"She is," David admitted awkwardly. "But she doesn't think much of me."

"No?" Kawani's tone expressed heavy doubt. "Why do you suppose that is?"

"Maybe because she knows what kind of a man I am."

"Maybe so." Kawani leaned back and regarded him thoughtfully. "But you strike me as a man in transition. I think when you see her again, she might see you differently."

"A man in transition." David chuckled. "That feels like an odd way to describe what's happened to me the last couple of days."

Kawani fixed him with a stern look. "Maybe you don't know, but every one of us has been where you are. You feel like one of us, so I almost forgot you haven't come through the smoke with us. But we understand it when you say your world is turned upside down. We have all had our worlds turned upside down here."

David realized suddenly that Simon's story of their flight from the Sacheth, the flight from their homes and families, had actually happened to them. He thought about everything Simon had told him, and he imagined Kawani and the others milling around the clearing going through those events. He felt ashamed for feeling sorry for himself.

"I kind of forgot that the story of the Remnant that Simon told me is your story," he admitted.

"It's all our story. And it's yours. You've been ripped from your home and everything you've known, and you find yourself dropped in with us. So find comfort in the knowledge that we share that. Everyone here understands, better than you think, what you're feeling. Though for you it is a fresher wound."

"There is a comfort in that." He smiled softly.

"You are here for a purpose, David." She suddenly grew serious. "I see purpose all over you. The Calling is all over your life."

"Until two days ago I would have said you're nuts," David confessed. "But the Living God seems determined to give me a crash course in the Calling."

"For some the Calling is something they pursue. But in your case the Calling pursues you. You can no more avoid it now, I'll wager, than you could forget about that girl you left behind."

"Well, I've made my choice," he affirmed with little conviction. "And tomorrow night I will leave with whoever else will come."

"You're going to lead us to the Mountain, then?" Kawani asked in surprise. "Do you really have an idea where to look?"

"Yes," he said confidently. "I believe I know where to look."

They talked about other things then, and Kawani introduced him to many other members of the group. He learned that there were a little over six hundred in the remnant of the remnant, although not all of them were convinced of the wisdom of leaving if the entire remnant did not leave with them. They would all meet the next night and decide once and for all whether they would stay or leave.

The sun was settling on the western peaks when David realized that Simon and Temian should have been back some time ago. He hadn't considered the possibility that something could happen to them, but as the sun started to sink behind the peaks he became determined to go look for them.

He was about to put his hand on Kawani's shoulder and tell her his plan when the two men came into the clearing leading his horses. Relief flooded through him, followed by a mix of apprehension and curiosity as Simon scanned the clearing of people and finally rested his eyes on him. David saw a shadow cross the other man's face, and the nervous knot, which had slowly loosened as the afternoon passed, returned with a vengeance. He watched both men as they handed off the horses and made for the fire that he and Kawani were seated beside.

"You found my horses. Did you see anyone else?"

Temian nodded and Simon shook his head slowly. Realizing what they had just done, Simon looked at Temian in surprise and the other man just shrugged.

"That *camp*"—Simon put heavy emphasis on the word—"was like nothing I have ever experienced. There was no one there, but there was something there."

"He was there," Temian interrupted. "He spoke to me."

"Who was there?" Simon turned toward him. "I saw no one there."

"I didn't see him," Temian admitted. "And I have not brought it up until now, but I heard the Voice of the Living God. He spoke to me. The entire time we were on the ground, He spoke to me."

"On the ground?" David looked at Simon incredulously. "What happened?"

"I no longer doubt any part of your story," Simon said, by way of answer. "We no sooner stepped in the clearing than we both felt this... what would you call it, Temian?"

"Presence." Temian spoke the word with emotion and layers of meaning.

"Yes, Presence," Simon nodded, lost in a memory he couldn't seem to articulate. "Anyway, we found ourselves on the ground. We were on the ground for... a long time."

"Did you see or hear Joshua?" David pressed.

"I heard the Voice of the Living God," Temian repeated, looking at David in a new way.

"What did He say?" David asked in curiosity, trying to ignore the look.

"I cannot say," Temian said. "I mean, I know what was said, but to repeat it would be... wrong."

"I saw things," Simon chimed in. "I didn't hear a voice, but I saw things. I know what I must do tomorrow morning. I know what I must say to the other elders."

A large crowd of eavesdroppers had gathered around them as they spoke. Many were suddenly looking eagerly towards the path. The thought of experiencing the Living God in a real and tangible way was a temptation they could not resist. Simon raised his hand for silence as everyone started asking if they could go.

"It is in the small clearing between here and the village," he told them. "You may go and see if you can find it. But I suspect that we only found it because of David."

Many took off down the trail immediately, hoping to find the side trail that would lead them to the camp on the hill. Simon and Temian simply watched them go and then turned back to David and Kawani.

"David," Simon started gravely, "I know you hope that your decision has already been made. And we will do everything we can to support you, but everything in me leads me to warn you that the choice He spoke of is still before you."

"No, I've made the choice," David insisted. "And I am not leaving this clearing until after the full moon tomorrow night."

"David!" Temian's sudden deep voice brought his eyes to the big man with a jerk. "What Simon says is true. You cannot escape the Choice. I do not understand what that choice is, but I know it's important for you. What you're doing feels more like running from it. But He won't let you. He knows it's too important for you to make it."

"I am not leaving this clearing until tomorrow night," David clipped each word for emphasis.

Temian shook his head. "Even if you did leave, know that I'll expect you back here to lead us tomorrow night. I will follow you through the Valley of Death and beyond."

Kawani looked at her brother in surprise. David realized in that look that the man was doing something out of character for him. But he just shook his head. He would not be leaving this clearing if he had any say in the matter. For him the decision had been made.

The two men sat with him around the fire and they remained quiet for some time. Soon the others who had gone in search of David's camp started to return. Apparently the trail was nowhere to be found. As the dusk deepened and night truly came on, the remaining stragglers

A BANNER EXTENDS

wandered into the clearing. The slope was utterly impassible, they admitted. If there was a camp up there, it was hidden and shut off to casual visitation.

Many gathered lamps and made their way back down the path to Kathik, seeking their beds for one more night. A good number of people remained, having already given up the comfort of the village in anticipation of their departure in the next few days. They kept a respectful distance between the four at the fire and themselves, but curious glances were returned every time David looked around.

"I'm afraid to sleep," he finally confessed, loath to break the comfortable silence around the fire.

"Why?" Kawani asked. "You're safe here."

"I don't think I am," he admitted with a chuckle, and then hurried to explain. "I'm not safe from Him. Temian and Simon are right and I know it in my very core. But I'm not going to make it easy for anyone to try to change my mind."

"Don't worry, David," Kawani assured him. "We'll watch over you as you sleep. We won't let anyone steal you away."

David smiled. He really had started to feel safe in the group. They all sat in silence again as the fire burned low. He sighed contentedly as he laid out his bedroll in the company of his new friends.

AN INEVITABLE APPOINTMENT

The morning sun was full on his face when he woke to the smell of woodsmoke and fish. He smiled to himself and let the peace of the clearing soak into him. The forest was absolutely still, without the slightest breeze singing in the trees. In fact, the only sounds were of the fire and the morning birds bathing happily in a small stream nearby. No sounds of the other campers stirring came to his ears. No sound of deep sleepers. No sound of the movement of bodies in bedrolls. Nothing but the birds, the small creek, and the fire.

David sat bolt upright. The peace of Joshua's clearing smothered all sense of panic and fear. But he still felt frustration and foreboding as he took in the small clearing with the fire and cooked fish to one side. The rest of the clearing was empty except for the birds. He didn't even have his bedroll, although his cloak was wrapped around him to keep away the morning chill.

"*No!*" he suddenly screamed. "*I chose!*"

The birds took off at the sound of his voice. He looked around the clearing again, but now it was truly empty. He felt his frustration rising in him along with uncertainty. He had chosen, hadn't he?

He stood up and went to the fire. The fish had been cooked to perfection and removed from the well-tended flame. He picked up the spit absently and tore off a piece.

"Where are you?" he muttered, feeling fear and despair lurking on the boundaries of the peace that all but smothered him in this place.

No answer came, but the peace did not waver. An idea came unbidden to his mind. The Living God was waiting. Waiting for him to prove his choice. He absently ate the fish as he thought about what Joshua had told him. There was someone else coming to test him. And he wasn't allowed to lie. And obviously Joshua wouldn't be there, because the choice had to be made without him present. That didn't make much sense.

"The Examiner won't come here," David realized out loud. "Because there is too much of His Presence here."

His voice seemed unnaturally loud in the sudden stillness of the clearing. The birds had all but gone, frightened off by his tirade earlier. No, he realized as he stood in the empty clearing, the choice wouldn't be made here or the remnant's clearing. It would be made in that small clearing at the bottom of the hill, when he turned left and forsook the temptation of the village.

"Fine." He nodded as he spoke out loud. "I will go down the mountain and make that left, and the choice I've already made will be proven."

He strode confidently out of the clearing, leaving its supernatural peace behind him. The path was still there and the morning sun cut through the trees to dance around him as if to celebrate the choice he was confident he had already made. He all but jogged down the hill and came into the clearing at the bottom. There sat the trail that led between the camp and the village. He kept walking toward the left, victory at hand.

"David." A strong voice stopped him in his tracks.

His brain screamed for him to continue. Screamed at him to not turn around. He stood frozen in place like a deer caught in the open. A feeling of fear and uncertainty replaced the confidence of just moments before.

"David," the voice insisted from behind him, "where do you think you are going?"

"I'm going to the camp of the remnant," David muttered, so softly he doubted the voice heard him.

"You go to death, child. But you have no idea why. You walk blindly to death's door, uncelebrated, unremembered, and unfulfilled. You go there because you think that is the better way, but you don't have a clue about what is better."

David shook his head. "I will not listen. You're trying to trick me."

"I'm trying to show you an alternative to dying."

The voice pulled at him with a power all of its own. It was so unlike Joshua's voice that at first David was repulsed by it. But as he listened, he sensed a truth in it. Death *was* waiting ahead, he knew. He didn't understand how or why, but he believed the voice. He slowly turned and saw the source of the voice. It was the figure he had seen the day before. Dressed like Joshua but not. A presence and sense of power about him, but veiled and unlike Joshua.

"Who are you?" David whispered.

"I am the one He spoke of to you—the one who tests," the man declared.

David felt something off about this man. He had an air of arrogance about him. David shook his head.

"But who are you?"

"You may call me Saucan," the man smiled.

The smile was unnatural to that face, David immediately realized. The man was tall and handsome with features that seemed timeless, but David could tell that Saucan was many things other than warm and friendly.

"There is nothing you have that I want," the young man declared, and turned to go.

"I can offer anything a young man's heart desires," Saucan declared. "Recognition? Child's play. Power? How much can you even handle? Love? With my help you can have the hand of any woman. You know so very little of the world you find yourself in, David. Let me be your guide, your right hand."

"You are a liar."

"I have been forbidden to lie. Did not He tell you so? David, I'm not offering you anything that is not already in you to become. I can see your mind; I know your thinking. You have the potential to be a great man, in this valley and beyond. Is that not even worth a look? Do you not see that you are being offered two great choices, equally tempting?"

"I choose the Living God."

"You don't understand." The man's voice wove through his mind like smoke through the trees. "Both choices involve Him. You are His creation; He will be glorified no matter what you choose. But if you don't understand what you are choosing between, it will haunt you right up to death's door. Let me just show you the way I'm offering."

"How will you show me?" David asked as he turned back.

"Give me your hand and we'll explore your deepest longing and potential together." Saucan extended a hand from beneath his cloak.

David felt a part of his mind screaming at him to say no, to turn and leave Saucan and the clearing behind. But it was drowned out by curiosity, and a deep feeling of his own desire for success and power. And what could it hurt just to hear this man out? After all, he could only show the truth.

Ignoring the scream of warning in the far reaches of his head, he reached out and grasped Saucan's outstretched hand. He felt power envelop and surround him like ice water, and everything went black as pitch.

───── 7 ─────

DESIRES OF THE HEART

avid's panic was intense but short lived. Saucan's hand was still holding his, and in his other hand a dim light suddenly appeared. The forest and sky were gone, and they both stood on a black floor, hard and cold as stone. Saucan waited for David to regain his composure.

Finally, David spoke. "Where is this place?"

"The beginning." Saucan's voice seemed deeper and more beautiful here. There was a power to it.

"The beginning of what?"

"The beginning of you. Here we will explore your potential. Your strength. Your power. Here we will build a future for you from your heart's desires. And I will show you what you will become with my help and guidance."

"But Joshua…"

"Joshua is not here," Saucan cut in. "This is about you and your potential. Once I have shown you what you are capable of, you may offer all of that glorious destiny to Him. But let me first show you."

"How?" David asked lamely.

"By letting me into your mind." Saucan raised his hands. "I can read you a little, but I need more understanding to show you what you are truly capable of."

David felt a brief wave of uncertainty and revulsion but it passed quickly into the darkness of the space around him. With a small amount of reluctance, he nodded. Saucan brought his hands to David's temples and stared into his eyes. David had the oddest sensation of falling, and then the darkness around them both burst into a dazzling array of scenes.

David looked in wonder around him as memory after memory played out before him at high speed. He was in his childhood room, watching himself playing. He was at the dining table with his family before his father had died. His father's funeral. Hunting with his brothers. Time seemed to dissolve as he swept through scene after scene, memory after memory. Some memories flew past so fast he barely recalled them and some memories he lingered in, sometimes uncomfortably long.

It could have been mere breaths, it could have been twenty years, but the images finally slowed and Saucan stepped back. A different kind of smile curled the corners of his mouth, failing to reach his eyes. He nodded in satisfaction.

"Are you ready to see what I can do for you?"

"What can you do for me?"

"I will not tell you; I will show you. I will show you everything you will become if you let me help you. But I need your yes."

"Yes, show me."

"Well chosen, David." The smile got suddenly colder, and Saucan reached up and touched David's forehead.

A blinding burning light forced his eyes shut even as the word *chosen* rang in his ears. Was that it? Had he accidentally made the choice? Was failure that easy? He felt consciousness leave him.

———

He woke up in the tent he had been given the night he'd walked into Kathik and announced himself to the surprised elders. True to Saucan's word, he had been able to articulate and argue his way into their confidence. His knowledge of the valley and its people, both now and into the future, amazed them. And with Saucan's help he laid out his new plan for the Amatta—a plan that would make the valley a mighty nation.

Saucan sat lounging in a chair nearby, regarding him.

"I failed Him," David lamented in sudden realization.

"You fulfilled His desire to save His people," Saucan corrected. "And with my help you will make this valley a mighty nation. Together we will make this a people that strikes fear into the hearts of any that oppose us."

"What happened to Simon and the others?" David's memories were not complete.

"Who knows—probably died in the northern mountains somewhere." Saucan shrugged. "They are in the past, the past is dead. This is your future."

David closed his eyes and the world spun.

"My Lord?" A voice beside him whispered in concern, and a hand reached out to steady him.

He opened his eyes and beheld the breathtaking view of the valley below from one of the parapets of the wall. Behind and below him lay the city of Kathik. The great walled city of Kathik, the building of which he himself had overseen. Farmland stretched out below the city walls, and the river glistened beyond.

He looked over at the man holding his arm. He knew this was his advisor, but he couldn't remember his name. He was surrounded by the members of the inner court and had been discussing something of import, but he had forgotten what he was saying.

Saucan stepped up and took his arm. With a wave he sent everyone toward the curtained exit.

"My Lord is still recovering from his ailment, but you have your instructions." They reluctantly left.

"Saucan." David shook his head. "Is this real?"

"Of course it's real."

Memories flooded his mind. His rise to power. His ability to manoeuvre through politics as easily as a fish through water. His plans for the city, now built. His slow rise to almost king-like status. How many years had it all taken? Five? Ten? There were gaps in his memories, but they were his memories.

"Does my lord see how much we've accomplished?" Saucan cooed in his ear. "All of this is yours—all of this and more."

"Is this real?"

"Doesn't it feel real? This has all emerged out of your abilities and potential. Your deepest desires made real. I have given this all to you because it was in you to give."

"What else is possible?"

"I'm glad you asked. Search your heart, David. What else do you want? You control the entire valley. You control the Koreb Pass. You've started trade hundreds of years before these fools would have. What other desires of your heart do you want?"

"A long life with a wife and family," David murmured, and closed his eyes.

"Let me show you what is possible," Saucan whispered.

This time the world around him really did spin, and he fell with a thud into a cushioned chair. More memories than before flooded into him—or was it *out* of him? He became aware of a great passage of time. With it, a maturity in governing and an increase in knowledge. He felt smarter, wiser than he ever had. He felt powerful. And he *was* powerful. King David of the Amatta. His name carried weight, not only here but out in the world.

With the help of Saucan he had made the valley a thing of beauty and wonder. The ore deposits of Pethe, which he had only known about as an exhausted legend, were rediscovered and mined. Great military defence works had been built along the Koreb, sealing the valley like a great fortress. Trade had increased. With Saucan's help, he had discovered deposits not only of iron but of gold and silver. Wealth flowed into the valley.

He'd brought others into the valley as well. Immigrants from the nations that the remnant had known came to live among them and take part in the prosperity. The Amatta was a great melting pot of cultures and knowledge. And at its hub he stood. It was all because of him. Saucan had seen it, but now he saw it, too.

An army stood garrisoned in the Koreb. He had been reluctant at first, but now he saw the value. And as the numbers of his soldiers grew, so did the realization that like a hunting dog, they would have to be exercised. A dozen targets lay on the war table. Maybe, one day, they would even bring the fight to the Sacheth.

The room around him stirred in hushed appreciation and he brought himself to the present moment. This was a long-awaited day. A day he had desired above all other days. He smiled in happy anticipation and opened his eyes.

His throne room was heavily decorated for the occasion and was lined with all of the most respected lords and ladies of the Amatta, as well as no small number of honoured guests from other kingdoms. It was not every day, after all, that the King of Amatta got married.

A stir at the far end of the room caught his eye, and a tall, veiled woman dressed in a white gown flowed gracefully toward him. His heart skipped and his pulse raced. Of all that he had built and accomplished, it all paled next to this moment. Something spoke clearly in his heart that this, above all else, was what his heart desired.

Everyone bowed as the future queen passed them. Most favoured of women, she was to be queen of the Amatta beside their beloved king, David. The silence was broken only by the sound of her dress across the floor as she came and stood at the foot of the steps to the throne.

With a beaming smile, he arose and descended the steps. Heart beating wildly, he gently grasped the veil in both hands and lifted it to behold the woman he would share everything with.

"You are a fool, David." Nebaya's eyes locked with his and revealed such a profound look of disgust that he staggered.

"I don't understand."

"If you think I'd marry you after what you've become... after what you have done to the valley. After the stench you've made of the name of the Living God." She shook her head vehemently. "Well, you are a bigger fool then I had ever imagined."

"I have everything I could ever want," David boasted, looking into her eyes. "I reach out my hand and it becomes mine. Why not you, Nebaya?"

"I am not yours for the taking." Her eyes flashed in anger. "You will destroy everything you touch."

David shook his head. "This isn't right. None of this is right."

A sudden hiss of anger and frustration sounded from behind him. Saucan all but flew down the stairs. He glared at Nebaya for a long moment and then grabbed David's arm.

"Pick another!" he hissed viciously. "Pick another. Anyone but her. Everyone else but her."

David shook his head in confusion and looked at Nebaya. She looked at him, her anger and disgust turning suddenly to pity.

"I don't understand," he repeated. Everything seemed to waver around him. Something stirred deep inside his soul. This wasn't who he wanted to be, was it?

"You must pick someone else!" Saucan's voice took on a note of rising panic. "She is poison to all we have built! She will bring it all to ruin!"

"But of everything around me, her love is all that I truly desire," David declared obstinately.

Nebaya reached out her hand and laid it on David's head. Saucan froze like a wild animal about to strike. David looked up into her eyes and realized the truth of what he had just said.

"Dear one," Nebaya smiled sadly, "I belong to the Living God. You cannot have me—not here, not now, not ever in this place."

"Be silent!" Saucan rose up suddenly in power, striking out at Nebaya.

"No!" David screamed. "You will not hurt her!"

The room exploded inward. Everything shattered like glass struck with a hammer. Nebaya caught his eye briefly and smiled sadly before she simply popped out of existence. The narrow broken pieces of his reality lashed out at him, cutting into him, shredding his body and mind and threatening to drive him mad with pain.

"Idiot!" Saucan hissed, leaning down to whisper in his ear. "Foolish child! Do you think what I was offering was a small thing? Do you think

I couldn't have done all that for you and more? Now you will have none of it! I will grind you down like the future you just gave up. I will make the remainder of your days so miserable you will wish you had never been born!"

David struggling for a response, but under Saucan's onslaught his mind spiralled into dark places and refused to think clearly. The other man's words rang true in him. He'd given up everything because he couldn't have Nebaya. Could never have her, in fact. She was lost to him forever.

"Nebaya," he whispered.

"What?" Saucan lashed out viciously. "That girl? Was she worth it? Was preserving that memory worth it, David?"

"I don't understand," David wailed, lost in the turmoil of his mind and emotions.

"You could have taken anyone else!" Saucan continued to rant, ignoring him. "There were beautiful women by the hundreds I could have given you! An entire harem's worth! If only you had opened your mind to the possibilities!"

"I don't want anyone else," David shouted back, suddenly realizing the truth of it. "Nebaya has had my heart since the first day I saw her!"

"Well, you can't have her!" Saucan grew suddenly in size and power, the veil that he had obviously placed over his appearance ripped apart by his sudden hatred.

Towering before David was what could only be a Maylak, or something very like one. But although this Maylak may once have been beautiful, he was now twisted by a hatred that was ugliness personified.

With great effort, the being brought himself back under control. As quickly as the Maylak had appeared, Saucan returned.

"What are you?" David whispered.

"You were not content to accept your potential with our partnership. You gave up all of the others so easily, but you hid her from me." Saucan shook his head slowly in disappointment. "And then you tricked me and let me put her into our vision. What a fine mess that made."

"I don't understand."

"I don't understand," Saucan mocked. "Of course you don't. I offered you power I rarely offer anyone. I offered you a throne. Everything I offered you was in my power to give! And you were too weak, too childish to see what I was offering. Third son of a pathetic family. What a disappointment."

David felt like his head was encased in mud. He couldn't think. He couldn't respond. Every word from Saucan pounded him deeper into a darkness from which he feared he would never wrestle free.

"Joshua," he murmured suddenly, reaching out with a faint tendril of hope.

"What?" Saucan stopped ranting and considered him. "He can't help you once the choice is made, you know. Once that is done, you are mine. And now I intend to destroy you."

The weight of what Saucan said fell on him. He wasn't lying—once the choice was made, he had to live with it. Anger rose up in him. How fragile was the moment of choice! How was he to have known that taking Saucan's hand would condemn him? He saw the thing before him now, evil and twisted. But he had not known before. The entire choice was unfair.

"Roll in your self-pity all you want, boy. It changes nothing."

"Joshua, help me," David whispered again in despair.

"He can't help you."

There was an edge to his voice that caused David's muddy mind to stop sinking. Was that a lie? David struggled to think. He knew only one thing for certain, he needed help.

"He follows his own rules," Saucan continued. "He gave you over to me and you chose to listen to me. You went to Kathik, remember? You were in Kathik. He himself told you that if you went to Kathik the choice was made. You might as well admit it: you've made the choice."

David struggled to think. Something wasn't entirely right with that logic, but Saucan wasn't outright lying and he knew it. He also started to realize that it was Saucan affecting his mind, muddying his thinking. He tried to fight through it, but it was stronger than he was.

I need help, he screamed into the darkness of his soul. *Living God, I need your help!*

"David!"

A new voice entered the conversation, and David looked up in shock to see Nebaya standing between himself and Saucan. She was dressed no longer in the wedding gown but in the clothes she had worn that day under the avalanche shelter. His heart jumped as he saw her.

"What is this?" Saucan sneered. "You cannot be here."

"No rules are being broken."

Saucan considered her, uncertainty in his face for the first time. David also considered her and struggled to understand what was going on. How could Nebaya be here? What rules were they talking about? Saucan continued studying her with his hatred on full display, but she just turned and knelt down beside David.

"Nebaya, what are you doing here?" David looked at her in wonder.

"I'm not here, silly," she laughed softly. "I'm a fragment of your imagination."

"I don't understand."

She shook her head. "You've said that a lot. David, people we meet in our lives leave a mark on us. Some good. Some bad. Those marks help make us who we are and become part of us. Do you understand that?"

"Yes."

"Good." She leaned down to whisper in his ear. "Saucan has corrupted your thinking, dear David. Every part that he couldn't corrupt, he has shut away from you. Anyone who served the Living God in your life is absent from this place. Everyone except me. He missed me."

"Enough," Saucan moved forward and grabbed her by the arm. With a great push he thrust her into the darkness surrounding them.

Just like that she was gone, swallowed by darkness deeper than night. But in a small part of his mind a space was clearing. He reached out and found a space in his thinking unmuddied and clear.

"Nothing but my faith and the choice," David muttered.

"How can you think the choice hasn't been made?" Saucan sneered as he stood over the young man. "You yourself know you were in Kathik. You saw it."

David remained silent for a long time. The turmoil in his mind increased and lashed at his thoughts, threatening to unseat his sanity, but he held on to the quiet place he had found. Saucan seemed to suddenly sense the place in his mind and poured all of his malice at it, but it refused to be swept away. One idea formed in him. One truth that seemed to stand, even in the onslaught to Saucan's storm.

"When is a lie a lie?" David mused.

"Do you think to banter with me, child?" Saucan sneered. "I am beyond your reach in this game. You are playing against the Master. I could have given you the desires of your heart, but I can just as easily plunge you into the depths of your worst nightmares."

"I didn't come here to beat you," David admitted. "I recognize that I can't. I can't even see through the web of half-truths and deceptions that you have spun all through my head. I am truly and completely outmatched by you."

David smiled then as the realization struck him, sneaking through the maelstrom of darkness in his thinking. Saucan's eyes narrowed and he prepared his greatest blow. His hands shook in anger and the darkness became an almost physical thing. David simply continued.

"I reject you, Saucan, and everything you're offering. I choose the Living God."

The darkness around him lashed out violently and Saucan's voice was suddenly all around him and even in his head.

"You are nothing! You will come to nothing!" he screamed. *"She will live and die a thousand years from now and you haven't the power to do anything!"*

His voice was suddenly gone, and David collapsed in a heap on the cool dirt of the forest floor.

"That is a lie," he wept, and knew nothing else for a long time.

8

REBORN

He did not know how long he lay weeping on the forest floor, but after a time he became aware of a growing peace settling on him. His soul, flayed by Saucan's wrath, was suddenly soothed and made still. He became aware of a familiar presence in the clearing with him and he sat up and looked around to find Joshua sitting on a nearby rock, watching him.

"Why didn't you warn me?" David asked softly.

"I did," Joshua reminded him. "I told you he'd try to make you choose yourself over the Living God."

"But those were Saucan's ideas," David started to argue and then paused. "Or were they?"

"He cannot create," Joshua corrected him. "He needed your mind, your imagination, and your desires to draw from. He is, as he said, the Master at what he does. He takes the unredeemed desires of a man's heart and twists them for his purposes."

"So everything I saw could have come true?"

"He is a master manipulator and deceiver. What you saw could very well have come to be, but the horror of that reality was hidden from you. In the end you would have been his tool for the final destruction of the remnant. And you would have destroyed everything that makes you David in the process."

"I'm sorry." David shook his head sadly. "I wanted to be better than I am."

"I'm proud of you, David," Joshua countered, and walked over to lay his hands on the young man's shoulders. "What Saucan revealed in you was only dark possibility. Whatever harm was done was done to your own opinion of yourself. And humility is not such a bad start, is it?"

"It felt so real," David admitted. "I felt it; I even felt that I had lived it."

"And knowing that you could actually have it, would you?"

David thought for a long time.

"In all of my memory of it, I never felt anything like I feel being here with you. I would give up all of that for this, to just sit here with you, even if it does mean dying uncelebrated, unremembered, and unfulfilled."

What happened next confused David greatly. Joshua laughed. The sound filled David with inexplicable joy, and he just stared in happy confusion.

"Come with me, David," he finally said, leading back up the slope to his camp.

David followed him quietly. When they got to the clearing with the small stream and pond there was no fire, but Joshua proceeded to wade into the middle of the pool and stood waiting for him. David shrugged and joined him. He found the water extremely cold, and the pool was deeper than he expected. He stood waiting as Joshua regarded him with a happy solemnity.

"David, in times past this was done as an act of confession and repentance. Do you submit yourself to the Living God, turning from your old ways and promising to serve Him and Him alone, all the days of your exceedingly long life?"

David looked at him in confusion and then nodded.

"Words, please, David."

"Yes. With all my heart, yes."

"This was an ancient custom, and it pleases me to restore baptism to my people." Joshua smiled happily as he seized David by his arms and plunged him into the cold pool.

The water rushed into his open mouth and nose and cut off a shout of surprise. Joshua released his arms and grabbed him by the hand. He shot up out of the water with a sputter.

"You went into the water a broken man of sin, but you come out a child of the Living God," Joshua continued without missing a beat. "Receive now the Spirit of the Living God."

Joshua breathed on David, and his entire being was filled with a Presence very much like the one that always hung over Joshua's clearing. Like a flood the Presence spread through him, sweeping away the hurt and despair left behind by his trial with Saucan. In an instant, the entire affair was laid bare and David understood what Saucan had tried and failed to do.

"You see, David," Joshua beamed at him, "Saucan did not lie. Your past life is buried in the water, and you have come out reborn in the Kingdom of the Living God."

"Showing is better than telling," David laughed.

"Indeed." Joshua helped him to the edge of the pond and he sat on the edge of the horse manger. "And now that I've shown you how, I want you to show others and teach them to do the same. But first sit with me awhile. There are still a few hours until the remnant's remnant will meet, and I delight in being with you."

David nodded, the Presence within him continuing to untangle the knots Saucan had made before his mind's eye. He sat, and together they enjoyed the soft sound of the creek and the clearing. After a long time, David spoke into their content silence.

"We need a better name than the remnant's remnant."

They both laughed, the sound carrying across the mountainside and over the valley.

9

THE FRAGMENTS

David and Joshua talked the remaining hours of the day away as Joshua explained what must come next. In the past David would have balked and questioned what he was being told, but events of this day had changed him. The Presence of the Living God within him confirmed everything he was being told. Finally, as the afternoon sun sank below the mountains above them, Joshua rose and bid him farewell.

"They will be waiting now," he said with a smile.

"But will you not come with me?" David asked one more time.

"I am with you, in here." Joshua put his hand over David's heart. "The Spirit of the Living God is the seal between us. And you will see me again when you've completed your journey. Now I have to go ahead of you and prepare a place for everyone."

A tendril of fear snuck through the young man's soul. The memory of Saucan and the ease of his deception pushed up from the back of his mind.

"Fear not, David." Joshua smiled as if seeing his thoughts. "Learn to walk with the Spirit within you and trust Him as you trust me. He will teach you as I would. Now go."

David nodded and without another word turned and descended down the trail in the glowing twilight. Reaching the clearing of his decision, he all but bounded to the left, not taking the risk of raising his eyes to the forest around him or the trail to the right. In little time he came to the thicket and the sound of a large commotion in the clearing beyond.

He paused briefly to listen. Simon's voice carried loudly over a chorus of other voices. Much of the conversation was muddled, but it was quite apparent the argument was about whether they should all leave or stay. Joshua's instructions were fresh in David's mind, and he smiled to himself as he passed through the thicket and into the clearing full of people.

Silence fell as all eyes turned to the new figure stepping out of the forest. Simon turned and closed his mouth mid-sentence, looking him up and down.

"I would ask where you have been all day, but for now I'll just assume it involved swimming in the river," he finally remarked with a half-smile. "We were worried something terrible had befallen you when your bedroll turned up empty."

"Something terrible did happen to me," David said simply. "Something terrible and wonderful. But that's a story for later."

"So you've made your choice, then?" Temian bellowed from the front of the crowd.

"I have. Have all of you?"

"We're still going over it," Simon confessed. "Although now that you're here, I'm hoping much of the dissent can be quelled."

"We'll see," David said as he scanned the clearing before him.

There were more people here than the day before. The entire six hundred appeared to be in attendance tonight to decide, once and for all, whether they would stay and rebuild their lives in this valley or push on to search for the Mountain of the Living God. David looked to Simon for permission to stand on the rock with him.

"You belong up here more than me, I think," Simon said, and then turned to address the crowd. "This is David, the man you have heard so much about in the last days. I believe he holds the key to our future."

David bounded up onto the rock with Simon and turned to face the people as the Spirit stirred within him. Everything that Joshua had instructed him came to the forefront of his mind and he felt a sudden overwhelming love for these people. These were now *his* people, and he was ready to do anything for them.

"The Living God has sent me to lead you to the Mountain," he stated up front. "And whoever would go with me is welcome. But I must also warn you, only those who truly wish to serve the Living God should come."

A murmur ran through the crowd. They had not expected that. This was different from any speech that Simon had given in the past.

"It is not enough on this journey to say that you love Him. It's not enough to say that you honour Him. By the end of this journey, each of you will be asked to lay down your very lives for Him. This calling is not for the half-hearted and the undecided. It would be better for such people to stay here, in this valley, and contribute to making it in every way a place that honours and serves the Living God.

"But if you wish to go on from here, knowing that the Living God awaits you at the Mountain, then be ready to lay everything else aside."

"Do you know where it is? Have you seen it?" someone in the crowd interrupted.

"I know where the Mountain is, but I have not seen it. The One who made the Mountain and the road will be our guide."

"What can we bring?" someone else shouted.

"Bring a cloak for the weather and a week's worth of food. Anything else will just weigh you down." David looked intently out at the crowd. "This warning comes from the Living God. We will all pass through the Valley of Death before coming to the Mountain. Those willing to lose their lives for the sake of the Living God will stand with Him on the other side. But those who would hesitate should not come at all, but stay here and serve Him in their own way."

A murmur rippled through the clearing, but no one responded openly. David looked out at them all, meeting uncertain stares with a look of encouragement and confidence.

"When will we depart?" Temian finally asked from the front.

"Tomorrow, at first light," David declared. "There is no need for discussion on my part. There is nothing here for me. I will go even if I go alone. Take this night to decide for yourselves what you will do."

Without another word he stepped down and passed into the crowd. He realized what he said was true. He wanted everyone to choose to come with him, but whether they did or not was up to them. And he realized he was hungry, having not eaten since the night before. The crowd parted for him and he headed to the fire to find food. Simon watched him thoughtfully from the rock. The people turned from David to Simon in expectation.

"I think we've heard everything we need to hear from him on this matter. He is right that each of you must now decide what you will do. As for myself," he declared, "I will go with David. From the very beginning, the Mountain was my goal. I am now more determined than ever to see the Mountain of the Living God, though it cost me everything—even my life."

Many in the crowd nodded, though a great many others still showed uncertainty. Simon understood much of what was going through their heads. For the better part of the last year, they had argued and discussed what they would do when this moment came. Now the message from the Living God spoken through David was simply this—they had to put action to their words. There was nothing more to say.

"Kawani and I will also go," Temian suddenly declared; his sister nodded. "We serve at the pleasure of the Living God. Anything is a small final price to pay to see the Mountain."

Many others then voiced their agreement. Simon regarded them all proudly.

"You have all heard what David just said. Many of you have heard David's story, either directly from him last night or from others today. From that story, you know this valley will see peace and prosperity for a thousand years. It is no shame to choose to be a part of the foundation of that success. Only the Living God knows what difference you can make here—what differences you are destined to make. Those of us that choose to go tomorrow must go prepared to pay the full price. If you cannot, if you are unsure, then I think you had best stay behind. This is the point of decision for our group, and there will be no maybes, no half-hearted okays. Let your yes be yes or your no be no."

The crowd murmured their agreement and started to break into smaller groups. Simon knew there would be many, many discussions long into the night. He also knew that not everyone would be going tomorrow. David's warning rang in his own soul, and he considered what lay ahead. With a sigh, he got down from the stone and walked over to Temian.

"Our new friend is newer still," the big man noted as Simon came alongside him. "Whatever happened to him today has remade him."

"Do you suppose he will tell us the story?" Kawani asked hopefully from his side, looking eagerly in the direction that David had gone.

"Let's go find out." Simon was determined to know himself. "We'll ply him with food and lure him into talking with a little fellowship."

The other two nodded and followed Simon toward the fire.

It didn't take much food or time to get David to talk about what had happened since he'd awoken in Joshua's clearing that morning. They sat around the fire in complete silence as David told them the entire story right up to his strange baptism in the pool. When he finished he simply trailed off in silence that no one broke for a long time.

"I want to be baptized," Kawani suddenly blurted. "Can you baptize me, David?"

"Yes," David nodded. "Joshua told me that everyone ought to be baptized and I should teach others to do it. But I have to warn you—it's an unnerving experience and not something to decide to do lightly. Not that he warned me about that at the time! Actually, I've just had an idea of where we can do it, if you can wait."

"Where is that?" Simon cut in. "I find myself wanting this strange bath myself."

"Two days up the valley there is a series of waterfalls…" David said tentatively.

"Yes," Temian nodded. "We call them the Gellah. The water issues from a hole in the cliff and falls in three drops to a pool below."

"Three? No, there are seven drops from the top of the cliff." David shook his head in confusion.

The others looked at each other and then back at him.

"David, I have been there. There are definitely three drops, and the falls don't go to the top of the cliff," Temian assured him. "But a thousand years can change even the course of a river."

A new idea occurred to David. A thousand years truly could change a great many things. Just look at what the Amatta would become in that time. At some point Gellah would go from three to seven drops. And there would be a cave behind the third fall in a thousand years. He shook his head.

"Anyway, the falls are there and the pool is a good stopping point before the real test begins. Tomorrow we'll make for the falls with whoever decides to come with us. We'll stop and baptize everyone in the pool of Gellah, and from there we'll search for the road up into the Valley of Death."

"Why wait?" Kawani pressed, her eagerness to be baptized plain on her face.

"Well, the two days to the falls will both sift out those who are choosing to go for the wrong reasons and allow those who take longer to decide to catch up with us. Two days of grace given before the choice is irrevocable. Because once we find the hidden road and set our feet upon it, there will be no turning back."

"Then there is our plan," Simon said. "I have to admit it's a relief to be presented with one and not have to make one up. Tomorrow the remnant of the remnant will set out on its final journey."

"Oh, about that," David laughed softly. "I have a new name for those of us who leave tomorrow."

"Oh?" Simon raised an eyebrow in surprise and glanced at the others. "Maybe you want the group named after you?"

"Well…"—David became suddenly self-conscious as the others laughed—"Joshua and I were talking, and we both agreed that 'remnant of the remnant' wasn't a great name. So he suggested the Klasma."

"Klasma." Kawani spoke the word softly. "I do not recognize it. What does it mean?"

"He said it meant fragments, or broken pieces. He meant it affectionately."

"Well, who are we to argue with that name, then?" Simon laughed. "And it is a better and more fitting name than the one we have. Very well; tomorrow the Klasma departs for the Mountain of the Living God.

They all laughed then. The crowds around them looked their way with eyes that spoke of longing and just a hint of jealousy. Simon waved the nearest group over and the four spent the night working their way group to group, talking, listening, and doing their best to help with the decisions that were not yet made.

— 10 —

FAREWELL AND FORWARD

The next morning dawned to find a large group, dressed for travel, waiting patiently to depart. David estimated five hundred at least had chosen to go with them. Another, smaller group was there to say farewells and see them off. Chief among them was a well-dressed young man about his age. The man approached the fire where he and Simon were having a quick breakfast.

"Ah, Samuel!" Simon greeted him when he was near enough. "Thank you for coming to see us off!"

"I did not have much choice," the man said sullenly. "Especially since you wouldn't leave me the journals back at the camp."

"No." Simon smiled. "I wanted to put the finishing touches on my work before I passed it on."

Simon reached into his pack and drew out a leatherbound bundle of parchment. He looked at it wistfully for several long seconds before handing it to the younger man. Samuel took the bound papers with a marked respect that he didn't show for Simon. He squinted at the front of the leather cover and then quickly stuffed the bundle into a pack he had brought.

"I can't read the title you've given it through this smoke," Samuel admitted, "But I will look after it and add it to our archives like you asked."

Simon nodded graciously. "Thank you, Samuel. It contains important history, even if you don't agree with how it concludes. And of course it falls to you as my successor to continue the office of Chief Archiver."

"And of course you convinced the elders that I was the best choice," Samuel said bitterly. "Despite the fact that you know I hate the politics and the talking and the constant need to deal with people."

"As I have already told you, Samuel," Simon said in exasperation, "you may make the office your own. Your primary role is to preserve and keep the record, after all. Assign someone else to deal with the day-to-day interactions."

Samuel snorted and then patted the pack that contained the papers. Without another word he turned and left. Simon watched him go and then turned back to the others with a sad smile.

"Do you wish he was coming with us?" David asked.

"Who? Samuel? Heavens, no!" Simon shook his head and laughed. "Samuel could not be happier to settle here, in this valley. His love is reading and study. But he has been a good friend in his own way, and I will miss him."

David nodded and looked around the clearing. Goodbyes were tapering off, and the crowd was getting restive. A stocky man of about twenty-five years approached them.

"Ah, and here is Duncan," Simon announced when he was close enough. "Are your instructions clear?"

"Clear enough," the man said as he stopped in front of them. "Wait for the stragglers and then make for the Gellah Falls. Be there no more than two days after you, or don't bother."

"That's it." Simon nodded and then turned to David. "I took what you said last night to heart and augmented the plan. If anyone can get the stragglers to be on time, it'll be Duncan."

"I cannot fault that planning," David said as he shrugged at the two men. "Would you like to get this journey started?"

"You're the man the Living God has chosen to lead," Simon said in answer.

David nodded and picked up his gear. With Simon in tow, he strode to the stone at the top of the clearing and bounded up onto it. Everyone stilled as they turned to look at him. He felt the sickly roots of uncertainty weave through his gut, but digging deeper he found the unwavering Presence from the day before. Confidence settled over him, along with a peace that passed understanding. He raised his hand—unnecessarily, since silence had already fallen.

"This morning each of us is starting out on a journey of faith. For everyone here but me, this marks the last part of a journey that started years ago as you fled death and destruction at the hands of a cruel enemy. I cannot truly say I understand how that feels. For me, this journey is an end as well, but it is the end of a self-centered life, full of vain pursuits. I look ahead to the conclusion of this journey—to the Mountain of the Living God, and to a new future full of hope and purpose. And I invite you to look to that future as well. To see this as rushing to a beginning, not an end. I know in my heart that God has a purpose for each of you. You are all the Klasma, the fragments gathered from broken nations long lost. You have a hope and a future. Are you with me?"

"*Yes!*" The crowd thundered as one in the clearing, their voices ringing over the trees and reaching even the village of Kathik as it stirred awake.

Without waiting, David stepped off the rock to the edge of the clearing where Temian and Kawani stood with the horses. They were unsettled, and sensed a journey ahead. At first he wasn't sure whether he should bring them, although to leave them behind seemed equally wrong. They were, after all, just as out of their time as he was. He smiled and passed the four of them with a nod. The horses were dealing with this new world better than he had, overall. He heard them turn and follow him down the path toward the river, and the head of the Amatta Valley where the Gellah Falls waited.

GELLAH FALLS

The journey up the river was familiar, and yet harder than he remembered. The reason for the difficulty was immediately apparent: there was no road. In his time, a well-maintained road ran from Kathik to the village of Bato, and then beyond to the falls and the Shaar Pass. Here, in this time, there was but a series of narrow paths that were obviously made by game, starting suddenly and then as suddenly disappearing.

David had almost immediately given over the role of leading after he ran the entire troop into a dell of dense thicket that they had to backtrack out of. From that point he admitted he wasn't fit to be a guide, pointing out the lack of the road he was used to. Temian and Simon just laughed and picked half a dozen others who were familiar with the trails ahead to lead the way. From what David could see, they were all better at bushcraft than he was.

"You have to expect that," Temian pointed out when he mentioned it. "We've been wandering the mountains for five years, often passing through valley and pass where no road goes. We've all but forgotten the luxuries of roads and bridges."

"I guess I didn't even consider that," David said flatly. "I'm just the opposite; I'm used to roads and bridges and staying in inns when I travel, which is rare. It's been just days since I was eating food that my mother's cooks had prepared and sleeping in my own bed."

"I don't remember the luxury of a bed or food not cooked over a fire!" Kawani laughed as she led Storm ahead of him. There was much amused agreement along the line.

"You must all think I'm spoiled and soft. And you'd be right, I guess."

"Of all of us, I think your loss is freshest, David," Kawani reassured him with a gentle smile, looking back at him. "But in the short time that I have known you, you have not struck me as spoiled and soft. You started off a little naive and lost, but your experience with the Living God has changed you in ways I think you do not yet realize."

The reminder of his experience just the day before made him reach down inside himself. The Spirit of the Living God stirred there, not really responding to his silent query, but reassuring him that He was still there, still abiding. David's thoughts rested on that Presence, that knowledge that the Living God was somehow with him. Joshua had said the Spirit would teach him. He wondered how.

Through communion and time spent with Him, the thought occurred. *By learning to be still and listen, you will start to hear the still small voice.*

The peace of the Spirit flowed over him as if to reassure him that the idea was good. He smiled and looked up to find Kawani looking back at him in expectation. He realized she had just asked him something.

He shook his head. "Sorry, Kawani. I was thinking about something. What did you ask?"

"I asked, what's it like carrying the Spirit of the Living God?" she repeated. "You mentioned last night that this man Joshua gave you the Spirit of the Living God. What is that like?"

"I'm honestly still trying to work that out," he admitted with a small laugh. "I feel this peace and this presence when I stop to reach out to it. In fact, that's what I was just thinking about."

"Do you think that I can have it, once I am baptized?" she pressed.

"I... well, I don't know, but I think so," he said uncertainly. "I mean, I had the impression that I was to pass this all on, so why not this part as well?"

"I want all the Living God will give me," she said.

"I think that would make Him very happy." The words were out of his mouth before he had time to form them.

Kawani beamed back at him happily and he smiled back. In his own head, however, he couldn't help but feel like those weren't even his words.

They camped in a large meadow by the river, and were back on the trail the next morning when it was light enough to see the trail ahead. There was an energy about the group that David found contagious. The decision to leave the valley had made them almost recklessly eager to get to the Mountain. David couldn't blame them. He himself felt like this part of the journey was just the beginning of something much, much greater.

As they marched up the valley the second day, the peaks across the river suddenly drew up close. From David's memory, he knew that the valley would narrow to no more than a quarter mile wide and stay that way for many miles before opening up into a junction of sorts. The Shaar Pass would rise up between the peaks on their right, and the valley would turn to the left and go for many miles until it ended in impassible mountains. The only way anyone knew beyond the mountains was the Shaar Pass.

His mind went back to the conversation about the Gellah Falls the night before last. He and his brothers had once climbed the cliffs to get above the falls. They had thought maybe they would find another pass beyond, but what they had found in following the Gellah Creek was a cold, deep lake bordered by a ring of snow-covered peaks. They had returned to the falls dejected and spent the rest of the day descending the falls one tier at a time, swimming in each of the pools and revelling in their bravery. All seven tiers. They had even stopped to thoroughly explore the third tier with its shallow cave behind it.

His sister's story of her experience the day they had lost her in the Shaar Pass came back to him. He recalled finding her by the fire near the falls. He and his two brothers had retraced their journey back up into the pass all of the way to the summit, but could not find the trail she insisted was there.

He went over the pass in his memory. There was just no way there was a trail leading up the mountain on the left-hand side of that pass.

It's there, the thought shot through his mind. *The path will be revealed.*

One more day of moving north and one more night sleeping beside the river. Finally, they came out of the narrow valley and he beheld the falls from a small rise for the first time. Sure enough, about a third of the way down the cliff from where it should be, a fountain of water was ejected from a dark hole and fell in three drops to the valley floor. He stopped in wonder as he realized that the hole was the cave. At some point in the next thousand years, something would collapse the exit to that cave and force the water to come down from the cliff above.

He looked to the right, and sure enough, the Shaar Pass rose from the valley floor and passed between two peaks to the wilderness beyond. His eyes strayed to the farthest peak, upon which would be the path that led up into the higher peaks beyond and eventually to the Valley of Death and the Mountain past it. The slope rising up with the Shaar was steep and broken. The forest struggled to cling to the slopes, and scree littered the base of the slope everywhere. Nothing about that mountain gave any sign of a path or way up accessible by a ten-year-old on horseback.

Simon came up beside him and followed his eyes to the mountain and pass ahead. "So there it is."

"Yes."

"I bet you're thinking that there isn't a path up the side of that thing." Simon's tone confirmed his agreement.

David just nodded again. His head told him exactly that, but something new was vying with that belief. He accepted, maybe for the first time, that his sister hadn't lied about that day. And if she hadn't lied, then there was a path. Who knew what that path might actually look like now, but in that distant future it was wide enough for a horse. He looked over to his sister's mount. It was that horse, come to think of it.

"It's there," he finally stated. "Somewhere on the slope between the treeline and the sheer cliffs of that far mountain. And it'll take us up and around somehow until it leads us away from the summit of the Shaar."

Simon stared at the mountain, his eyes tracing the line that David suggested. Finally he just shook his head and gave David a shrug. They both knew they were trusting the Living God to show them a path that neither of them, in either of their times, had seen. And between them, only David even knew someone who had seen it.

"At no time has it ever been said that the Mountain is easy to find," Simon said quietly. "We will go as far as we can with our natural eyes and thinking, and then we'll simply move beyond that into the realm of faith."

"Simply?" David laughed. "Simply that? Well, I guess you are right, Simon. Three days ago I would have said we're all crazy. Look what three days can do to a man."

They set up camp around the base of the falls as the sun set over the distant peaks that marked the far end of the valley. David looked down the length of the wilderness toward that end. There was nothing down there, he knew. Nothing but trees and streams and the Valley River as it was robbed of its power one tributary at a time until it reached its own headwaters at the base of the glaciers that hugged the mountainsides so many miles away.

Temian came up as he looked west, and watched with him as the last slip of sun slipped behind the peaks.

"Will it look the same in a thousand years?" he asked finally.

"Strangely, yes," David said after a moment. "There is nothing up there but trees and wild game for miles and miles. It's wild and broken and bordered on both sides by mountains. There's no exit to the valleys beyond. And of course at the end there are those two mountains and the glacier rising up between them. But no one returns from there."

"Are you telling me that no one in all the long years between now and then has explored beyond that glacier?" Temian asked incredulously.

"As the legend goes, two friends tried. They left mid-July and bragged they would find the Mountain of the Living God and bring back proof. Only one of them returned to the valley, starved and half mad at the end of August, missing most of his fingers and toes to frostbite. As he told it, they had managed to climb the glacier, only to find a great lake of broken ice with mountain peaks like islands sticking out for miles and miles beyond their view. Emboldened, they had started out into it when a great bottomless ice fissure opened beneath them. One was lost to the darkness, but the other was saved by a ledge. It took him a long time to climb out, and even longer to get back down the glacier. It's a tale we're told as young men to warn us of the dangers of old ice in the mountains."

"I am familiar with the dangers," Temian nodded. "It sounds like our brothers and sisters of the Amatta never really overcome their contentment to stay in the valley."

"Well, those that do get the itch to leave take the Oath and join a merchant guild caravan," David explained. "That usually gets rid of the desire after a time. And of course we like to explore the world around us, but even then we don't wander very far. The farthest out from the valley I've been is three days beyond the Shaar, and I know of no one who has gone farther, personally."

"I myself have walked to the foot of that glacier," Temian nodded west. "And I helped explore seven days beyond the pass behind us. I did not climb the glacier, myself. It is old and full of hidden death, like your legend so clearly highlights."

"Seven days beyond the Shaar?" David marvelled. "What did you see?"

"Forest and mountains, rivers and game, but no sign of another soul," Temian said wistfully. "And the farther we went, the more we felt like we were walking away from the Mountain, not towards it."

David nodded. The world seemed suddenly so large and empty, except for the five hundred souls camped around him. He stilled himself and tried to listen for the Spirit within. A deep sense of peace flooded over him with a tint of expectation that sent a thrill through him.

"Tomorrow morning we'll have a baptism service," David declared. "Let your sister know so she doesn't come hunting me down."

Temian laughed. "Tell her yourself. Here she comes."

"I've picketed your horses, David," Kawani called out as she approached. "Now I want to be baptized!"

"Tomorrow morning," David laughed. "You will have to wait until tomorrow morning—and then I promise, no more waiting."

"But why?" the young woman demanded teasingly.

"Because I do not think you will be the only one. And it will do no good to have everyone crowding around the pool in the dark; someone will drown."

"Fine," she declared. "But I want to be first."

"You shall be first!" David declared through more laughter.

"Good!" She nodded and pointed back the way she had just come. "Simon has a fire going and I'm hungry, but he sent me to tell you two."

Temian and David laughed and followed her back to the fires of the camp. A sense of peaceful expectation settled over them all as night fell completely on the valley.

— 12 —

A Baptism of Water

The sunrise was still behind the Shaar Pass when Duncan and a small band of stragglers wandered into the camp. They were tired and footsore, having made the two-day journey to catch up in just under a day. True to his word, Duncan had brought in the stragglers on time.

David watched as the two dozen or so young people spread out to find various groups of friends and rest their exhausted legs. Duncan came over to their fire with a smirk on his face and another man in tow.

"That'll teach them not to be late," he declared as Simon handed them each a bowl of oatmeal. "I ran them like livestock most of the way here. But no one had to be left behind. Even Varanel here kept up."

"So I see." Simon's voice sounded a little brittle. "Although I never would have expected him to actually join us. What brings you here, Varanel?"

David looked the new man up and down. He was fairly tall with a fair complexion. Blond hair hung down and got in his eyes. He had a familiar look about him, but David couldn't place it.

"I decided I was wrong to dismiss you," Varanel admitted. "And then I heard about this David fellow and his story. To be honest, that still wasn't enough, but then I had a dream the morning you left and I decided that I had to come."

"A dream, you say?" Simon's eyebrows shot up. "What kind of dream?"

"It was unlike any dream I've ever had. And in it, I believe I met the Living God. He told me things that may be important to your success."

"What kind of things?" David cut in.

"I'm not comfortable saying right now," Varanel said as he turned to look David up and down. "You must be David. I'm here to help; that's what I can tell you."

"That must have been quite the dream," Simon said dryly.

David looked between the two men. There was something between them—some bad blood, as his father used to say. David felt a stirring in his gut about Varanel, something that didn't fit. He also had an odd feeling that he needed to protect this man, but that didn't feel right, either. Here was a man who said he'd met the Living God in a dream, and David needed to know more.

David decided to break the silence that had fallen on the group. "Everyone is welcome. And Varanel has decided to join us of his own accord. If he still wants to come with us up into the pass after this morning, I don't think we should hinder him."

"What do you mean, 'after this morning'?" Simon caught something in his tone.

"I am not sure." David looked down into the fire and searched for an explanation. "It's a feeling I have. The Living God wants to do something today. Something that will set us apart from others. I mean more apart than we already are."

They all looked at him, questions on their faces. Varanel had a look of sympathetic support as he just nodded. David felt something stir in his gut that he almost thought was jealousy. He thought about how he could explain himself better, but finally he just shook his head and waved them all off.

"I'm new to all of this, remember. I have no honest idea what is going on, or even what is going on in me. I know things I cannot explain."

"Well, we're all new to this." Temian gestured to encompass David and the valley around them. "So I guess we all have to trust the Living God. What is the plan for this morning, David?"

"Well, I'm thinking we'll gather everyone around the lower pool," David said, hoping no one would realize he was making this all up on the spot. "And I'll baptize Kawani, you, and Simon to start. That way you three can help me with whoever else wants to be baptized."

"Even with four of us, it's going to take a while to baptize everyone," Simon said.

"You can baptize me, as well," Varanel offered eagerly.

"Well, only those who want to be baptized should be baptized, for starters," David warned, ignoring Varanel's eagerness. "We can recruit a few others to help us as we go along. The ceremony is very simple."

"Enough talk!" Kawani boomed out in excitement. "Let's get this done!"

"Since you are so eager to get started, go out and tell everyone we will begin as soon as the sun clears the mountain." David shook his head to cut off her protest. "You'll be thankful for the sun when you come out of the water. That pool is going to be cold!"

"Come with me, Varanel!" Kawani demanded as she got up to leave. "You can tell me about your dream."

Varanel held up his bowl of food awkwardly but Simon simply took it and motioned him to go with the eager woman. Shrugging, he smiled at David and then followed Kawani out into the camp. Simon watched him go with hard eyes.

"Of all the people I swore would never join us, he was at the top of the list," Simon finally muttered.

"It is exceedingly odd to find him here," Temian agreed, but turned his eyes to David. "What do you think, David?"

Surprised, David just shrugged. What did he actually think of this late addition?

"Honestly, I don't know," he finally admitted. "My thoughts are muddied and confused about him, and I find his declaration of having a dream to be a little off."

"Varanel having a dream of the Living God is a little off," Simon agreed. "Back in the village he was a fawning, lazy bureaucrat dreaming of greatness."

"Yet there is something familiar about him," David mused, stung by Simon's harsh words for reasons he couldn't put his finger on.

"Maybe you see a bit of your old self in him?" Temian offered as he studied David's face thoughtfully.

"A bit of me?" David was immediately taken aback but then thought about it. "Maybe that's it. Maybe he reminds me of myself."

"From your description of the way you were tempted, I can assure you that Varanel would have gloriously failed where you passed," Simon snorted.

"Maybe." David felt a little irritated. "But the Living God rescued me from that. Maybe he's done the same or is doing the same with Varanel?"

Simon shrugged. "Maybe. But there is a difference between you two at the heart level—mark my words."

"We shall see." David felt suddenly challenged to prove Simon wrong.

Over five hundred young adults stood around the lower pool of Gellah Falls, waiting for David, Simon, and Temian as they made their way up from the camp below. Curiosity mixed with eager hunger was on every face as they parted to allow David to approach the water's edge. Kawani waited there, dressed in shirt and trousers, along with Varanel and half a dozen others.

The Presence of the Living God suddenly fell on David as he looked at the awaiting faces.

He raised his voice as he turned slowly to address the ring of people. "Brothers and sisters of the Klasma, welcome to a new beginning! The Living God himself has joined us here this morning to mark this turning point in each of your lives. You have been called out of many nations. You have fled before a ruthless enemy. You have wandered for years on a vague command and promise. The Mountain of the Living God is one final test away.

"But today is not about that test. Today the Living God wants to invite you into a new promise. He's offering you adoption into a new family. Today He is asking you to set aside your old lives, your old hopes, your old dreams. In return he offers you a new family, a new Kingdom, a new purpose. The Klasma, the fragments of old, will be fitted to gather into something new."

David removed his cloak and quickly stripped down to shirt and trousers. Bracing himself, he stepped out into the broad pool and waded out until he was in just over his waist. The biting cold of the mountain water caused him to hold his breath. He turned and motioned Kawani to join him.

"Days ago, I was given this ceremony by the Living God, when he appeared to me as a man named Joshua. He instructed me that I was to pass it on to any and all who wished to join me. Through this act of baptism, we surrender ourselves and acknowledge that we belong to and serve the Living God."

Kawani stood beside him with a questioning look.

"I'm going to dunk you," he whispered. "I've never done this before, so any help you can give me would be appreciated."

She nodded, her smile beaming as he clasped her hand and put his hand behind her back.

"Kawani," his voice carried out over the water, "do you submit yourself to the Living God, turning from your old ways and promising to serve Him and Him alone, all the days of your life?"

"I do!" she declared.

David pushed her back into the pool and then pulled her up again. The words that Joshua had spoken over him only days before were on his lips, even before she was fully upright.

"You went into the water a broken woman of sin, but you come out a child of the Living God! Receive now His Spirit."

The Presence of the Living God welled up in David, but seemed to explode in Kawani. Light seemed to radiate off of her as a spray of water from her hair caught the sun. She raised her hands as if to grab the sky and broke into song almost immediately. Her voice carried high into the cliffs, and everyone simply stared at her. David didn't recognize the words of the song, but he immediately understood it. It was a hymn to the Living God, and it rose from a soul finally alive and set free.

There was sudden movement around the pool and David had to raise his hands to stop the crowd from coming as one to be baptized. The hunger in the air was palpable.

"Let me now baptize Simon and Temian," he said quickly. "And they can also start baptizing others. I promise that everyone who wants to will be baptized this morning."

David motioned quickly to the other two men as they stripped down to their shirts and trousers. Kawani continued to sing, stopping only to laugh joyously before breaking into new verses. Simon waded out first, and David met him a little way from Kawani.

"You ready?" David saw the man's uncertainty as he watched Kawani from the corner of his eye.

"I do not understand what this is," Simon admitted. Then he tapped his gut. "But I know down here that it is the Living God."

David nodded. He asked Simon the same question he'd asked Kawani. Simon nodded.

"Words, Simon," David laughed.

"Yes!"

David plunged him into the pool.

Simon came up out of the water and David proclaimed the words that Joshua had spoken over him. Simon stared right through him like he didn't see him. David looked at him, concerned, and was about to call his name.

Leave him, a voice that wasn't a voice spoke to him, *I am showing him the truth of me.*

David shook his head. But a peace fell over him concerning Simon and he turned to Temian. The big man's excitement was almost greater than his sister's.

"I'm going to need your help, Temian," David said. "I can put you under the water but I'll never lift you back out without your help."

Temian nodded in understanding. David asked the question. Temian's voice boomed out across the water with his "yes!" David plunged the man into the pool and then began trying to pull him back out. Temian stayed under and almost threw David's footing on the stone bottom. He panicked briefly, and then the large man suddenly burst up out of the water with a great shout of joy.

"Great is the Living God! Worthy of all honour and all Glory!" His voice carried and harmonized with his sister's song as it lifted up the cliffs and across the valley.

David proclaimed the second part over Temian, completely drowned out by the other man. He looked over to the shore and saw that Kawani's little group had started organizing the people. Obviously she'd been planning and preparing for how they were going to organize so many baptisms. Kawani waved for one of her helpers to join her. David watched as a woman named Hanah waded out eagerly.

Kawani proved to be a good student, and in the span of asking the question she had the other woman under the water and then back out. Her voice sounded like the manifestation of joy as she declared her friend to be a child of the Living God. The other woman was weeping and hugging the tall woman tightly. Kawani looked over her friend's head to seek David's approval and he simply nodded. He didn't have to worry that Kawani would need further instruction.

"Come, Brother David." Temian slapped his shoulder. "There are many brothers and sisters to baptize, and many hands will make lighter work."

"What of Simon?" David looked over at the other man, who seemed lost in a trance. "We should get him to the shore. Whatever the Spirit of the Living God is doing, we shouldn't just leave him to freeze in the water."

Temian motioned to two men already wading into the water eagerly. They reluctantly went over to Simon and started to lead the oddly catatonic leader to shore. David quickly assured them that they could jump back to the front of the already huge line at the water's edge when they had him settled.

So began a process that seemed to stretch out into a timeless day. One by one a young person appeared before David. One by one they answered the question and were plunged into the cold pool. And one by one as they came up, they received the Spirit of the Living God.

The reactions coming back up seemed as varied to David as the people themselves. Combinations of peaceful, joyful, awed, and worshipful. Each person seemed to respond to the Spirit in their own way. Others took on the responsibility of baptizing their friends, and the pool was ringed by a dozen people receiving those still eager to become a part of this new family.

David paused to look around at the people in the pool with him. Joyous laughter and praises to the Living God echoed off the rocks and all but drowned out the falls behind them. The sun was several hours past noon, and the crowd of the waiting had dwindled to only a couple of dozen.

He watched as Varanel was baptized by Kawani. The man came up out of the water with a sputter, a look of wonder and something that almost looked like fear in his eyes. He smiled and thanked Kawani and then headed to the shore. David watched him make his way to a secluded spot, where he just sat down and stared up at the mountain above them.

David's thoughts were interrupted by the realization that someone was waiting for his attention. He looked down at the young man in front of him.

"My name is Kai," the man introduced himself. "I wish to be baptized. I surrender everything I am and everything I have to the Living God. I will serve him all the days of my life."

It felt like the Spirit of the Living God wanted to jump out of David's chest in response to the man's eagerness. He nodded and grasped the man by the shoulders. The memory of his baptism at the hands of Joshua came to his mind, and he plunged the smaller man deep into the pool. He barely had to pull to bring the man back up, and he declared him a child of the Living God. He released Kai, but was enveloped in a great bear hug.

"I will follow you as you follow him, David," Kai assured him.

"We will serve the Living God," David said awkwardly.

Kai nodded, a smile beaming from ear to ear. He looked around the pool and then announced he'd go prepare lunch for them.

David nodded and then looked around to confirm that they were almost done. Temian waded over to him, slung an arm over his shoulders, and started heading toward the gravel beach. David submitted to the unspoken guidance and they waded numbly to the shore.

"I can't feel anything below my waist," David said as they sat down on the sun warmed shore.

"Something warm to eat will be most welcome," Temian added. "But first we should check on Simon. He never returned to the pool."

"The Spirit was doing something different with him. But let's go see what he can tell us," David said.

They staggered to their feet and made their way up out of the bowl that held the pool. There were many people still hanging around and they found the going slow as each little group greeted them and spoke encouraging words. It did not take them long to find Simon, sitting beneath the shade of a tree overlooking the valley. There was a small group surrounding him but no one was talking. Simon shifted his gaze from the valley to them when they approached.

"Joshua sends his love, David," Simon said softly when he was close enough. "Now that I understand who he is, I find that declaration to be... everything."

"You saw him?" David found himself looking around for the other man.

Simon nodded. "I did. He took me away to meet him. It was like I simply left my body behind. I didn't understand before, but I do now."

"Understand what?" Temian pressed.

"Who He is," Simon admitted. "He was there the entire time, in the ancient writings, but we lost the ability to see Him, to know Him. It's His spirit that we carry now. He's restoring a people unto Himself."

"Simon, who is Joshua?" Temian asked.

"You know already." Simon shook his head in wonder. "Even when I say it, you'll realize that you know. David knows, although he does not understand the significance of who Joshua truly is."

David's thought flew back to that first night when he had met Joshua. The realization that he had felt. The awe that he had beheld God in physical form.

"He is the Living God in human form," David spoke out loud.

"How can that be? God is not man." Temian shook his head.

"And yet this man Joshua is just that—in nature the Living God, in form a man," Simon said. "I came up out of the water and immediately found myself standing before Him. He was dressed in white and His eyes shone like fire. He just studied me for some time and I couldn't say anything. I was frozen there.

"Finally he asks 'Do you know who I am?' I found I could talk and I said 'You are the one that David called Joshua.' He nodded and then extended His arm to a book laid open on a pedestal nearby. 'Do you know what this is?' He asked me. I went over to the book and looked down. To my shock, I realized I was looking at a passage of the holy texts. 'These are the Holy Texts,' I said in awe. 'Complete as you would understand them,' Joshua nodded.

"I reached out hesitatingly to turn the pages. There were many more texts than I had ever known bound into that one book. I knew that we had lost much of what had been written, but seeing that book, I finally understood how much. Joshua then came close and closed the book and put it into my arms. 'This book is a small record of who the Living God truly is, Simon.' His voice grew in power and flooded over me. 'Knowing what is in the texts helps you to learn about Me, but my desire is that you *know* Me. My desire is that everyone who would be called by My name would know Me.'

"The room dissolved into blinding light, and the book in my arms seemed to melt into me. His voice was everywhere, inside my head, ringing in my ears and thundering in my body. 'I will write My story on your heart, Simon, so you will be first among the Klasma to never fear losing My Word again.' And then stories and images passed before me, and I knew no passage of time until a short while ago. And then you two came up, and here we are."

They were all silent for a long time. There was a peace between them all. Finally, Temian stirred with a question.

"It's not that I do not believe you, Simon," he said. "I just don't understand how this Joshua is the Living God. What I mean is, why does the Living God represent Himself as Joshua?"

Simon thought for a moment, searching deep within his own thoughts to try to formulate his answer.

"Joshua is the bridge between the Living God and us. His name in ancient tongue means 'The Living God Saves.' He has other names; I remember them spoken, but He has chosen that name to be known to us. And it's through Joshua that we will find the Mountain of God and be able to go beyond."

"What is beyond the Mountain?" David asked in wonder.

"Everything," Simon smiled. "I do not even understand my own answer, but my heart says everything on this side of the Mountain is a shadow of what lies beyond."

"I thought the Mountain was the goal," Temian said in weariness.

"It is, Temian," Simon smiled at his friend. "When I say beyond I truly don't see it as walking past the Mountain into the ranges beyond. It's something both greater and completely different. But for us all right now, the task is to get to the Mountain."

"My heart is peaceful but my head is confused," Temian admitted.

"Welcome to the struggle," Simon laughed softly.

They were interrupted by Kai with an armload of food. They relieved him of his burden and they all sat back down and took turns talking about what each of their baptisms were like. Each story was a little different, David noted as he ate happily, but they all involved a meeting and feeling of what they collectively agreed was the Spirit of the Living God. The Presence that he realized had been with him since that afternoon in Joshua's clearing was now apparently with everyone else. And he didn't feel an ounce of jealousy, he mused.

The rest of the afternoon evolved into a celebration. The camp below the falls was full of new songs and shouts of praise. David and the others were quickly drawn down from their high spot to join in, and David marvelled at what he saw. It was much like a rowdy evening in a good pub, except there was no wine, no cider, and no walls or roof. Over five hundred people rejoicing in this strange new life they had been baptized into.

Gone was the weight of their past lives, the loss of family and homes. They were a new family, bound by the Spirit of the Living God into a new kingdom. And they were unrestrained in celebration of that reality.

Kawani seemed to be the party's master of ceremonies. She couldn't stop singing—she wouldn't have stopped singing even if she could have. Going from group to group, she would get everyone raising their voices. New songs, old songs made new—she was a fountain of joy and energy. She came over to David and embraced him.

"David, thank you for your obedience, Brother." She wept happy tears on his shoulder. "I am alive for the first time, free of my heaviness! I want to sing until my voice quits."

David was at a loss for words; he awkwardly hugged her back. He found himself struck in that moment with a loneliness and longing for his time, his Amatta Valley. The image of Nebaya in the common room of the Dancing Dove flashed through his mind. He sighed and gently let Kawani go. She released him and looked into his eyes. Her expression softened in compassion.

"I forget, you feel like you've been one of us for years, but for you the loss of family and friends is days old." She squeezed his arm, and a thought seemed to occur to her. "But they are not dead, they are only far, far ahead. And there is something in that. Something to hold on to."

She returned his confused smile with a beaming smile of her own.

"That puts a new song in my head. We love you, David. You are one of us. We are now family, and we have an Eternal Father."

David laughed then as she spun away and started singing a song about family lost and family found, and the Living God binding them all together in eternity. He sat back down and watched the celebration in a new contentment. He belonged here, even if he missed his time. And somehow he knew Kawani was right; his time wasn't gone, it was just a thousand years ahead.

── 13 ──

A BAPTISM OF FIRE

The light that surrounded Ra'ah was excruciatingly bright. At first it had burst forth from the great Maylak in front of him, sweeping everything away like a flood. But as the moments passed by, the light slowly grew all around him to match. He was encased in a world of pure light.

Slowly four dimmer forms spun out of the light and formed a semi-circle that included him. They were oriented around a point before them. A Presence descended over him. It was like the Calling he often felt inside, but as it increased there was a sense of dread about it. The light seemed to split like a curtain and Ra'ah felt the Presence come down on him like a great iron blanket. He fell to the floor with his face pressed into the cold stone as the unmistakable, indisputable Presence of the Living God stripped away every selfish ambition, every vain conceit, and left him utterly bare and defenceless against the One who judges all.

RA'AH.

His name wasn't spoken audibly, but filled him and the space around him with frightening power. He shuddered at the reality that the voice, if it could even be called that, was able to destroy him utterly. His mind spiralled downward in fear and met a surprising force rising up from the depth of his soul. His spirit—long ignored, often abandoned, underfed and crushed by daily life—arose within him in response to his name.

"Here I am, Lord," he croaked a whisper. "Do with me however you will."

The Presence shifted, never growing weaker, but suddenly he was cradled in an encompassing blanket of love that didn't hide the true nature of the One before him, but rather justified him before it. A love that protected better than armour, stronger than death. He swooned under it.

Ra'ah. I have seen your heart and I am pleased. The voice coursed over him and through him. *I knew you in your mother's womb and have set you apart as a shepherd. Go and raise up other shepherds to look after my flock.*

"I will do whatever you ask, though I do not know how," he said brokenly.

A hand touched his shoulder and he looked up to stare into the face of love.

ANGELIS.

Angelis shook under the power of the Presence that filled her and surrounded her in a liquid light. She knew immediately that she was in the Presence of the Living God. She knew she could be destroyed instantly in a wave of beauty and power. She knew above all that she was broken and unworthy to be here. And she accepted all of it because she was in the Presence of the One she loved more than life. And He knew her name.

"Your servant hears you, Lord," she whispered.

The voice's words filled her and surrounded her like a warm blanket. *Daughter, see today I am putting a new song in your heart and a new story for you to tell. And then I am going to send you to the nations to share them both, that all the world would come to know me.*

"Oh, Living God, yes." Ange's heart leapt in her chest. "Your servant hears you!"

She looked longingly up into the very face of love.

Daskow lay on the floor shaking in the Presence of the One. His soul laid bare, his every thought known, he shook at the realization that nothing in him or about him justified his life. He was by all rights dead already and awaiting judgement at the Living God's pleasure.

DASKOW.

"I am here." Daskow forced himself to speak. "All that I was, all that I am, and all that I ever could be is yours."

I know, Daskow. The voice swept him utterly out of awareness of his body or surroundings.

He found himself pulled through a universe of images. He couldn't even put an idea to what he was seeing. An explosion of violence and light with no sound. A burning ball of fire hanging in a star-filled void. An orb of incredible beauty spinning in the same blackness. And suddenly he was watching people, nations, city after city that rose in splendour to fall in flame and ruin. He would have been driven mad, he suddenly realized, but he was being held by the One. The images stopped as suddenly as they started.

I am the First and the Last. Your hunger for knowledge begins and ends with Me. I have heard the cry of your heart, and it pleases Me to give you what you have asked. What I teach you, be diligent to teach others. Teach nothing that I have not taught you, however, and pass on the warning.

Daskow sensed the shift in the Presence around him, and he tentatively looked up into the loving embodiment of all Wisdom and Knowledge.

Nebaya lay face down under the Presence of the Living God. Soul laid bare, she made no attempt to hide herself or who she was. She made no pretence in what she might deserve. She trusted entirely in the goodness and holiness of the One who had brought her here. To live would be mercy and love. To die would be justice but still love. She recognized almost immediately in the power of the Presence that in all things the motive was love.

But not a fuzzy love. It was an all-consuming love, terrible in its power and its ability to transcend feeling. It made the word almost foreign. In the Presence of the Living God was a love that would not refuse to sentence justly. Would punish rightly. Would mourn the loss of the accused without staying that One's hand.

NEBAYA.

She became as a dead woman under the weight of the voice that was everything but simple sound. She wondered if she could even speak; she wondered if she'd ever speak again. She was suddenly and acutely aware of how unclean her words often were. She was loath to speak now. She could not speak in the Presence of the Holy One.

She felt burning heat against her lips, pain like fire that passed into her, burning her chest and her throat. Her vocal cords were suddenly on fire. And the heat burned into her very soul, skipping memory to memory across a lifetime of quick words and hot retorts.

See, I have cleansed your lips. Now I can put my words in your mouth.

"Great is the Living God and greatly deserving of all praise," she whispered, surprised she could say anything after the fire.

I have chosen you, daughter, to be first among the nations to speak My words. I will raise around you a company that you will train to hear Me and speak as you do. And remember: in whatever you say or do, let it be done in love.

"Teach me, Lord." Nebaya's heart leapt in her chest and she looked up into the face of love.

Anatellia shook under the Presence of the Living God. The light was like liquid fire, burning her without consuming her. She knew she should be destroyed in this Presence. No, much more than destroyed—obliterated. She'd dared to serve the Living God. Now she understood the word "terror" and found it woefully weak.

ANATELLIA.

The voice that wasn't a voice washed over her like a wave of fire, burning away all thought and pretence and leaving her single of mind. Even should she cease to be, she would serve the One who spoke her name.

"Your servant hears, Lord," she gasped.

What would you give to serve Me, child?

"Everything," she declared.

Everything is a lot more than you understand. How will you give Me what you do not understand?

"By giving it to you a piece at a time, as I come to understand it," she said.

Understand, child, that what you give I will take and use.

With the words came a flash of understanding. She saw the trap that she herself had built almost immediately. It wasn't clever, but it had worked on her since she'd fled her mother's house so many years ago. She would abandon the Anatellia she was to serve the Living God, by wandering the valley as some new Anatellia. She really would give everything to serve the Living God, but she had actually convinced herself that the Living God would take what was offered and destroy it. In place of the old, He would give her a whole new life in return.

Her mind raced through a dozen arguments. The horror of who her mother was molding her to be came to the front of her thinking, forming an image of herself that she had tried desperately to destroy. That could not be her calling. That person could not be who the Living God wanted.

The Presence around her simply waited. She saw the horrible truth. The Presence shifted around her and filled her, but would not touch that image that mocked her.

Will you truly give me everything, child?

"I will. Take it." She had one choice she would make. All other choices were anathema to her very being.

The Presence of the Living God moved into that space that she had guarded for so many years. A new revelation wormed through the hardened image of herself that she hated so much. This truly was her calling: not to be what her mother had tried to make her, but to become the woman that the Living God had called her to be. A leader, a strategist, a servant of the people. She saw so clearly her role in the group of five: how the Living God had kept and nurtured what she desperately wanted to destroy to spite her mother. A wave of sorrow washed over her. Sorrow for trying to destroy herself.

A wave of peace washed through the Presence, and she looked up through tears to see the face of love looking back at her.

A VERY HIDDEN ROAD

The camp of the Klasma woke with the sunrise, full of hope and eagerness. Every one of them was sure they would be on the final road to the Mountain of the Living God by nightfall. Even David stared excitedly at the tree-lined slope of the mountain that rose up alongside the Shaar Pass. The path was there and with five hundred sets of eyes they would find it.

They broke the camp into groups of twenty-five, and then each group chose a leader. Those leaders gathered excitedly around David as he recounted in detail his sister's story and their own attempts to find the trail. He went over the layout of the pass above them and explained that the trailhead had to be somewhere between their camp and the top of the pass where he and his two older brothers had realized that their sister had become lost.

He pointed up. "Somewhere on that mountain is the trail that will lead us to the Valley of Death and the Mountain beyond."

Once they had a plan and each leader understood his group's place, the leaders returned to their groups and everyone headed up the slope into the trees and the pass. David thought the plan was simple: spread out and climb. Eventually they would come across the trail as it ran along the slope, leading up above the pass and eventually around the mountain. With this many eyes, even the most hidden trail ought to reveal itself.

He took a small group consisting of Kai, Varanel, and Simon up into the pass to get a look at the summit. He knew there was no path out of the pass at the summit, but he wanted to see if he might be able to spot the trail climbing up into the mountain peaks from there.

It took considerably longer than he remembered to reach the top. A thousand years of hunters and adventurers would make a pretty clear trail, but the pass was a heavily wooded nightmare now. After getting them caught in the third thicket in twenty minutes he finally gave up the lead to Kai, who was a much better tracker and woodsman. With Kai's leading they got to the summit around noon. They came out of the trees into a relatively flat meadow that extended for a couple of hundred paces and gave them unobstructed views of both sides of the pass. Simon looked up the slope and whistled.

David followed his eyes. The summit looked very much the same as in his time. The mountain that they were currently searching towered up on their left. Another peak rose in front of them to the right. Between them rose an impossibly steep and narrow cut that disappeared far above them in a series of cliffs. According to Anatellia, the narrow valley continued far up into the mountains beyond, with a narrow track clinging to the left side.

David scanned the mountainside for any sign of a trail. He recognized the zones that it had to be in, but nothing revealed the path. He also realized that the trail had to be well above the tree line by the time it came into the pass in order to be able to climb over the broken rift between the two mountains. Varanel moved to stand beside him as he studied the mass of rocks in front of them.

"You're saying there is a trail up that?" Varanel asked incredulously.

"I believe there is. A trail wide enough for a horse and a ten-year-old girl."

The other man snorted as he studied the slope with its cliffs and overhangs. A seasonal creek obviously flowed between the two ridges but it was dry now. After several long minutes of consideration Varanel continued. "Most of us would break our necks trying to climb up into that from here. And you said that in a thousand years, no one has found a trail up there except your sister."

A sudden realization struck David. "Well, what I meant was that I had never met anyone except my sister who even claimed there was a path up there. But that doesn't mean no one else has found it in a thousand years. It just means that no one found it and then returned to talk about it."

"Equally distressing." Varanel gave David a significant look.

"We'll find it," David reassured him. "You'll see."

"And I hope it will not be the last thing I see," Varanel shot back gently.

To David's disappointment, they searched all that day without finding any trail that led them above the pass. They scoured the ridge all the way up into the pass but every hopeful lead led back down into the pass or simply dropped off a cliff. The mountain sides were simply too steep, with great rock overhangs cutting off ascent and loose rock threatening to turn ankles or send the searchers sliding down the slopes of the mountain.

Dusk brought everyone back to camp, dejected and forlorn. The excitement of the morning was all but gone. The leaders sat in a great circle around the fire and discussed their findings. The mountain, it was agreed, was quite an inhospitable pile of stone. Covered by scree and overhanging cliffs both above and below the tree line, it threatened everyone who set foot on it. If there was a trail leading up into the high country it was highly probable that it didn't exist yet. And many doubted it could even exist after a thousand years of wear and change.

"Is it possible it's on another mountain, or another slope?" Temian offered.

"What I know," David said in exasperation, "is that a ten-year-old girl on a horse got separated from her three brothers at some point between the river where we had last seen her and the top of the pass where we realized she was missing. It was foggy and rainy and she admitted that her horse was doing all of the guiding. So I have no idea where they wandered between the river and the summit."

"Is it possible she and the horse wandered past you all in the fog and ascended some path on the other side of the pass?" one of the leaders asked.

"Not at all likely, for a couple of reasons." David shook his head. "First, the trail in my day cuts through very similar forest as you see today. She could not have simply slipped into the forest and passed us through the brush without making a lot of racket. And we were there to hunt, so we were listening carefully anyway. Second, we had set a rather brisk pace up into the pass. If she had wandered off the trail, climbed the slope, overtaken and passed us before we noticed her missing at the summit meadow, she would certainly have been aware of it. From her story, she was lulled in the saddle by a horse that never gave her a reason to pay attention. At least not until she was some way up the narrow trail."

"And you believe her?" Varanel asked quietly. "I mean, there was fever involved, if I understood your telling correctly. Can we trust her account?"

"I do," David admitted. "And it was the exposure on the mountain trail that got her sick. And I just... well, I feel it's true."

"It's just that it would be easier if we had someone or something to corroborate the story," Varanel pressed.

"The only other witness is that black horse picketed over there." David gestured toward his horses. "Because that's her horse, and the only other creature I know of who has passed that way. Good luck."

There was then uncomfortable silence for some time. No one wanted to suggest that David's story was somehow wrong or inaccurate, but even he was forced to consider that it was a second-hand story, and a lot of information simply wasn't available.

Simon finally cleared his throat and everyone turned expectantly toward him. "I suggest we expand our search tomorrow. We'll start at the bend of the river and move up both sides of the pass. I understand David's reasoning for focusing on that mountain above us, but let's eliminate all possibilities."

"I feel like we need to trust the Living God," Kawani cut in. "We all believe the trail exists. We know it's well-hidden. So well-hidden that David knows of only one person in a thousand years that has seen it. What made us think we would find it simply by looking for a day?"

"What makes us think that looking for two days will be any different?" Varanel countered.

"I cannot speak for all of you," David said softly after a long silence. "But I will keep looking until I find that path. I know it's up there somewhere. And I have no other path to take. So tomorrow we will search as Simon suggests and continue to trust that the Living God will reveal the path to us."

"And if he doesn't?" Varanel said.

"Then I will go to sleep tomorrow night still knowing that He is the Living God. And I will wake up the next day and keep looking." David felt his frustration break loose. "I have only really known Him for a short time, but He has known each of us all of our lives. I do not believe He will keep the path from us, but even if He does I will continue to try to do this one thing that He's asked of me. Because in this one thing I find more hope and fulfillment than a lifetime of my own selfish ambitions."

"It's easy for you—you haven't left behind family and friends," Varanel retorted hotly.

David felt his blood burn. He opened his mouth to respond but a hand grasped his arm. He looked down to see Kawani look up at him with understanding in her eyes. She just shook her head gently and he sat down.

"Varanel"—Temian's tone was full of rebuke—"David has lost his entire world, or have you forgotten his story?"

"It's true that I have been plucked out of my entire world," David said before Varanel could respond. "And I've been thrust here, with all of you. And the one who has done this to me has made Himself known to me. Even if I were to try, I could not be resentful to Him. To be honest, I have allowed myself little time to work through what has happened to me, or where I am, or even where it all might lead.

"But in all of it, all of this, I have one wild, crazy belief. A hope that refuses to die inside of me, like the stubborn embers of a fire. I have experienced the Living God. I have met Him in the man, Joshua, who is not a man. And I hold to this wild and crazy idea that in all of this there is no loss that surpasses His purpose for me—for all of us. My hope and future lies ahead, up that mountain—on my hands and knees if I have to. But you all have to wrestle with what you will do and how far you're willing to go."

There was a wave of silent nods around the fire. There was really nothing else to be said and they all knew it. Slowly they left the fire and went to spread the news of the plan for the next day.

An attitude of determination seemed to replace the eagerness of the previous day. The group leaders met at David's fire and worked out a grid that would cover both sides of the pass all the way to the summit. One by one, the groups left to continue the search until David found himself alone with Kai in the camp.

He sat in silence and traced the tree line up the mountain and into the pass. Going over Anatellia's story in his head, he tried to reconcile her story with what he could see. But the fact was that they hadn't found a useful trail anywhere on the mountain. And above the tree line were treacherous cliffs and scree slope, consistent with his sister's story.

In frustration he got up and started climbing up toward the falls. Kai followed him like a loyal puppy, respecting his desire to be in silence, but not to be alone. They picked their way around the bottom pool and climbed up into the steep cliffs past the first and second falls. Shortly, they found themselves beside the pool below the third waterfall, staring into the rush of water as it poured out of the cave set deep into the side of the cliff.

This cave was definitely not yet the grotto familiar to David—in this time, it was narrow and full of the rushing mountain river. He contemplated trying to climb up into it and quickly discarded the idea. There was a small amount of cave roof visible above the water, but the flow was too swift and too deep. It would simply sweep him into the pool and then almost immediately over the second and first falls. And that would end his service to the Living God fairly quickly.

He looked across to the mountain that now partially obscured the pass where the Klasma were even now searching for his mystery path. There was something nagging him, something wrong about the mountain—or was it something else? He shook his head and sat down in the sunlight on the shore of the pool. How could there be a trail that no one could find? How could his sister's story be correct, and yet over five hundred people searching couldn't find her trail?

He lay back, suddenly very tired. In minutes he was sound asleep.

He woke with a start to find himself in shade. The sun had moved across the sky as he slept, and it was now obviously afternoon. The dream that woke him up immediately started to fade, but he shivered anyway. He'd dreamed of his sister, ten years old, daydreaming as her horse plodded through a forest thick with fog. He tried to shout at her to pay attention, but he found he had no voice in the dream.

The horse, for its part, had driven him crazy with its wandering. Smooth as the fog itself, he watched as the horse simply wandered through groves of trees and meadows, often doing great wide circles that drove the dreaming David crazy. At first he thought the dream was trying to tell him something, but the third time the horse passed the same fallen tree he realized that the horse wasn't leading him anywhere.

He stretched and stood up. Kai was nowhere to be seen, but that wasn't really surprising. He had probably figured David wasn't going anywhere and had gone back down to find lunch.

David walked to the cliff edge and stared out at the valley below. The view was the same but different. From up here he could see the mat of forest stretching out below him and flowing up the sides of the mountains. He looked across the valley for the knoll of trees on the other side of the pass that his brothers always called "the Wart." Sheltered yet offering a view, it was always a great spot to camp.

His eyes did fall on a knoll, but it was too high on the mountain, above the treeline. He looked in confusion farther down the mountain but couldn't see the Wart. Realization slowly dawned on him. This forest was a thousand years too new. He understood that trees, although long-lived, didn't last a thousand years. Much of the forest of his Amatta Valley was tended wilderness. Throughout the long centuries there had been fires. Woodsmen in every generation had culled wood from the length and breadth of it. That was why the valley forest seemed so unexpectedly foreign to him.

And now as he looked out off the top of the falls he realized that there was a problem with their search for the path. The trees were lower on the slopes here, for whatever reason, than they would be in a thousand years. So the path was actually higher on the mountain, above the current treeline. And so it must start climbing out of the pass earlier.

He started back down the falls to the camp below. As he reached the pool at the bottom of the first waterfall, the sun suddenly disappeared behind a cloud and the ominous roll of thunder echoed into the valley. Looking up, he saw the mass of darkness coming over the peaks above him. A summer storm had snuck up on them and was about to remind them just how small they truly were. He all but ran back into the camp to prepare.

He caught Kai leaving the camp just as he entered it. The look of relief on the young man's face told David he had been coming to get him. He felt a sudden surge of appreciation for this unexpected friendship. Kai fell in beside him as he hurried into camp.

"No one should have left their gear lying around, but let's check," David said. "There is nothing worse than a wet bedroll."

"Already being done," Kai assured him. "I was just coming to get you before you got stuck on the cliffside in a storm."

"I don't deserve your devotion, Kai," David laughed.

"None of us deserve what the Living God has given us," Kai laughed back. "As for me, well… you're stuck with me!"

David laughed again, and they made their way back to the shelter of the fire to wait out the storm. The wind had picked up and another peal of thunder echoed in the valley. The trees where they had set up camp were large and seasoned, and David settled in to ride out the storm under their protective boughs.

He didn't have to wait long. Mountain storms were notorious that way. At least down the Amatta where the valley widened, you could see them coming and prepare. In this narrow part, they almost seemed to leap over the peaks to fall on the unsuspecting.

Lightning arched across the sky in great sheets and the thunder followed almost immediately behind. The forest that had grown dark as the storm settled overhead was lit up with flash upon flash. Kai sat near the fire and stared up in wonder at the sky above, oblivious to the need for shelter until the rain suddenly broke over them in a torrent.

David watched from under the shelter of the trees as Kai laughed and caught the rain in his mouth. He really was carefree to the point of being oblivious. Even as the lightning increased to the point that David couldn't tell where one clap of thunder ended and another started, Kai refused to come under shelter. He got up and started dancing around the fire, arms raised in worship to the Living God. He stopped only briefly to add fuel to the fire to keep it from being doused.

David watched the other man and realized he was feeling something he would never have expected in a thousand thunderstorms. He was jealous. The realization made all other thoughts flee out of his mind. He was jealous of Kai's child-like display of adoration to the Living God.

Something stirred inside of him. The presence that he had come to recognize as the stirring of the Spirit within him rose up in curiosity and seemed to touch the jealousy, sending the feeling scattering out of his head. David realized that he didn't have to be jealous—that jealousy was something from another life. With a laugh he pushed himself up and joined Kai in dancing around the fire. The storm became a display of the power of the Living God.

The storm passed as quickly as it had appeared, and the two men pulled a log over to the fire to sit and try to dry off. There was a deep sense of peace over the valley as the storm rumbled in the distance, heading toward the broad Amatta and the new settlement of Kathik.

Groups started returning almost immediately; their calls through the forest seemed loud in the post-storm calm. David and Kai simply sat and waited, neither of them too eager to break the strong presence of the Living God that had come to permeate their campsite.

Simon found them sitting there some time later. He stepped into the small clearing and stopped to stare at them. They stared back and waited.

"None of the groups coming back have anything to report," Simon finally declared. "There are a few that are preparing to go back. There is a large group planning to move beyond the pass in the morning."

David felt the stirring within him. There was clarity in the plan. He just nodded and offered a spot on their log.

Simon looked at him questioningly. "No thoughts?"

"Lots of thoughts," David said. "But for now let's just sit and let the Living God speak to us."

Simon was about to retort but just stopped. He nodded and came around the fire to sit with them. All three sat in silence for some time.

Simon looked at the ground and shook his head. "Why does it look like someone's been dancing around the fire?"

David and Kai broke out in laughter.

"You wouldn't understand," David said finally.

They were saved having to explain by the arrival of Temian, Kawani, and a dozen other group leaders. Everyone was soaked and dejected and came to encircle the fire.

Kawani looked at the three men sitting on the log and shook her head. "You three have the only fire left in the camp," she scolded. "You need to share the flame."

"It's not my fire," David teased. "It belongs to the Living God. And you may take freely of it."

"Share the log, little brother." Kawani made them shift down so she could sit beside him. "I'm in no hurry to run off with the fire right now. Did Simon tell you that some people are planning on going back?"

"Yes."

"And you're going to let them?"

"Let them?" David said. "I have no right or authority to stop them. And I do not believe it would be wise to. The opportunity to turn back is almost gone and this may be the last one."

"Maybe we have not found the trailhead because there is still hesitation in the group?" Temian mused out loud.

"Maybe," David agreed and looked around. "I think we need to offer anyone who is hesitant to continue the opportunity to return."

"But that doesn't help us find the trail," the woman named Hanah pointed out in frustration.

"I am more confident than ever that we will find it," David said. "But once we do, there is no turning back. We will either pass through to the Mountain or we will die in the attempt."

Many of the leaders looked at him with uncertainty, but everyone kept their peace.

"Let's tell everyone to meet us at the lower pool just before sunset," David continued. "We'll offer that those who want to go back can leave tomorrow morning."

"And what about the plan to look beyond the pass?" Simon asked.

"We will not need to: the trail head is here, on this side," David said confidently.

Simon shrugged. David realized he wasn't asking for himself, but for the ears of the leaders around the fire.

"I'll address that idea tonight as well." David looked at Simon, but spoke loud enough for everyone. "Let's go out and tell the others the plan."

They all nodded and drifted away from the fire in small groups, leaving the four on the log alone with their thoughts.

"There is such a presence of worship in this campsite," Kawani suddenly blurted. "I've been trying to figure out how to describe it, but that is the closest description I can come to. Does anyone else feel that?"

"Mm-hmm," David nodded. "Kai and I noticed that earlier."

Simon's snort was cut short as Kai deftly bumped him off the end of the log. Kawani looked down the line of friends quizzically.

"Next storm, Kawani, next storm," Kai said reassuringly as he pulled Simon back up onto the log.

Kawani knew she was missing something but she just shrugged. She started singing softly to herself, and when they looked at her with encouragement, she sang the verse louder. David realized he recognized the tune, but she had changed the words, turning an old nursery song into a hymn of praise to the Living God. They let her sing it through once, and then when she started over, they joined in. Their voices flowed through the trees and after a while they heard voices return from other parts of the camp. After a while she stopped and listened with joy as her song continued through the forest. Harmony and melody entwined and the song grew a life of its own.

She stood up and picked a brand out of the fire.

"Time to spread the fire," she whispered.

With a wave and a skip she left their campsite, her voice rising to blend with the choir all around them.

The sun was hanging above the mountains at the far end of the valley when they all finally gathered in the great bowl of the lower pool. David watched them all gather from a rock by the water. The sound of the falls drumming the water drowned out much of the chatter as everyone waited for the meeting to begin.

Simon came over the edge of the bowl from the direction of the camp. His eyes scanned the crowd until they locked with David's, and he nodded to confirm that they were all there.

The Spirit of the Living God had been prodding David all afternoon, reminding him of what had already been said. As he stood up on the rock and held his hands up for silence, he went over in his head what needed to be said now.

"Everyone, I know you are all tired and discouraged." His voice, buoyed by the acoustics of the natural bowl, carried from one side to the other. "And some of you are ready to give up and return to your friends and family who stayed behind in the valley."

He saw everyone looking around; a few people were nodding. He marvelled at how quickly they had become discouraged. He had to admit that before his encounter with Joshua he would have gone right along with them. But that experience had changed him. Hadn't it changed them as well?

The presence of the Living God suddenly fell on him, and the next part of his speech was swept from his mind. He realized later that the words he spoke instead weren't truly his.

"I tell you now, any of you with that hesitation in their heart, you need to leave. Go with our love and blessing, but go. If anyone takes the path ahead with a double mind, they will surely die. It is better for us all if you return to the remnant with what you have learned and experienced. Who here can say what influence you will have in the future of the valley? But not all of you here now are supposed to go forward. Decide now and be certain in your hearts."

David looked at the faces staring at him. In many eyes he saw fierce determination, but in some there was embarrassment and doubt. These were the few that his message was for.

"It is not a failure to return," he comforted them. "The Spirit of the Living God provides the faith and courage to continue. In some of you, that faith and courage isn't there. Consider that He does not wish you to continue. But having received the baptism with us, being bound with us in the Kingdom of the Living God, you too can contribute to that kingdom.

"And who can say other than the Living God whether your influence keeps the memory of the Living God alive for a thousand years? Without you, my sister and her friends might never have been out wandering the valley, might never have been trying to answer the Call. And what is the Call if it's not the desire in each of our hearts to serve and experience the Spirit of the Living God? Those who return to the remnant tomorrow are my ancestors. You will be reminders to them of something more, something that they stop just short of."

"But would we not be stopping just short as well?" Varanel called out. "Would we not be doing exactly what you accuse the remnant of doing?"

"Weren't you all baptized?" David asked.

The people nodded.

"Didn't you all receive the Spirit of the Living God upon baptism?" he pressed.

They all nodded, some shouting in agreement.

"Then you all must turn to the Spirit within you and ask, 'Am I to stay or go?'" David concluded. "You have come this far, but now there are those who realize they do not have, or rather they have not been given, the ability to go on. But it's not an issue of failing to go on or turning back. Those who return are not going back. They are going forward to help preserve a people—the people from whom I have been plucked out. A people who will once again be called to the Mountain. I'm standing here as proof that you will make a difference, that you will succeed. Those of us that continue, it is *our* influence that is a mystery to me."

There was much nodding and murmuring after that. David raised his hands one more time to bring silence.

"Take the time to pray, to seek the Living God, each of you. Tomorrow we will say goodbye to those called to return. And I know we will find the path after that."

He stepped down off the rock and headed through the crowd toward the rim of the bowl. Kawani and a few others joined him. Kawani had a guilty look on her face, but David did not think it was doubt about continuing on. He came out of the bowl and looked back at the pass with its elusive trail. In the light of the setting sun the mountainside was bathed in fire, the trees on the lower slopes casting long shadows against the rock. He squinted. There was something moving on the mountain above the treeline.

"David..." Kawani stepped up beside him, her face bathed in the sunlight, "I have to tell you something. It's about the horses."

"They pulled their pickets during the storm," David stated quietly and flatly.

"Yes, but... how did you know? No one else does."

David pointed past her shoulder toward the mountain and the pass.

"That stupid horse is two for two," he said.

They all turned to follow his gesture. High above the treeline, two dark shapes were moving across the impossible steep slope of the mountain. A black shape leading a grey shape. Kawani gasped.

"The trail is higher than the treeline in this time," David explained. "The trailhead doesn't start in the pass; it must start in the forest somewhere below us where that ridge comes to meet the cliffs of the falls."

Kawani shook her head. "I don't see any trail where they are walking. How are we going to find them with night approaching?"

"We aren't. They'll either turn around on their own or just keep walking until they find the Mountain themselves."

"What if they fall off the trail in the dark?" Kawani asked anxiously.

"Seriously, Kawani," David said in exasperation, "they are out of our reach either way. Usually, I'd say horses are smarter than people. My horse is a regular trail horse in the mountains. But Storm has always been another story. If it wasn't my sister's beloved horse, Mother would have sold it long ago."

15

THE MOUNTAIN OF THE LIVING GOD

E ven after the blinding radiance disappeared around him and he felt his feet come to rest once more on solid ground, Ra'ah found that he could not see properly. Like stepping out of the sunlight into a dark, windowless room, he found himself blinking and trying to get his eyes to adjust. The last image in his head had been of the most glorious, beautiful being he had ever seen, and it seemed burned into his sight and memory.

"Where are we now?" Ange's voice murmured from beside him. "I can't see anything."

"Close your eyes for a minute," Daskow said. "Wherever we just were, the light was very, very real."

Ra'ah closed his eyes as his friend had instructed. His vision may not have been working, but his ears were just fine. He heard the breeze through grass and a stream nearby. He heard the song of mountain birds. He even fancied he heard conversation far away—perhaps there was a village nearby.

He opened his eyes tentatively and found he could see around him, although everything was still quite blurry. He saw the other four standing beside him. They were on a road. He saw the streambed in front of him and across it a lush valley that rose to tall peaks.

"Living God," Daskow breathed reverently.

Ra'ah nodded. He wondered if everyone had experienced what he had. The presence, the voice, the image of the man. Had they all heard the words the Living God had spoken to him?

He blinked rapidly and found the blurriness disappeared quicker. He breathed in the pure, fresh mountain air. He looked up at the mountain across the valley from where he stood. It was tall and imposing, but it still looked like any other mountain.

"Ra'ah, turn around," Ange whispered.

He turned around and gasped. They stood on a broad paved road that led straight through a pair of city gates into a walled city that made Kathik look like a farmer's barn. Nestled between two great spurs of the massive mountain, with white stone walls that spread from either side of the gates from ridge to ridge, the city climbed up the mountain slopes, clinging in stone tiers, almost to the very summit.

"The Mountain of the Living God," Anatellia declared in awe.

The mountain was in every way more than he had expected, but the City… the City was like nothing he had ever dreamed. Nowhere in his collective memory had he heard of such a place. *Why, this city could hold a thousand Kathiks,* he mused. He pulled his eyes from the dizzying heights and looked at the valley stretched out below the mountain. Cultivated fields full of grain could be seen extending down the long valley, and buildings were dotted everywhere; to the right of the City, nestled against its walls, were enough buildings to be a village.

The gates into the City were wide open, and he could see into the lower parts of the City to reveal a wide road and many, many buildings, right up to the distant first tier where the City started climbing the steepening mountain slopes.

In everything he was seeing, in everything he was taking in, something suddenly struck him as odd. He turned to the others as he worked out his question.

"Someone is coming out of the gates," Daskow interrupted him.

16

Into the Valley of Death

D
awn saw the entirety of the Klasma gathered at the river to say goodbye to over thirty of their number. This small group of men and women had decided that they simply were not called to go farther, and taking David's warnings to heart, they said their goodbyes and gave farewell hugs through tears. The clouds above them hung heavy and grey, as if the sky would shed tears of its own.

David took the opportunity to speak to every one of them, encouraging them that they were going to make a difference. They had to make a difference. He found it almost amusing that he could be hugging and saying goodbye to someone who could be a great, exceedingly great grandparent. There was some laughter when he mentioned it, but still so many tears.

David could put himself in their shoes. He understood how torn they must feel. But deep in his heart he knew they could not come. That if they did, they would be mourned anyway. He looked up at the mountain behind them and wondered if any of the others staying might be lost before they reached the other side.

They all watched as the small group of returning Klasma waded the Valley River and set off back to the remnant. Once they were gone out of sight, the crowd turned to the leaders expectantly. David had sent word to all that they were to strike the camp and be ready to move, and they were eager to see what came next.

"Well, thank the Living God for yesterday's rain," David told his friends. "Let's go find out how those horses got onto that mountain."

The night before, David had gathered with the other leaders and told them about the horses. They were all a mixture of incredulous and stunned. The good news, they all realized, was that horses don't hide their tracks. And especially after a good rain, those tracks would be quite evident. So the plan that morning was quite simple: find the tracks leading from the camp and follow them to the trailhead.

They returned through the camp and found the trail easily enough, but the hoofprints led at first away from the mountain. The groups spread out from that point and made their way up the slope. The trail returned quite suddenly under David's feet and cut back up the slope toward the falls. It dead-ended in a scree slope.

"Now where?" Varanel muttered from beside him as Temian, Kawani, Kai, and Simon spread out along the fan of rocks.

David shook his head and looked up the slope. The slide of scree filled a small flume, with cliff on the left and treed slope on the right. He started walking along the slide to the right and found signs of the horses again. Excitedly, he followed hoofprints around until the scree slope flattened out and then fell off a short drop of fifteen feet. Imprinted in the stone was a clear sign that the horses had crossed there.

"Good place to break a leg," Kawani noted as she looked at the slope.

"Horses made it; so can we," David assured her.

Proving his point, he stepped out onto the scree. The stones shifted under his feet but didn't slide. The slope wasn't steep enough. Carefully he made his way across the twenty strides between him and the brush on the other side of the slide. He stepped between two tall shrubs that dangled broken branches, indicating the horses' passage. Before him was a clear line across the steep slope of horse hoofprints, angled upward straight and true.

"What do you see?" Kawani asked from behind him.

He crouched and stared in wonder at the grass-covered slope in front of him. A trail, evident only by the flattening of the slope as it rose up the mountain, became evident to his eyes.

"I see a trail," he said dryly.

Kawani pushed through the bush to stand beside him and stared up the side of the mountain. Her foot came off the narrow trail and she slid a bit before regaining her footing. David took several strides up the trail, following the horse prints. To his right the mountain rose steeply, to his left it dropped away to the trees below. But in a strip no wider than his shoulders, the grade was level enough to keep a traveller from sliding down the slope.

"Amazing," he marvelled.

"Nothing uses it," Kawani pointed out as she squatted to look past him up the trail. "Not even animals. That's why we couldn't see it—it blends in."

Kai came through the brush, with Simon and Varanel in tow.

"Everyone's starting to gather down there," Kai pointed out. "Do you want them up here?"

David shook his head. "No, not yet." He pondered the next move. "We will have to lay out some ground rules first. Five hundred pairs of feet on this slope are going to tear it up something awful."

"David…" Simon waited for his attention and smiled encouragingly once he got it. "This is not our first climb. We've done over four years of this."

"I'm worried none of us has done something like this, Simon," David confessed, although he returned the smile.

"Is this really it?" Simon asked the question on all of their minds.

"I believe it is." David pointed at the grass-covered slope. "In a thousand years, imagine the trees that could cover this slope. I could see my sister and her horse wandering up here in a heavy fog. And once here, there'd be no place to safely turn on horseback."

Simon pointed at the sky. "The next question: do we go back down and wait for better weather?"

David looked up at the heavy grey sky pensively. His eyes followed the trail up to where it topped a small ridge and disappeared from sight. Could he scout ahead? Was that allowed?

"I say we go on. We've found the trail; let's get this done," Varanel declared hotly.

"What will rain do to the trail?" Kawani's eyes strayed to the foot mark she'd made when she stepped off the path. "I don't particularly relish the idea of getting caught high on a mountain in the pouring rain."

"Kai?" David looked at him. "What do you think?"

"It is not raining now," Kai pointed out. "It might rain in an hour, or it might never rain. We could set camp back up and sit in the rain for days. Or sit there waiting for it to rain for days."

"You are absolutely no help," David shook his head.

"I think it's your decision, David," Simon said. "You were given the job of leading us. What does the Spirit say?"

David closed his eyes to shut out as much distraction as possible. The presence that he associated with the Spirit of the Living God seemed distant on the side of the mountain, drowned out by his own anxious need to get going. He didn't really want to lead any more, he realized. He never really had. He'd just been swept up into it. Now, faced with a choice that could get many of them killed, he really didn't want it. He opened his eyes and looked up the trail.

"From my sister's story, the trail up into the high pass took less than a day. It hasn't rained up to this point and may not actually rain at all. So I'm with Varanel on this one. Let's get this done."

They all nodded.

"David, you lead the way. Kai and I will get everyone organized down here. Looks like we're going single file," Simon said.

"Okay—and send Temian ahead to join me," David said. "Just in case we need someone with strength."

David ignored the looks that Varanel and Kawani gave him as he studied the trail ahead, looking frequently up at the sky. He felt the hesitation in himself and worked to push it aside. Simon disappeared back through the bushes, shouting orders to the people on the other side. Within seconds Temian came through the brush. With a nod and not another word, David started up the path.

The path climbed steadily and drew up against the mountainside on their right. On their left was a steep slope that more often than not ended in a sudden drop. The grass cover grew thinner and thinner as they climbed, until finally it was gone completely. They walked along the path—a narrow ribbon of stone with cliff on one side and a steep drop on the other. And steadily they ascended above the pass.

The Klasma were stretched out behind David for over a mile. He led, with Varanel right behind him. Kawani and Temian followed after.

He looked out and realized that they had already come abreast of the summit that was still some distance ahead. He could make out the thin line of their trail rising over and around the mountain, taking them up into the narrow cleft above the summit itself.

He heard Kawani call his name and turned to see her pointing up. He looked up and saw the wall of cloud as it rolled down toward them. He adjusted his cloak and tightened his collar. The other three did likewise and Temian turned to pass the advice down the line. It was going to get colder and more damp from this point on.

David turned and continued the ascent.

The valley and pass below had long disappeared into a world of grey mist and hard mountain stone. David's visibility was reduced to barely two hundred paces. But the trail continued. He studied it as he went. It was obviously not natural—rising steadily upward without outcrop or jutting stones. There was also very little debris on the trail, which he attributed to the slightly overhung cliffs above them.

After several hours in this grey world, two things were apparent. The first was that they were in the steep narrow draw far above the summit. A darkness loomed out across the emptiness on the left that could only be the cliffs of the mountain opposite. Second, it was apparent that the trail had steepened considerably.

David wondered again how his sister had ridden a horse up here. He shook his head as he looked over the edge of the trail to see that there was now nothing but a drop into darkness on their left. The rain and fog on that day must have been thicker than this, he realized, or his sister would surely have panicked. He considered whether this was the Valley of Death that they were in now. If it was, he was confident that just up ahead would be the summit of the pass and then the Mountain of God beyond.

As if to mock his light heart and hope, the skies chose that moment to open up.

They climbed doggedly through the steady rain. The wind in the steep narrow canyon seemed to swirl in cyclonic eddies that threw the rain sideways at times. At the beginning, David had hoped the overhanging cliffs above them would give them shelter, but as the wind picked up it drove the rain right into their faces. Over time the rain turned to a sharp, biting sleet, which was not an improvement.

David hung close to the cliff wall and surveyed the path ahead in deep apprehension. The trail levelled out and turned sharply to the left at this point. David watched as the wind blew the sleet sideways across the path. He felt the body of Varanel press close, and leaned back to listen to him.

"We can't stop here," Varanel said above the wind.

"We're about to get the wind full in our faces." David pointed ahead. "This might be the most sheltered spot left on the trail for all we know."

Kawani leaned over Varanel's stooped form to look ahead as well. She just shook her head and looked at him expectantly.

"We cannot stay here," Varanel insisted. "How much farther until the top of this pass?"

"I don't honestly know. But it's got to be close, considering how far we've climbed."

"If we stay, we'll freeze to death!" Kawani shouted. "We're committed now."

David nodded. They couldn't stay here, obviously. He turned and carefully made his way toward the sharp turn. Luckily, the sleet wasn't accumulating, but the temperature at this altitude was dangerously low. He pulled his hood down across his brow and went around the corner.

The wind blew sleet directly into his eyes, and he stopped to wipe them clear. The gale was much stronger here, pushing against him at an angle that forced him back toward the cliff. He looked to see if the others were following, and then bent himself into the wind and pushed forward.

David eventually realized that the storm was getting worse. He had been making his way up the trail in a cold, wet daze for longer than he could track. The sleet had at some point turned to snow that collected on the path several inches thick. The wind whipped around him, cutting into his cloak and making his fingers numb. He looked back to see huddled forms come to a halt in a single file row behind him.

Dear Living God, he thought, *are we going to die up here?*

Suddenly, out of blinding grey, something rose in front of him. He gasped before he realized what it was: the trail rose steeply at this point, climbing out of sight into the snow. He put his foot to the snow-covered slope and slipped.

Wild fear gripped his heart as he collapsed to the trail, keeping himself from sliding off into the void. He stayed there on his hands and knees until Varanel crawled up to him.

"Are you all right?"

David nodded. He looked up the trail that rose steeply in front of them. The snow covered it completely. The rock scraped clean by his boot glistened in the icy cold.

"We've got to turn back," Varanel shouted.

David shook his head. They couldn't turn back. They had to push on.

"I'm going back!" Varanel was becoming hysterical. "We can try again when the storm passes. But we're going to freeze or fall to our deaths if we stay here."

"No!" David yelled back. "We can't turn back!"

"I am!" Varanel knocked David's hand away and turned to go back down the trail.

In horror, David watched as the man lost his footing on the snow-covered stone. Windmilling in desperation, Varanel grabbed hold of

Kawani's arm as she tried to steady him and he fell off the trail, pulling her down with him.

David felt fire flash through him. Time slowed, and he propelled himself flat across the trail just as Kawani was disappearing over the edge herself. His hand caught a fistful of fabric and he gripped it tightly, twisting it so that it wrapped around his hand as the weight of his falling friend almost dislocated his shoulder. And then new horror struck him: he was sliding off the trail with them.

17

A Meeting Before the Gates

The people that walked toward them from the gates of the City confused Ra'ah greatly. From a distance, he had thought they were Maylak arrayed for battle. But when had Maylak ever utilized horses? Not that these were riding; rather, each one led a horse. There were maybe three dozen of them, and they were following two figures walking in front. One of these leaders resembled the others in appearance, but the other had a radiance much like the light they had just passed through.

His eyes were drawn to this man, for man he was. Dressed in radiant clothes that moved on him like the armour of the Maylak, he was holding an intense conversation with the man who walked beside him. The cadence of his voice, without distinguishable words, carried the distance between them and filled Ra'ah's heart with delight. The memory of his experience just moments before and of staring into the face of Love itself came sweeping back to him. He didn't understand how, but this was the man he had seen in that other place.

He returned to consider the others walking with the man of light. They were not Maylak, he realized, but men and women. Although they were dressed and looked so alike to the Maylak that he still wasn't completely sure. The man of light had turned his attention to Ra'ah and his friends, and his escort fell back as he approached.

Ra'ah heard fabric rustle, and out of the corner of his eye, he saw Anatellia kneel before the approaching man. The act seemed right and he followed suit. They knelt in silence as the man regarded each of them.

"Welcome, dear friends, to the City of the Faithful," he smiled at them.

"You are Joshua," Daskow said in awe.

"In the flesh," the man laughed. "But that is a conversation for another day, my boy."

"We have come as the Living… as you have asked," Anatellia stumbled.

"A lifetime of thinking is hard to rearrange," Joshua said. "But yes, I have called you here."

"But we're not finished the task we were given, Lord," Ra'ah said awkwardly. "Surely you will send us back?"

"Be at peace; I will not keep you long from your task. I have only brought you here so that I might better equip you. The enemy is aware of you and your mission, and he moves to make a quick end of this troublesome five." Joshua smiled again. "But, as ever, I am ahead of him. I have equipped each of you with an awakened purpose. I have given you a full measure of my Spirit. And I am sending back an honour guard to protect each of you."

He motioned toward the soldiers waiting behind him, and they moved forward. There was something ageless about the man Joshua had been talking to, and yet something so very familiar. He looked at each of them as if remembering old friends, and then his eyes rested on Nebaya. Ra'ah was taken aback at what he saw in the man's eyes.

"Hello, Nebaya," he said softly.

"David?" Anatellia's voice spoke a wealth of confusion.

"Hey, little sis." David's gaze shifted to his sister. "Have I got a story for you."

I'm going to die, David thought as he slid in slow motion off the edge of the trail. *This is how my life ends.*

The fistful of cloak suddenly got lighter. In cold realization, David understood that Varanel could no longer be hanging on to Kawani, whose hand was now gripping his arm like a talon. It wouldn't make any difference in a matter of moments because there was nothing on the trail for him to hang onto. He would slide after the other two, and they would all be dead.

Something heavy fell onto his legs a moment later, and his slide was arrested. He had all but forgotten about Temian. He could hear the big man calling back down the trail for help. He realized then that he had his eyes squeezed shut. He opened them to see Kawani's petrified face looking up at him. His reassuring smile froze on his face as he looked beyond her. For the briefest of moments, the snowfall slackened, the wind ripped the fog away, and he beheld the bottom of the gorge a thousand feet below.

"What?" Kawani screamed up at him.

He shook his head and locked eyes with her.

"Nothing," he shouted. "Just hang on; your brother is going to pull us up."

It was an eternity before David felt hands gripping his body and pulling him back up onto the trail. Kawani followed after, and they all huddled in a tight pile against the cliff wall. Temian checked them both over as best he could, and wouldn't stop until he was convinced neither of them were hiding injury.

"Do you think Varanel might be alive?" Temian leaned close to David's ear when he asked.

David just locked eyes with him and shook his head. Temian understood. They both turned to look at the steeply rising path in front of them.

"Three options." Temian held up his cloth-wrapped fingers. "Go forward, go back, go down."

"Down is death," David said flatly. "Varanel fell trying to go back. We have to go forward."

"Can we walk up that?" Temian asked incredulously.

David looked at Temian's wrapped hands. He knew they had to go forward. He also knew that walking up that slope would likely be fatal if anyone slipped. And they would take anyone on the path down with them. But there might be a way up that slope other than walking.

Temian saw him looking at his bound hands, and then reached back into a pocket on his pack and produced strips of cloth that he started to bind around David's hands.

"What's your idea?" he asked as he worked.

"We crawl up, clearing the path as we go."

Temian regarded the steep path. "Crazy. If it's frozen, then it'll be insanely slippery. If you lose your grip on that, you'll come down and sweep everyone off behind you."

"That's why I'll go up first, and you'll follow a good distance behind me. If I slip and can't catch myself, I'll just roll off before I crash into you," David said.

"You'll just roll off?" Kawani cut in from the side where she had been eavesdropping.

Temian rubbed the sleet and snow off of the trail under them. The rock was wet. He nodded to David. David slipped carefully past him and then crawled up to the slope. With a sweep of his arm, he swept the slush off of the trail into the grey abyss. He crawled up onto the slope and rested on his knees and the balls of his feet. The rock felt solid. He bounced on his heels. The rock didn't slip under him. He swept the next section clean and carefully continued forward. Free of snow, the slope provided surprising good traction.

He gave a thumbs up to the siblings behind him and then set to work clearing a trail. It was not long before he was in a routine. The path continued to climb dizzily above him, spinning slowly to the left. The wind had picked up again and blew snow into his face. His body became sore and cramped after a while, but he didn't dare stand up or stretch—and still the path climbed.

Exhausted, half blind in the snow, he swept his arm out to clear yet another section and slipped. He felt his exhausted body slide, and he feebly lashed out to grab whatever he could. A hand caught his and pulled him up the slope with surprising strength. He looked up into the face of a smiling man dressed in warm furs.

"Hello, David!" the man laughed. "Well done climbing that in this snow."

"Do…" David looked around as other figures appeared out of the snow. "Do I know you?"

"No," the man said. "But we were sent from the City to help you once you managed to get this far."

"The City?" David tried to shake off the confusion in his mind.

"Don't worry, you're just a little frozen. We've got fires set to warm you all up and get you down the other side."

"The others!" David made to move back toward the steep trail. "There are others."

"We know, David," the man assured him as he deftly steered him away from the cliff. "We've been sent, remember?"

"Joshua?" David's thinking was getting thick.

"Yes, Joshua." The man was almost treating him like a small child now, leading him away from the cliff and toward a fire set to the side of a narrow cleft in the peak where the trail continued beyond the summit.

They pressed a warm cup into his hands and commanded him to drink. He mechanically took a sip. The warm liquid had an amazing effect on his body and mind, and he drained the cup in one long sip. He handed it back to one of those watching him and looked around.

"I did not know anyone but Maylak dwelled on the Mountain of the Living God," he said as he stared back toward the cliffs.

"Everyone who climbs the pass through the Valley of Death thinks that, to be honest," his rescuer chuckled. "We did too, but we were not the first, either."

"The others need to know I made it," David said anxiously.

"There is another not far behind you," the man assured him. "And many others yet behind that one. They are coming."

"How do you know?" David asked in confusion.

The man looked at him in amusement. "The Spirit of the Living God tells us. Did you think you were alone for that entire climb?"

They were interrupted by a small commotion at the cliff edge. A voice cried out in suspicion and surprise, and reassuring voices responded to him. Finally Temian's voice rang clearly through the wind and snow, calling David's name.

"Here, Temian!" he called. "I'm over here."

The big man appeared through the snow, a look of uncertainty on his face as he peered at the men and women with David.

"It's okay, Temian," David laughed. "They are the welcoming committee, sent by the Living God Himself."

Temian nodded and took a cup offered to him. His uncertainty drained away as he drank it.

"We will need to move you all through the summit and down the pass to the other side." The man turned back to them from the cliff. "There is no possible way all of you will fit in this narrow area."

"Temian will take the first group through," David volunteered his friend. "I will stay here until the last one comes up."

The man smiled and returned to the cliff edge. Temian and David waited anxiously, trusting and hoping they would see the faces of their friends.

Anatellia looked awkwardly at the others as David crushed her in a bear hug. The man certainly reminded Ra'ah of David, but he wasn't the David they had just left under the avalanche shelter only a short time before. This man was older. But an ageless kind of old. In fact, Ra'ah couldn't pinpoint what age this man was.

He looked out over the men and women in front of them. They all had the same ageless look about them. Young and in their prime, but something spoke of wisdom and time spent living.

"Okay, put me down," Anatellia finally had to tell him.

"I have missed you." David wiped a tear from his eye.

"Missed me?" Anatellia looked at her brother askew. "We just saw each other."

There was gentle laughter from some in the group of warriors. Joshua raised his hand for silence.

"There is much to be said, and many stories to be told. But I encourage you all to be about your business as soon as possible. This is a time of refocusing and renewed commitment to your mission. I have instructed David in all that you need to know."

"Oh please," Angelis begged, "can't we stay but a little longer? I would love to explore the City and talk with you."

"Child, I would love that very much, but now is not the time." He smiled at her. "When you return we will walk through the City together and you can sing me some of your favourite songs."

Ange nodded. The thought that Joshua would want to hear her songs pleased her greatly.

Joshua suddenly burst into radiance so blinding that the five had to shield their eyes. The others simply stared at the light in loving devotion.

I am very pleased with the five of you. Joshua's voice surrounded them like water. *Each of you should remember what I have spoken over you. David and his Thirty will be my protection over you and nothing will harm you. Now go and bring my people back to me.*

The light faded suddenly, and they were alone on the road with David and his troop. He looked at each of them with the happiness of a man seeing friends after a long separation.

"David, seriously." Anatellia stared at him. "What's going on? You're changed; we can all see that. It's like you've aged, but how is that possible?"

David looked back at the men and women with him, a sad smile on his face as he exchanged looks with them. Finally he shook his head and looked long at his sister.

"We've got a spot to stay the night just down the road," he offered. "Let's get walking and I'll tell you a story that you just aren't going to believe."

18

A Night at the Mountain's Foot

"**A** thousand years?" Anatellia repeated for the tenth time.
She looked up at the mountain above them before looking at the others. Anatellia wasn't the only one struggling with David's story. They all stared at him like he was insane. They would have dismissed him outright, except that he was so clearly different.

The man that Ra'ah and Nebaya had ridden with out of Meletsa just that morning had been a boy compared to this man in front of them. Ra'ah kept studying his face. It was David's face all right, but it was undoubtedly aged. The word "timeless" kept repeating in his head. He was also considerably more fit than the carousing young nobleman of just a day before. Ra'ah exchanged incredulous looks with Daskow and Ange before glancing over at Nebaya. Her face was completely unreadable to him.

"Time on the Mountain of the Living God moves differently," David repeated.

"But a thousand years…" Anatellia shook her head. "David, you'd be dead."

"There is no death on the Mountain, Anna," David said.

"But a thousand years!" Anatellia's voice rose in pitch.

They had walked to this village nestled at the foot of the mountain just below the City wall, and David had spent most of the evening telling them everything that had happened after the bright flash had separated them. He spoke of Simon and Joshua and the Klasma. He told them about the Gellah and the search for the trail up the mountain. He told them about the harrowing climb through the Valley of Death. But he had barely gotten to their arrival at the Mountain and entering the City of the Faithful before the questions started flying.

Daskow was fixated on the fact that David had actually met Simon the Apostate. That elicited laughter from not just David but more than a few of David's companions. He referred to them as his fellow Klasma, but they kept a measure of distance out of respect and understanding for what this reunion meant for David.

The others had questions as well, but they quickly deferred to Anatellia, who was completely astonished by the story her brother told. She kept making him go over the story again and again. She kept staring at him like he had stolen her brother, like he was hiding him somewhere from her. She simply couldn't get past the thousand years.

"Look, Anna," David held up his hands to stop her from going off again, "I will explain this as simply as I can. The Mountain and the City that you see are not at all what they seem. This is the Mountain of the Living God, but what is a Mountain to One such as Him? In truth, this is where the Kingdom of Heaven meets our world. The City was built long, long ago by a people that have long since passed beyond. The Presence of the Living God dwells in this City and even out into the valley. Those who choose to dwell in the City dwell ever in that presence. There is no death here, but in many ways there is no time. I remember a thousand days that passed one like another, but I've forgot a hundred times that many."

"But how can that be?" Anatellia's voice broke. "I feel like I've lost my brother. I don't know this man in front of me."

"But you do." David reached out and wiped a tear from her cheek. "I'm still your brother David. You're just letting fear cloud your eyes."

"You must have learned so much," Daskow marvelled softly. "Seen so much."

"You remind me very much of my friend Simon, Daskow," David smiled sadly.

"Can I meet him?" Daskow looked around at the Klasma, trying to pick out Simon.

"I'm afraid you will have to wait. Over the years Simon has retreated deeper and deeper into the City, until he almost never leaves the Temple area. It will not be long before he passes beyond the City."

"What is beyond it?" Ra'ah asked in confusion.

"The Kingdom of Heaven," David said simply. "Remember how I said this Mountain is where Heaven meets our world? The Temple is the threshold. Pass through the Temple and you will find yourself beyond this world, in the Kingdom of Heaven."

"What's it like there?" Ange asked eagerly.

"I do not know," David laughed. "You see, no one comes back."

"No one?" Ange's eyes grew large. "Can I go into the City and see the Temple? Just a quick trip?"

"No, none of you can be allowed into the City." David shook his head. "It is far too dangerous."

"Dangerous?" they all repeated in confusion.

"The most terrible kind of danger," David said sombrely, without a hint of humour. "You think of danger as something that could hurt you or kill you. I tell you, that City has claimed many of our friends, brothers, and sisters whom we will not meet again until we all pass beyond."

"What is this danger?" Anatellia pressed, eyeing the City like it was suddenly a threat.

"Desire." David spread his arms wide. "Desire to be with the Living God. Desire to never leave His presence. If you pass through those open gates, you may very well never leave."

"You've left." Nebaya spoke for the first time.

"I have clung to a vision for my life that has kept me here, in this world." David locked eyes with her. "We all have."

Nebaya held his gaze for a long silent moment and then looked away. David continued to look at her for some time until one of the Klasma called out his name. He looked up and waved a tall woman over.

"I'll let the others introduce themselves as they want, but this is Kawani," David introduced her, and then pointed to each of the five. "Kawani, this is my sister, Anatellia, Daskow, Ra'ah, Nebaya, and Angelis. Angelis is the one I told you about who has all of the stories and songs."

Kawani nodded to everyone in turn but eyed Nebaya a little longer before giving a big smile to Ange.

"Little sister," Kawani's voice was melodic, "I've been waiting so very long for a fellow voice to sing with."

"Surely there are many singers among you," Angelis giggled.

"None that love it as I do," Kawani admitted.

"Kawani is in charge of getting you all settled for the night," David explained. "She's got a cottage set aside for your needs and your gear is already stowed there."

Ra'ah, Daskow, Ange, and Nebaya all started to move to follow the tall woman. Anatellia stayed where she was. David waved for them to go and once they were gone he looked at his sister in expectation.

"The... Joshua said you were our protection?" Anatellia's voice expressed doubt.

"Yes." David gave her an appraising look. "I know it's difficult to catch up with all of this, but you need to trust what I've told you."

"There is an army coming to destroy the Valley and you've been sitting here making eyes at that girl for the last thousand years," Anatellia said flatly.

"Anna..." In that one word, David's tone carried humour and, to Anatellia's surprise, no small amount of rebuke. "I am not my own, to do as I please when I please any more. I belong to the Living God. I am His. And Kawani is as much a sister to me as you are. She does not have my heart."

He raised his hand quickly to forestall any response. "There is something else you need to understand. I have not been idle here in the City, waiting all these long years to pop back out and surprise you all. We have been preparing. We have been training. When I haven't been looking after you and your silly horse, at least.

"Did you think it was the Maylak who found you fevered on that mountainside when you were ten? And let me tell you how much of a miracle it was that you and that horse even made it through that valley. We lost a score of people up there ourselves. You were a sick mess, I can tell you. But it was all I could do not to take you in my arms and crush you to me. Temian told me I shouldn't have gone, and he was almost proved right."

"You were there?" Anatellia felt a lump in her throat.

"I was," David nodded. "I shouldn't have been, but I needed to see you. I have missed you, dear sister!"

She found herself wrapped in a great hug. Her memory went back to that day when she was ten. He had been there. He had watched out for her even then.

"Mother is going to lose her mind," she laughed through tears.

"Mother has bigger problems," David growled ominously.

She pushed him away and squeezed his arms. "These are definitely new."

"I've learned more than a few things in the long years of waiting. The Sacheth have responded to the threat you and your friends have presented by sending a force ahead of their army with all speed— murderers and assassins all. But Joshua set us aside from the beginning as his response. I am not boasting when I tell you that nothing will harm any of you. Seeing you finish your mission is our purpose."

"I think you have a secondary purpose." Anatellia's eyebrows rose.

David's mouth shut with a thump. He looked at his sister for a long time and then just shook his head and smiled.

"That is a story I'm not ready to tell my sister," he admitted. "I am not the same man you knew, but Nebaya still sees yesterday's David."

"Oh, I don't think she does," Anatellia laughed softly. "Something has changed in her. And she was staring daggers at your sister friend."

"I am not at all worried about Kawani," David assured her. "But if you love your brother, stay out of this Nebaya thing."

"I'm a neutral observer!" She raised her palms in surrender.

David shook his head. "I don't really believe that for a second."

Kawani showed them to the cottage that they were to stay in. It would have been the home of an elder back in the valley, Ra'ah realized. But here it was just an extra dwelling. For the entire walk there, Daskow had been asking Kawani questions, and Ra'ah listened intently. From Kawani's answers he learned that no, no one really lived in this village; it was no more than a place to meet and store goods that were headed down the valley. There were farmers, and they lived in their own houses. There were other villages, and the population outside the villages fluctuated from generation to generation. Yes, people still married and had children. And no, she had never gotten married.

As promised, their packs had been brought in and left by the door. David found the inside felt more like a barracks than a home. Food was set on a long table in the middle of the room, and beds were arrayed around the outer walls. Ange immediately commandeered a bowl of wild berries and dragged her bag to a bed. Nebaya picked up her gear and found a place in the back corner. Daskow's almost constant questions ended as he started grazing at the table.

"Did David marry?" Nebaya's voice cut through the room.

"No," Kawani stated flatly.

Kawani locked eyes with Nebaya across the room. Ra'ah felt a sudden tension, highlighted by the long silence that fell across the cottage. It was as if the two women were dueling with unseen weapons.

"That is surprising," Nebaya finally said.

"Not if you truly knew him," Kawani said flatly. "But his heart has been for the Living God and very little else since the first day I met him."

"You're right," Nebaya admitted, "I never actually met that David."

"You should take the time. But now is the time to rest. We'll be leaving very early in the morning for the Gellah."

Kawani turned and left, leaving the four in awkward silence. Finally Ange popped up and set the half-empty bowl on the table.

"There's no way I'm going to be able to sleep. I'm going to get to know these people. Who's coming with me?"

Daskow shook his head and flopped down on an empty bed with a plate full of food. Nebaya remained on the bed she had chosen and just stared into the fire. Ra'ah was overwhelmed and exhausted, but he still realized Ange was right. He grabbed his pack and slid it to one of the unclaimed beds, then offered Ange his arm and they slipped out of the cottage door to catch up with Kawani.

Ra'ah and Ange spent most of the evening and part of the night laughing and talking with the Klasma. Many of them had gathered around a communal area a little way from the cottage. Stone seats and wood benches were interspersed around a stone-lined pit and a well-banked fire burned merrily. Kawani's brother Temian welcomed them with a booming voice and introduced everyone gathered around the fire. Ange introduced herself and Ra'ah to all of them in return.

Kawani sang a song for them that made Ra'ah's heart soar, and then Ange, being a quick study in all things musical, picked up the song and together they filled the village with music. Ra'ah fancied he heard even more voices raised in song, as if coming from a great distance—maybe from the towering walls above them. The presence from his vision earlier in the day stirred around him and through him. He wondered if anyone else felt it.

"If I had to guess, I would say you are from Bato," a man named Kai suddenly spoke from beside him.

"Well, yes, but…" Ra'ah was flustered. "How do you know about Bato?"

"The Amatta may know very little of the Mountain of the Living God, but we know a lot about the Valley."

"But how?" Ra'ah asked. "I mean, surely you don't venture out of your valley?"

"For many, many years we didn't," Kai acknowledged. "But with Joshua's permission we built the Gellah road, and now we can."

"So you've been spying on us?" Ra'ah found that idea odd.

Kai laughed. "No, not spying. There is no information we could have brought back that He did not already know. But we have had friends in the valley, and from time to time we would exchange messages with them. And our group needed to learn the layout of the valley and the people. We couldn't protect you five very well if we didn't do a little reconnaissance in advance, now could we?"

"Protect us?" Ra'ah asked in confusion. "I thought the Maylak would protect us."

"Ah, you've met a Maylak?" Kai looked at him with new respect. "Few even among us can say that."

"What do you mean? Don't they live here as well?"

Kai shook his head. "Maylak are of the Heavenly Kingdom. They serve the Living God day and night without ceasing. If they live anywhere, it is beyond this place. But to go back to the question of protection, the Maylak do not fight flesh and blood. The dark creatures that have chased you are an abomination of spirit. But what even now descends from the far pass into the Amatta is a threat of living flesh. And that is what we have trained for."

"I don't understand," Ra'ah admitted.

Kai looked at him with a mixture of pity and compassion. "You probably understand more than you realize. But I imagine you never imagined yourself sitting here, in this place, when you woke up this morning. Tell me your story, son of Bato," Kai asked. "And then I'll try to fill in the blank areas."

Ra'ah chuckled at being called a son of Bato. He was not a very good representative of his village. But he told Kai his story and the man listened patiently as Kawani and Ange sang together in the background.

19

DOWN THE VALLEY OF LIGHT

R a'ah's head had barely hit the pillow before a knock at the cottage door revealed it was time to pack up and go. In very little time they found themselves at the edge of the small village staring at an already prepared escort.

The horses the Klasma were leading weren't for riding after all; rather, they were carrying supplies from the City to what Kai had told Ra'ah was "the project." He seemed amused by the name but wouldn't tell Ra'ah any more about it, other than that it was a surprise.

Of the three dozen Klasma, only thirty of them were part of their honour guard. The others were tradesmen headed to the Gellah with them. Kai had been true to his word the night before and had filled in the gaps for Ra'ah. As Master Dunhamai had warned just that morning, there was an advanced force rushing ahead of the Sacheth army. Their purpose, Kai informed him, was to kill the five meddlesome kids stirring up the valley and stop the flight before they had a chance to gain momentum. He had been greatly disturbed by that revelation, but Kai just laughed and assured him that no one was going to harm them.

He went on to reiterate that Maylak did not fight flesh and blood— that task fell to them. And to that end they had been trained, for more years than Kai had bothered to count.

That was something that struck Ra'ah as odd. These people had started to train as their protectors before Ra'ah had ever been born. Trained in the very City that towered over them now. Violence seemed out of place here and he couldn't shake that idea. When he mentioned it to Kai, the man just shrugged. "It's not as simple as that," he had said.

They started out immediately and set a good pace away from the mountain. Kai had told Ra'ah the night before that the plan was to get to the Gellah as quickly as possible so they could spend a day ensuring arrangements were on schedule to receive the first of the refugees coming up from the Amatta. Ra'ah was greatly heartened to hear that people would not simply be milling around the falls waiting for help.

He slipped in step with Daskow, who was trying to study the surroundings in the dim dawn light. "You were right about the cave," Ra'ah said.

"Hmm?" Daskow shook himself out of his own thoughts. "The what?"

"The cave, behind the falls?" Ra'ah reminded him. "There's a doorway of sorts there."

"Well, we did think so." Daskow nodded. "I look forward to seeing it with my own eyes."

"I'm just glad we don't have to try to go down through that valley of death up there." Ra'ah nodded to the mountains at the far end of the valley.

"I've never heard of anyone actually going the other way," Daskow said.

Ra'ah realized that he hadn't either. He wondered if it was possible. He looked around at the others. Ange was up ahead with Kawani. The two had become fast friends the night before. Anatellia and Nebaya were walking together in silence just a little behind them. The Klasma were spread out along the road and to either side of them. He saw Kai in deep conversation with David. Temian was in the front. A woman named Hanah was following close with Kawani. About a dozen other names floated with faces. It was going to take him a while to remember everyone.

"I wonder if this valley has a name?" Ra'ah mused.

David came up behind them. "It is called the Valley of Light. Because no one can bring darkness into it."

"The Mountain of the Living God, the City of the Faithful, the Valley of Light—who picks these names?" Anatellia jabbed.

"I'm told they are translations, little sister," David said. "I had nothing to do with their naming."

"You'd think with all the time you've had on your hands you'd have learned a few new languages," Anatellia said flippantly.

"Ganito?" David turned to her. "Je li ovo dobro? Of wat hiervan? Honestly, it's hard to practice them all without a native speaker. And the Amatta has lost its language diversity centuries ago. We're all stuck speaking the orthodox tongue."

"You haven't lost your ability to show off," she noted.

"Or his ability to shine horse flop," Nebaya added. "How do we even know that was another language?"

"Three," David cut in. "That was three other languages. And to be honest I have forgotten far more than I remember. The first few years I wanted to know everything I could."

"You can forget, then, even here?" Nebaya asked.

"Some things you forget, some things you let go of, some things get set aside until they are needed." He shrugged. "The higher into the City you go and the longer you stay, the more gets burned right out of you by the presence of the Living God. But the Spirit is a Refiner's Fire wherever we go."

"It is so strange hearing you talk that way," Anatellia said. "My favourite brother finally hears the Call."

"Heard, answered, and baptized into." David shook his head. "Now I cannot imagine a day without Him."

They walked in silence for quite a while after that. They were walking past farms with workers in the fields. Great gardens of vegetables and cultivated berry patches were everywhere. And as they passed, the workers looked up to wave and watch them go. Ra'ah was struck by the normality of it all. If he hadn't known where they were, he would have thought he was back in the Amatta.

Midmorning passed, and though the Mountain of the Living God continued to dominate the sky and land behind them, they entered into a part of the valley that felt much more like the valley they had come from. Along one slope, Ra'ah even noted what looked to be a mine. He looked back at David and pointed toward it.

"The mountains around here are rich with ore and such," David answered his unspoken question. "In this valley you may pursue what interests you like. There are a few who love working with metals and such. In fact that is our first stop, at the blacksmiths."

"Oh?" Ra'ah couldn't hide his surprise. "What are we picking up there?"

"Our weapons," David said.

"And here I thought you were going to defend us with your bare hands," Nebaya said.

"We've trained with about everything over the course of time," David explained. "But to be honest there is no need for weapons here, so we had to have them made."

"What did you train with if it wasn't weapons?" Ra'ah asked curiously.

David picked up a stick from the side of the road, and in a rapid series of thrusts and flourishes demonstrated his skill. Ra'ah and the women were impressed. Kai watched his friend and leader for a while and shook his head.

"Of course, very few of us like the sword," Kai spoke up.

"Why is that?" Ra'ah looked over at the man.

"Because there are very few options with a sword that don't involve seriously harming or killing your opponent."

"I would think that's the point!" Nebaya snorted.

"It is no small thing to kill another person," the woman named Hanah answered. "We have trained very long and very hard to be good enough that we would not have to kill, except as an extreme last resort."

"It seems our enemy will not hold to the same reverence in regard to killing all of us," Nebaya said.

"But that is not justification for us to be callous with their lives," Hanah countered. "In the end we all answer to the Living God for what we've done—and what we've taken."

Nebaya pressed further. "I fear our enemy has the advantage of not caring about any of that. In the end we may need to learn to take lives in order to preserve the innocent. We have not known war in all the history of the valley, but war is coming."

"Nebaya…" David's tone carried gentle rebuke. "Except for me, every one of this guard has seen war. They have lost family, friends, and homes to war. You are speaking of what you do not truly understand to people who do understand, but they are still committed to standing between you and the coming violence."

"It is odd," Hanah added, staring Nebaya down, "that a valley built by refugees of war should forget so easily the cost that was paid for their peace."

"A lot is forgotten in a thousand years," Anatellia cut in. "Some of that was accidental. Some of it deliberate."

The conversation was interrupted by a call from ahead. Ra'ah looked up to see they had arrived at a great courtyard in front of an open building. The sound of hammers on metal could be heard from inside. A bulky man with thick arms was waving at the approaching group.

"Barak!" David called out from the group. "How's our order?"

"Done, and good riddance to it." The man waved them over. "You know I hate doing this kind of work!"

The big man called into the building and helpers scurried out with bundles and hand carts. Ra'ah stood to the side with the other four and watched as their escort went through the offered gear. The weapon of choice, much to his surprise, was an iron-clad walking stick. A few swords were passed out too. And there was also a cartload of arrows, although not a bow in sight. David looked at the cart of arrows pensively.

"I told them to bring the bows and quivers here," Ra'ah overheard David saying to the big blacksmith.

"What can I tell you, David?" Barak shrugged. "They provided the quarterstaves in good enough time. And the arrow shafts. We had them kilned and fitted a week ago."

"They feel good." David hefted a staff in his hand. "Are they going to hold up?"

"They'll turn a blade and break stone without snapping," Barak assured him proudly. "They're lighter than those practice sticks of yours, though, so be ready for that."

David shook his head. "Kawani'll take my head off for sure with one of these. She's already frighteningly fast."

"Kids playing with sticks!" Barak snorted. "But these will keep you all safe and the sharp things at bay. I made you this as well." The man reached into a cart and brought out a sword. The leather-wrapped hilt and the scabbard were a dull black. There wasn't a marking or decoration on it. David gripped the hilt and drew the blade.

"It's perfect. Although you could have given it a little decoration."

"I don't decorate weapons," Barak growled. "I'd rather decorate a hammer or a chisel."

"You do," David pointed out sagely. "You decorate everything."

"Anything but a weapon." Barak shook his head. "I will not glorify anything forged for harm."

David smiled as he lifted the blade to catch the light. "It's for protection."

"Protection through harm." The big man shook his head again stubbornly. "If you want protection that doesn't maim, check these beauties."

He turned and plucked a silver-white shirt from a cart that a helper just rolled up. The shirt sparkled in the sunlight. He held it up for David to study.

"That's a chain mesh shirt," Barak said proudly. "Light and tough, it'll turn a blade at any angle except straight on."

"I'd rather not let a blade get that close," David said. "How many of these have you made?"

"Twelve," the blacksmith admitted. "They're time consuming and we weren't sure you'd be interested."

David sheathed the sword and took the shirt in both hands. He hefted it and looked at the big man in surprise. The smith nodded proudly.

"You weren't kidding about them being light," David marvelled. "We'll take them and decide who gets them later. And look, here is our tardy bowyer."

A wagon pulled up, drawn by two horses. The man driving it had an apologetic look about him, and he barely stopped before whipping off the tarp covering the back. Lining the bed of the wagon were approximately three dozen bows and quivers.

"You are late," David chided.

"Take it up with my leather-worker. He's obsessed with making everything beautiful."

They started passing out the weapons from the back of the wagon. Kawani grabbed two sets and walked deliberately over to Nebaya. Without a word of explanation, she handed over one of the bows.

"I have one." Nebaya lifted the bow and covered quiver off her shoulder in demonstration.

"No offence to the bowyers in your valley," Kawani said, "but this bow shoots like nothing you've ever handled. Unless, of course, your bow has sentimental value."

"It's just a tool." Nebaya shrugged and took the bow from the other woman.

She ran her hand along its beautifully detailed surface. The carvings were of animals and trees. The grip was wrapped in leather and fit her hand well. She removed the hood from her quiver and pulled an arrow. She forgot which arrows were in her quiver until Kawani gasped.

"Those are beautiful," the tall woman said, looking at the white arrow in Nebaya's hand with admiration. "Where did you get them?"

"From a Maylak," Nebaya said, and offered her the arrow.

Kawani accepted it, but looked at her with an appraising eye before turning to examine the arrow. Several others who had seen the arrow come out of her quiver walked over eagerly for a closer look.

"I'm surprised you all aren't using them," Nebaya said. "I mean, they are from here, aren't they?"

"No, Nebaya." Kawani shook her head as she studied the arrow. "This was not made here. This comes from beyond."

"Well, they worked really well on the dark wolves. And, frankly, just as well on the Sacheth." Nebaya shrugged and took back the arrow, returning it to her quiver.

"I didn't know you had encountered the Sacheth already," Kawani said.

"Ra'ah and I had the misfortune of meeting a few up in the Koreb pass, just yesterday morning." Nebaya shook her head. "It's hard to believe that was only yesterday."

"Do you want to talk about it?" Kawani asked softly.

Nebaya looked at the other woman. A cluster of emotions passed through her. But there was something sincere about the tall Kawani that frustrated Nebaya's attempts to dislike her. As if reading her thoughts and emotions, Kawani took her by the arm and drew her aside.

She spoke so nobody else could hear. "Nebaya, you need to understand something about me, woman to woman. We are not enemies, you and I. Whatever you think you've seen between him and me, know that I am his sister and nothing more. And I would be as a sister to you, if you would let me."

Nebaya stood completely still, stunned silent by the other woman's directness. Her brain was a scrambled mass of confusing emotional reactions. She opened her mouth to respond and shut it with a snap. She looked into the other woman's eyes, expecting to see pity in them, and found patient understanding. She took a deep breath and simply nodded.

Kawani nodded back and took Nebaya's old bow from her. She looked at it in admiration before she pointed to the new bow in Nebaya's hand.

"You'll find that bow to be as accurate as this old one of yours, but it has a better range for very little increase in draw. Grab an extra string or two off the wagon as well, and help yourself to a quiver if you want something more fancy. Although you don't strike me as caring all that much for fancy."

Nebaya nodded, thankful that Kawani wasn't going to push the conversation. Someone brought a quarterstaff over to Kawani, and she set aside her own bow to heft the metal-tipped rod. She stepped away from the others and the staff started to spin and dance around her as she tested its balance and weight. Nebaya watched in fascination at the speed and grace of woman and staff. Kawani looked up and smiled, thumping the staff onto the ground and leaning it toward her.

"Want to try?" Kawani offered almost playfully.

"I'd only crack someone in the head," Nebaya admitted, admiring the other woman's ability. "Although I understand what Kai was referring to now. I wouldn't want to come anywhere near you if you were swinging that."

"A well-trained warrior with a quarterstaff has many advantages over a swordsman or woman."

David came over carrying one of the silver-white mail shirts. He looked at the bow in Nebaya's hand and then offered the shirt to her.

"I would be very happy if you'd wear this," he said to her, and then quickly added, "I think every one of you should wear one. It adds one more layer of protection."

"Where's mine?" Kawani teased.

"You and Hanah can share." He shot her a look. "And grab a knife or two from Barak. They're all-purpose and we can't guarantee that the fights ahead won't be at close quarters."

Nebaya took the shirt from David and held it up. It was surprisingly light, with a high collar and cording to draw it snug it around the neck. She hated clothing that touched her neck. She handed it back with a head shake, but he refused to accept it.

"Please wear it, Nebaya," he said softly. "Do this one thing for me."

She shrugged and stuffed it into one of her pack pockets.

"I'd rather have one of those staffs," she said.

"And if I put one in your hands, would you eventually think you could use it to defend yourself?" David asked pointedly.

"I'll teach her," Kawani cut it from over his shoulder.

David nodded and walked over to where extra weapons were leaning. Kawani watched him choose one, and then she leaned in to whisper fiercely to Nebaya.

"I will teach you," she assured her. "But if you ever so much as think to use what I teach you against an enemy, I'll crack you one myself."

"Don't you think I can fight?" Nebaya asked defiantly.

"I have no doubt about your ability to fight," Kawani laughed suddenly, "but it takes more than the ability to fight to win one."

David returned with a staff in his hands and held it out to Nebaya.

"They are good for support, balance, carrying things, and clubbing anything up to and including a bear," David informed her. "Kawani is a good teacher. She'll show you its other uses."

"I won't disappoint you," Nebaya said before she had time to think about it.

David stared at her for a long moment before turning and walking away.

"Come on," Kawani hid a smile, "Let's get some strings and a few short blades for me."

Nebaya nodded, but her eyes stayed on David's back as he moved through the guard.

20

THE GAP

They departed from the blacksmith soon after and made their way at a good pace. The broad valley narrowed as they went down it, and bent gradually to their right. David pointed at a rip in the stone of the mountains between two great peaks and declared that to be the entrance to the pass that led to the Valley of Death. About midafternoon they came to a crossroads where a road came down from the pass high above.

They continued walking into the slowly setting sun and finally came into a gap where two other valleys came down and met the Valley of Light. A road from each descended to meet their road, and there David paused.

"There are no roads or usable passes leading out of those two valleys, although the country is beautiful and the land available for the taking." He pointed up the two valleys, and then pointed to a deep ravine cutting into the cliffs that rose behind them. "This is our path here."

The small river that had flowed the length of the valley with them joined two others, and together they plunged into the ravine. A paved road left the crossroads where they stood and followed alongside.

"David's very proud of this project," Kawani whispered loudly to Nebaya.

"Well, yes, I am," David answered even more loudly as everyone but the five laughed.

They entered the ravine and Daskow immediately perked up. The river rushed alongside the road in a deep channel for some way into the ravine. Daskow looked over and David nodded.

"Wait till you actually see what we've done, Daskow," David said. "It took the engineers years to work this all out, but when they did... well, you'll see."

The ravine plunged deep into the cliffs until everything was in shadow. Suddenly the river itself crossed under the road and disappeared into a dark aqueduct. After crossing the river, the road itself descended into a cavern mouth that, as David explained, had once run with water.

"Almost a quarter mile that way"—David pointed in the direction the river now flowed—"is Gellah Lake. The three rivers feed the lake all year round, which is why the falls never dry up."

"And this cave?" Daskow pointed excitedly down the road.

"Leads almost straight to the third fall," David crowed triumphantly.

"Honestly, you'd think he dug it all himself," Kawani teased.

"And who spearheaded this project, Kawani?" David asked.

"You did, David," Kawani said in a coddling tone.

"No one else wanted the job," Kai quipped. "And you were so obsessed with those seven tiers."

"Daskow!" David ignored the jabbing. "Can you believe Gellah Falls only had three drops for the first half of Valley history? I never read anything about that!"

"You never read," Anatellia joined in on the jabbing. "At least not before yesterday. Well, my yesterday, anyway."

Daskow came to David's rescue. "I never knew that, either. It was probably just considered a natural event."

"Exactly!" David's voice echoed down into the cave. "And that reminds me: we need to leave the horses here with a couple of lucky handlers. Just do what we did last time."

"Why are we leaving them?" Anatellia asked.

"Because two dozen horses made an almost unholy din going down the tunnel," David shook his head. "You just can't imagine the noise."

The big man named Temian picked half a dozen people to deal with the horses and David led the five into the cave. Inside, the cave was probably six or seven paces wide and the roof was at least six feet above the head of the tallest of them. Torches appeared in metal brackets at regular intervals and the smell of damp rock filled their nostrils as they descended. The road ran for the most part along the same path that the river once had, but the way had been graded so that horses and carts could travel it.

Anatellia stopped at one point and closed her eyes. Ra'ah stopped with her and waited. Finally she opened her eyes and they continued. "It's just like I remembered it when I was ten." She shook her head. "But it's different knowing it was made by these people and not Maylak. And it's much different knowing it's a cave in the guts of a mountain and not just a ravine."

Ra'ah nodded. He wasn't a fan of caves, he had just realized. The spacing between the torches left long shadows. He shivered and wondered how deep they were and how much farther it was to the rockfall that marked the end of the cave.

The answer came quicker than he expected. From ahead came the light of multiple torches, and the cave narrowed, the path rising up while the ceiling dropped. A great set of iron double doors was set in a heavy timber wall that blocked their path ahead. There was no rockfall anymore.

"The rock wall door was removed," David said by way of explanation. "Which is a sadness, because it was such an amazing feat of engineering. But Joshua ordered the way to be opened, so here we are. The doors are mostly to keep the noise of the falls from making it impossible to communicate in the tunnel."

Ra'ah could hear the falls from behind the door, but when David lifted the latch and pushed the doors outward, the roar filled the cave. A mist-laden wind blasted past him and down the tunnel. David stepped out onto the other side and they followed.

The waterfall side of the cave had been drastically altered from what he remembered. Large stone blocks paved the floor of the once natural and rough cave. The road literally continued out from behind the falls and a waist-high stone wall had been built to prevent people from falling into the pool. The last light of dusk was just fading from the sky, and Ra'ah and the others looked out over the valley to see it had been taken over by a hundred torches and fires like giant fireflies. On the forest floor. The site caused them to stop dead on the road.

"I don't understand," Ra'ah sputtered as he looked at the fires below. "Have refugees already started arriving?"

"No," Kai answered from just behind him. "That's us."

"Us?" Ra'ah's confusion increased.

"What I mean is, these are people from our side, from the Valley of Light and the City," Kai explained.

"What are they doing here?"

"They are setting up a camp and fortifications," David answered from the front of the group. "We've opened the front door, but not everyone is going to be able to come in, at least not right away. So we are setting up a refugee camp and ramparts around the falls to discourage unwelcome guests."

A dozen more questions filled Ra'ah's head but David just held his hands up pleadingly. "Can your question wait until we've settled in the barracks and have some food in front of us?" he begged.

"I am hungry," Ra'ah admitted.

David led them down the road that had sprung up to replace the path that visitors had used for years to get to the third fall. It was apparent to the five that construction on this side of the falls had been ongoing for some time, although David insisted it had not been as long as they thought. The stone road suddenly transitioned to a wooden boardwalk as they passed the bowl that surrounded the first pool, and buildings rose up against the hill. David dismissed the guard and led them into one large building with the sound of voices coming from within.

The building was obviously a community mess hall and the tables were half-filled with a large variety of people of various ages. The conversations stopped as the patrons looked at them with various degrees of curiosity. At one table toward the back, a man stood up and shouted David's name.

"Duncan!" David waved the man over as he guided them to a large empty table. "I've brought the supplies you requested."

"Not nearly enough of them, I'll wager." The man strode through the tables. "We've already had some eager stragglers arriving. And my chief engineer is planning on moving the fortifications."

"Moving them? Where?" David's attention shifted suddenly.

Duncan spread his arms wide. "Across the valley. Basically cut off all access to the pass, the falls, and further up the Amatta, by drawing a earthworks line across the valley from slope to slope."

"And how does he suggest we defend that?" David shook his head in frustration.

"By removing access to it from the down valley side." Duncan shrugged. "The man is smarter than all the others put together. He seems to think it can be done."

"Sure," David said, "but can it be done with the people we have and the time we have?"

"He believes so," Duncan said softly, "but he's waiting for your go ahead."

"Let me get some food for our friends here and then we'll go talk to him," David sighed. "Oh, everyone, this is Duncan. He's one of the Klasma. Duncan, this is my sister Anatellia. And Nebaya, Daskow, Ra'ah, and Angelis."

"It is a pleasure to finally meet you all," Duncan said, tilting his head in greeting. "Sorry I've got to abduct David for a bit."

They all nodded. A young woman came over with some mugs and a pottery jug full of something steaming. She smiled at them all and placed the dishes on the table, and then scurried off to the kitchen. David waved in apology and then left with Duncan. The five found themselves alone in the room full of strangers.

"I have never felt so swept off my feet in my life," Ra'ah said. "And I'm counting the last ten days."

"And I feel the need to get my feet back under me," Anatellia agreed. "But I've been too preoccupied with what happened right after we met that big Maylak."

"You mean in that other place, with the light and the almost unbearable Presence?" Ange whispered. "I thought I was the only one who experienced that. Did you hear what He said to me?"

Anatellia shook her head. Ange looked at the others, but they all shook their heads as well.

"Well..." Ange pursed her lips. "Did He tell you He was going to put a new song in your heart and a new story to tell, and He was going to send you to the nations?"

They all shook their heads.

"What did he tell each of you?" Ange pressed. "Come on, I shared."

"I'm a shepherd," Ra'ah said hesitantly. "And I'm supposed to raise up other shepherds."

"I'm a teacher." Daskow's voice was low but it carried over the table. "He showed me things I do not understand and told me He was going to teach me, and that I should teach those things to others."

Nebaya and Anatellia stayed silent. The other three waited until it was obvious they weren't going to talk. Ange let out a frustrated noise.

"We shared with you!" She gave the two women her crossest look.

"Maybe another day." Anatellia shook her head. "I'm still working through it all."

Ange turned her look full on Nebaya. Nebaya simply stared back. The girl came back from the kitchen with a tray of soup bowls and bread. They thanked her and Ra'ah started passing out the soup.

"Well, Kawani said she's a worshipper," Ange started in again. "She said that she knew it from the moment she was baptized."

"What is that?" Ra'ah felt something jump deep down within him.

"She said it's something they all did when they first came to the Gellah, before they went up Anatellia's trail." Ange gave Anatellia a look. "David introduced it to them."

"David?" Anatellia said. "How did He learn it? What is it, even?"

"And why didn't he include it in his story?" Nebaya asked.

"She didn't really explain it," Ange said. "But it involves getting dunked, and then the Spirit of the Living God comes down and doesn't go away. She said she would show me if I wanted. I think we all should get baptized."

"The practice of baptism is old," Daskow spoke up. "It was popular for many centuries in the valley, and then it fell out of favour."

"Why?" Ange asked.

Daskow shrugged. "I do not know. But there are no surviving holy texts that reference baptism. So the practice probably got purged."

A half-dozen of their guard entered the common house and made for a table. Kawani, Kai, and Hanah were with them. Before anyone thought to stop her, Ange waved Kawani over.

"Hello everyone," Kawani greeted them. "How's the soup today?"

"We just got it." Ra'ah motioned to the half-empty table. "Would your group like to join us?"

"I can go check," Kawani offered.

"Before you go…" Ange glanced at the others. "Could you explain baptism for us?"

"Ange told us that David taught it to you…?" Anatellia's eyebrows expressed her disbelief.

"Joshua taught David, and David taught us," Kawani explained. "It's simply an act of setting aside the old life and submitting to serve the Living God."

"And it involves getting dunked." Ange nodded as if that was exactly how she had described it to them.

"Ange tells me the valley doesn't practice baptism," Kawani said. "Would you like to be baptized?"

"What purpose would it serve?" Nebaya asked bluntly.

Kawani locked eyes with Nebaya and held her stare. The contest lasted well past awkward and Nebaya finally dropped her eyes away. Kawani then looked at the others in turn.

"It seems to me"—she was choosing her words with care—"that five young people wandering the valley desperately looking for purpose in the Living God might naturally want to declare that hunger and desire through baptism. As I said, baptism is just an event where you set aside the old life and commit to serving Him."

"I would like that," Ange said.

"So would I," Ra'ah agreed.

Daskow nodded.

Anatellia looked up at Kawani, and they stared at one another for a long moment. "Why wait?" she finally asked.

Kawani shook her head. "We will have plenty of time tomorrow. There is no sense everyone catching pneumonia or twisting an ankle climbing around the pool in the dark."

"I thought we'd be leaving first thing tomorrow." Anatellia frowned.

"Something's come up," Kawani said. "But I'm sure your brother will be along to explain. It's not really my place. If you'll excuse me."

She walked away and rejoined the others at their table.

"What is with you?" Ange turned on Nebaya. "You're ruder than normal with her. And she doesn't deserve that."

"I don't want to talk about it." Nebaya pushed her bowl aside and stood up. "I need some air."

She left all of her gear at the table and walked outside.

"Should one of us go after her?" Ra'ah asked.

"No." Anatellia shook her head. "She needs to be alone with that."

"With what?" Ra'ah pressed.

"Ra'ah, one day you are going to make someone an amazing husband," Anatellia laughed.

Ra'ah's mouth snapped shut. He tended to miss things related to relationships with women. The others often laughed when he failed to recognize a person's interest in him. He always considered himself a rather poor choice for anyone's interests, especially with his wandering around the valley and not settling down. He looked towards the door through which Nebaya had just left.

"I always thought we'd all just grow old together wandering the valley." He gave an exaggerated sigh.

"If Matron Willard gets her way, you'll be married within the year," Ange laughed.

"What?" Ra'ah felt his face flush.

Anatellia nodded. "Oh yes; she interviewed us quite thoroughly. She's on the hunt for a suitable woman for you."

"That's not funny." He looked to Daskow to help him out.

"Don't look at me!" Daskow raised his hands in surrender. "I was more than happy to keep her scheming focused on you."

"And when was this taking place?" Ra'ah demanded, horrified.

"When you, Nebaya, and Amon went to help that woman with the wolf bite," said Ange. "And come to think of it, we never got to hear what happened there with all the craziness that's happened since."

"First things first." Ra'ah felt his heart race. "What exactly are you all planning with Matron Willard?"

"We aren't," Anatellia corrected. "Matron Willard has taken it upon herself as a good adoptive mother to find you a suitable wife. And Daskow is right—we were all more than happy to keep her focused on you."

Ra'ah glared at them as they all broke out laughing.

21

A New Beginning

Nebaya strode back up the hill in search of a place to be alone. The new settlement around the falls felt unbelievably crowded to her. She passed down into the bowl of the first pool and made her way to the water's edge. There were no torches down here, at least.

What is my problem? she shouted into the vaults of her own head.

As if to mock her, her thoughts brought David to mind. She lashed out at the image in her head, and picking up a rock, she threw it at the pool. It skipped into the darkness and struck the other side with a crack. In the dark shadows of the far side of the pool, a figure stood up and looked toward her. She almost dropped to the rocks in the hope that she wouldn't be noticed.

The figure began making its slow, unsteady way around the pool toward her. She looked up at the edge of the bowl and then back at the figure. She didn't feel a threat from it, nor did she believe a threat could have made its way into the camp of these people.

Did I hit them with that rock?

The dim features of an old man took shape as he came within feet of her and regarded her silently. She wondered if she should apologize. She also wondered how long he'd stand there in the dark staring at her before he spoke. A wilder idea occurred to her that he might be a little crazy.

"Your anger is misplaced, child," the man stated matter-of-factly.

"You…" She bit back an angry retort and took a deep breath. "You don't know me, sir. But I am sorry for that rock. I did not know you were there."

"That is the nature of lashing out in anger, though, isn't it?" The old man chuckled. "We often cause harm where we never consciously intended to."

"I'm sorry," she mumbled, and turned to go.

"Why go now, child?" The old man's voice was soft but commanding. "Now that you've interrupted my prayers we might as well sit and talk awhile."

"I did not mean to..." she stammered.

"You did not mean to," he repeated. "Well, that may be true. But what did the Living God mean to do?"

"I don't know what you mean," she said.

The man sat on a stone outcrop nearby. "People always think the course of their lives is about their choices, what they meant to do. Rarely do they consider what He might be doing. You came down here to be alone and throw angry rocks. You didn't realize that He brought old Timothy down here to pray."

"I really am sorry." She felt the opportunity to escape the conversation was rapidly closing.

"So you've already said," Timothy acknowledged. "But you don't realize we're beyond the rock now. The Living God has set up an appointment with you and old Timothy here. I see the fire in you, the Hand of the Living God is on you. But you are like a wild mare, unwilling to take the bit and bridle and be led by Him."

"Now see here..." Nebaya retorted hotly.

"No, child," Timothy cut in softly. "This is not the time for angry replies. This is the time for setting aside that anger. You've carried it long enough."

"You think it's that easy?" Nebaya asked bitterly. "That I can just forget all of the hurt and all of the disappointment and stop being angry?"

"I think that all He is asking is 'Are you willing to try?'" The old man's eyes shone in the darkness. "Are you willing to say yes to Him when He asks for that anger?"

"Yes, of course, yes!" Nebaya almost spat in frustration.

"Have you been baptized into Him, child?" the old man asked.

"No," she said in confusion.

The old man got up, removed his cloak, and waded out into the pool.

"What? Now?" She could see the dark outline of the man in water up to his knees, waiting for her.

"You are not a person who waits when something needs to be done, are you?" he asked patiently. "Or do you wish to go back on your word to Him?"

"You're getting on my nerves, old man." Nebaya took off her robe and waded out into the water after him.

"Have you ever witnessed a baptism?" the old man asked.

"No," she said shortly.

"This is how it goes," he explained in a patient tone, as if to a child. "You will kneel. I will ask you a question. You will say yes. I will direct you forward into the water. You will come out of the water. I will pray that the Spirit of the Living God come to dwell with you. Any questions?"

"No," she repeated as she knelt in the water. "Ask your question."

"Do you surrender yourself to the Living God, forsaking your anger, your hurt, and your past life, to serve Him and Him alone?"

"Yes, I…" She was cut short as he pushed her forward into the water.

It seemed an eternity before he pulled her back out. She sputtered and spit water.

"You went into the water with everything you were. In the water the old is buried. You come out born anew as a child of the Living God," Timothy said.

"I feel no different," she admitted.

"That is between you and Him." Timothy's head nodded in the dark. "Receive now the Spirit of the Living God."

A fire seemed to fall on Nebaya. The presence that she had felt the day before seemed to settle in her belly. It was like a consuming fire inside of her. And it came for what she had said it could have. She hesitated, for the briefest of moments, and considered hanging on to her anger. It was like a warm blanket that protected her. But protected her from what, exactly?

The pool, the old man, the roar of the falls behind her were suddenly gone. She stood in a high country clearing with a beautiful cabin. There was a woman singing an eerily familiar song hanging laundry on a line. The laughter of a little girl could be heard around the corner of the cabin, and the deep voice of a man calling her name.

Nebaya's heart leapt in her throat. She moved slowly around the line to look at the woman hanging laundry. The woman stopped singing suddenly when she noticed Nebaya.

"Hello, honey." The woman smiled. "My goodness, you've grown."

"You aren't here." Nebaya shook her head. "You're dead."

"Is that what you think?" The woman looked at her sadly.

"I know it." Nebaya tried to hold her emotions, tried to keep herself together. "The fire took you."

"Sweetheart…" The woman reached out for her. "There is no death for those who serve Him."

"No, you and Dad died in that fire!" Nebaya reached out to pull the blanket of her anger around her, but it wasn't there.

"What's this?" A man stepped around the edge of the cabin and stopped when he saw her. "Nebaya?"

"Daddy?" The weight was too much, and she broke.

The pain that she had protected herself against all those long years flooded through her, whipping past her soul like the fire that had stolen everything and everyone she had loved. She fell on her knees, bent over in agony. Hot tears poured down her cheeks to fall onto the dirt in front of her. Without access to her anger, she was defenceless. She was going to be destroyed.

Arms encircled her. The long-remembered smell of her father's sweat. The flowered smell of her mother's soap. The pain lanced through her consciousness into the darkest depths of her soul, and like lightning in the dark sky, it lit her up and revealed her darkness.

"I'm sorry," she sobbed as the arms held her. "I'm so sorry."

"You've carried this for too long, my sweet Nebaya!" Her father's voice broke. "It's not yours to carry."

"Lay it down, sweetheart," her mother begged.

"I will," Nebaya wept brokenly.

A wind blew through her, a presence stronger than her father entered the clearing with them. There was a smell more beautiful than her mother's soap suddenly on the wind. A third set of arms wrapped around her, even as she felt her parents' arms slip away. In desperation she reached out to hold them, but they stepped away out of her reach. The arms now around her held her fast. She turned her head and saw through tears the face of love from her vision—the face of Joshua unveiled.

She turned back to her parents and watched as they and the cabin and the clearing became indistinct and dissolved into radiant light. The last to fade was a little girl, running and playing across the clearing to her parents. The little girl turned at the last moment and looked into Nebaya's eyes. It was like looking into her own soul.

"I will never see them again." Nebaya's voice cracked.

Joshua's voice was like a soothing balm. "Yes, you will, child. They wait for you beyond this world, in the true Kingdom, which is in Heaven."

"I am nothing without my anger," she lamented. "I am defenceless."

"I am your Defence," Joshua admonished.

Nebaya shut her eyes. "I am weak, Lord. How can I be what you want me to be?"

"This weakness is not the end of a story," Joshua laughed. "It's the beginning of a greater story. Now I will teach you a better way."

David strolled absently down from the tunnel door and went over the internal checklists in his mind. Seeing his sister and the others had brought back some long-buried memories. He marvelled that, after all these years, the feelings had stayed dormant but lurking. His life before the Living God had plucked him out of it shouldn't have remained that prominent. But here he was working through the old insecurities, rifling through old emotions and ideas.

A house is only as strong as its foundations, the thought popped into his head unbidden.

He nodded. That was very true. And he wasn't going to rebury the old feelings. Better to dig them out and replace them with better foundation.

He stepped off the road and stared across the bowl of the first pool to the newly rising moon. *There is something stirring in the Spirit tonight,* he mused. The falls felt different since the last time he'd been there. Mediators had been sent from the City to pray over and dedicate the land to the Living God. He acknowledged it was something he did not understand, but he knew better than to bad-mouth it. The presence of the Living God was stronger here than it ever had been.

He caught movement down by the pool. By the light of the moon, someone was stumbling out of the water. He shook his head. Whoever it was had gone in clothed—probably didn't watch their step in the dark and fell in. Another thought occurred to him—maybe they had fallen from above. He made his way down to check on them. The figure turned toward him as he approached, hair hiding the face in shadow as the moon rose behind them.

"David?" a soft, familiar voice whispered.

"Nebaya?" David's confusion was complete in finding her, of all people, coming out of the pool.

She moved toward him and stumbled. He reached out instinctively and caught her, drawing her up against his chest to steady her. He braced for the immediate push away, but she just lay her head against his chest. He froze in confusion and uncertainty.

"Nebaya," he repeated softly. "Are you all right?"

There was a long moment of silence as he stood there awkwardly, holding her by her arms. Her hair was wet, and soaked through his cloak and shirt. He felt the old desire, long dormant but awakened since he had first seen her again in front of the City. The ache of his heart was a distraction.

"You remind me of him," Nebaya finally said, and pulled gently away. "More now than you ever did."

He held his breath, holding the moment like it would shatter and blow away. He didn't know who she meant, but the way she said it won over his heart right then and there. He let his breath out slowly in a whispered prayer to the One who hears.

"What were you doing in the pool?" he finally asked.

"Timothy..." She looked around as if he should be right there. He wasn't. She shrugged. "A man named Timothy baptized me."

"Baptized you?" David said incredulously. "At night? And alone?"

"Yes." She nodded as she searched for the cloak she had set aside.

He watched her as she fumbled around. It was certainly Nebaya in front of him. But it also wasn't. She was different—there was a vulnerability around her that was very unlike her. It was like coming to a rose bush expecting thorns, and finding none.

She picked up her discarded cloak and swung it around her shoulders. "I'm cold," she stated flatly, and started up the slope of the bowl.

David shook his head and followed her up.

22

A Restive Pause

R a'ah awoke the next morning with a start. The sounds of a busy camp outside the bunkhouse came through the walls with the sound of the river, but that wasn't what had woken him. He could make out sunlight sneaking through a few cracks and the room was gaining a warm stuffy feel that spoke of a summer morning well underway. He sat up to shake the last cobwebs out of his head and then heard the sounds that had stirred him from his slumber: a rapid series of cracks and short encouraging shouts from somewhere nearby.

He jumped up and put his shoes on. He hated always being the last one up. He hurriedly opened the door and stood there blinking in the midmorning sun for several long seconds. He caught his breath as he stared out over the massive work that he had glimpsed the night before, spread out below and around him. The engineers had taken great care to design and build this new settlement to fit into the forest around it, but the sheer scope of the project still scarred the once pristine valley. Ra'ah pondered, and not for the first time, how many people actually lived in the Amatta and how many would heed the warning.

The sound of wood striking wood caught his attention again, and he looked over to a nearby grassy clearing where Nebaya and Kawani were faced off against one another. Nebaya was listening intently as the other woman explained something about the quarter staff, watching the woman's hands shift and grip the leatherbound wood with practiced ease. The others were nearby, watching the exchange with interest.

Kawani gave Nebaya a sharp command and the staff in Nebaya's hands swung down toward the other woman suddenly. Ra'ah bit back a cry of surprise as the tall guard casually deflected the attack, giving quiet instruction as she did so. Nebaya's staff became a flurry as she pivoted it and struck from all sides. Kawani nodded and kept talking as she effortlessly deflected and blocked the attacks.

Ange looked away from the exchange long enough to wave Ra'ah over. He slowly joined them, not wanting to take his eyes off the strange dance that the two tall women were performing. The others acknowledged him with quick nods as the fight continued.

"Your entire mindset is only on attack," Kawani scolded Nebaya. "You must also be mindful of defence."

"But if I keep you defending, you cannot attack."

Suddenly Kawani's staff shifted and Nebaya's attack slid to the side. Nebaya had been expecting a block and her eyes widened in surprise as the other woman's staff shot out and hit her just below the ribs. She staggered back, and Kawani's staff flicked out and cracked across her knuckles. She cried out and backed up further, waving the other woman off. Kawani simply planted her staff with a thud in front of her.

"Point made," Nebaya gasped. "Point made."

"You have a lot of natural ability," Kawani said. "But for you it is important to realize that the person whom you are facing has more training and more experience. Our purpose for being here, for being your guard, is to be the barrier between you and those who would harm you. Always defer the battle to us. And that goes for all of you."

They all nodded. Ra'ah had been shocked by how quickly the sparring had changed. Nebaya had been fast on the attack, but Kawani had demonstrated a speed that he doubted anyone could have defended against.

"How does a quarterstaff stand up against a sword?" Daskow asked quietly.

"The staff has longer reach, more force at twice as many ends, and can deliver quicker blows than most swords." Kawani shrugged. "No swordsman with any sense would come within range of us when we carry these."

"Hopefully we never have to test that," Daskow said.

Kawani just shrugged again. Something passed across her face that made Ra'ah uncomfortable. Her gaze suddenly shifted to a small knot of approaching people, and he followed her gaze to see David with a group of the Klasma and a woman of unfathomable age.

"Everyone, I'd like you all to meet Tecany," David said. "Tecany is the chief builder of the Gellah camp. She oversees all of the engineers and craftspeople."

They all nodded to the woman, who tilted her head in acknowledgement. She struck Ra'ah as a person with a dozen different things on her mind. Her eyes took in everything, and nothing was missed.

"We were just going down to the new defence works to talk with the builders," David explained. "And I thought I'd invite you all along, since we're also going to meet the first official group up from the valley."

"Already?" Daskow asked in surprise. "They must be a scouting group from Cardaya."

David nodded. "Yes. And an old friend is with them."

"Oh?" Anatellia's face reflected everyone's surprise.

"I will introduce him when he gets here," David assured them.

"I was kind of hoping we were going to get baptized." Ange looked eagerly toward the falls in the opposite direction.

Kawani's laughter filled the clearing like a fresh breeze on a hot day. She all but glided across the clearing, moving more like a dancer than a soldier. She wrapped her arm around Ange and maneuvered her toward the road that headed down valley. Ra'ah suddenly realized he was staring and jerked his gaze away, only to catch the gaze of David. There was a twinkle in his eyes and a small knowing grin. Ra'ah felt his face flush, and he fell in step with the group as they headed for the defence works down the valley.

"Be careful." David's whisper was close and full of gentle humour as he brushed past. "Her brother is very protective."

Ra'ah's stomach fell. He opened his mouth to deny what David was suggesting but no words came out. He shut it with an audible thump and set his eyes to the road in front of them.

The sheer number of workers in the valley started to make itself apparent as they walked. Crews were busy at a dozen projects. Teams of horses pulled wagons of cut timber over cobblestone roads laid out across the Gellah Falls side of the river. Carpenters and masons were everywhere, laying foundations and framing up walls on either side.

They arrived at the junction where the road from the falls met the road coming across the river and up into the pass, and a great foundation clearing had been made. Ra'ah looked at it curiously.

"It's coming along nicely, thank you," he heard David answer the ageless woman walking beside him.

"What is?" Ra'ah blurted, wishing he had been eavesdropping better.

"The inn!" David pointed triumphantly. "I had to fight hard to make it a priority."

"A terrible drain on resources." Tecany's voice was deep and commanding. "But I serve a greater Wisdom than my own."

"Everything seems so permanent," Anatellia marvelled. "You're building a city, not a refugee camp."

Tecany nodded. "Indeed. Because we *aren't* building a camp. We are building a gateway city."

Ra'ah looked around him in shock. He took in the workers, the buildings, the foundation for what he now knew was an inn. He tried to picture what it would look like. The image of the Crossroads and the Willard's Ox Inn flashed in his mind. This inn was going to be larger than even that one.

He looked forward and realized the river crossing was just ahead. The road split and descended the riverbank to the riverbed. A solid wooden bridge spanned the river right next to the ford, crossing it in five spans anchored by stone pilings. A short way downstream was another construction in progress. Great stoneworks were built on either side of the riverbank, and three great stone pillars rose from the riverbed. Ra'ah stared in wonder at what could only be the roots of a stone bridge, much like the one down the valley that connected the city side with Cardaya and Pethe.

"It seems that your priorities may be a little skewed." Anatellia's voice carried rebuke.

Tecany's icy glance toward Anatellia carried its own sharp rebuke. David's chuckle was strained. There was silence in the group for a long moment.

"We all serve at the pleasure of the Living God, child," Tecany finally said. "We of the City have long desired to set our hands to a project such as this. Many of us stayed and did not pass beyond because of the promise of this opportunity. To serve Him with our gifts is the greatest form of worship we can offer."

"I meant no disrespect," Anatellia apologized. "I am just worried about the thousands of people coming north in the next few days."

"We are not unaware," Tecany said shortly. "Every head will have a bed. And by winter every family a home. As more of your people arrive, more hands become available. We built all of this without their help; imagine what we can build with it! And here are young Duncan and Master Peter."

Two men were waiting for them to cross the bridge. Duncan, the man they had been introduced to the night before, and another man, equally as ageless as Tecany, but his entire appearance reminded Ra'ah of how a man might look if you rolled him down a mountainside. He eyed them all from under a heavy scowl.

"Peter!" David greeted him. "I've never seen you happier."

"I'd be considerably happier if Tecany would give me my workers and the resources I asked for." The man's voice was like gravel underfoot.

"You will get what you want when we've completed a sufficient number of barracks," Tecany dismissed him. "But I came down here myself to tell you to make due with undressed stone. You can make it pretty later."

"Pretty!?" Peter roared. "I'm trying to make an unbreachable defence, not build a tavern."

"Master Peter…" Tecany's tone became like the stone they were arguing over.

The man nodded curtly. "I know. Practical, not perfect—but it doesn't mean I like it."

"If you have time, I will show you the other quarry sites we've found for you," Tecany offered.

The gruff man nodded, and started back over the bridge with Tecany. The rest of them watched as the two moved out of hearing, and then Duncan turned to David with a smile.

"Those two love their jobs!" Duncan laughed.

"They definitely know their jobs. Even when they seem to conflict. What other news do you have for me?"

"Shall we walk?" Duncan extended a hand down the road.

Ra'ah's attention slowly drifted away from Duncan and David's conversation as he studied the changed valley around him. This side of the river looked remarkably different from the other. Large wooden buildings lined the slope. Many of them looked like the bunkhouse that they had been housed in the night before. In addition, there were storehouses at regular intervals. The road was paved with heavier stone and reminded him of the roads around Kathik, built for heavy wagons.

The arm of the mountain came around toward the river just ahead, creating a natural narrows as it met a similar arm from the other side. Looking ahead, Ra'ah was shocked to see great excavations on both sides. As they got closer, the view of the gap opened up and a large construction of moved earth and stone surrounded the road and river.

"What are they doing?" Daskow asked in surprise.

Duncan turned his head as they walked. "We are building a walled defence. A wall on this side and a weir and pool tucked up into the cliff on the other. When we're done, the only way past this spot will be climbing across the cliff like a goat on that side, or through the wall and gate on this side."

"Somehow I didn't think they'd chase us up here," Anatellia mused as she looked at the excavations with the workers milling like ants. "But I also didn't think we'd be stopping here. Can we really stand against them, even in this place? How many of you are there?"

"About five thousand," Duncan said. "And we've been eager to get started."

"What you need to understand, Anna, is that our greatest defence is not our strength or skill in battle: it is the Living God we serve." David gaze came unfocused across the river. "Not everyone fleeing north will be able to approach the Mountain or enter the City. Only those who know Him can approach Him."

The thought struck Ra'ah. How was he able to approach, then? Did he know the Living God? The Living God certainly knew him. Something stirred within him, an answer of sorts. Yes, for his part Ra'ah knew the Living God. Not well, but he knew Him. And a hunger growled deep inside his heart. He wanted to know Him better.

"I hope the Sacheth know they aren't allowed to approach Him," Anatellia muttered.

"Sis"—David's voice was low and carried a soft rebuke—"before all this is over, you will see how silly that statement was."

"I truly hope so," she whispered.

They approached the earthworks, which rose in a slope to either side of the road. The road continued level through them, and on down the valley. When they reached the summit of the slope, they could see down the valley for another half mile. The trees had been cleared in a great strip between the river and the steep mountain slope, leaving a bare field of grass, stone, and mountain flowers. It reminded him of the Valley they had all left.

The hill they were on ended suddenly. Ra'ah peered over the edge to see a great stonework wall starting to rise from the valley floor. Daskow peered over with him in interest.

"Are you going to be done in time?" Daskow asked.

"We're all in the hands and timing of the Living God." Duncan smiled. "We'll have enough of a deterrent built to turn the hearts of the Sacheth, I'm sure. If they've forgotten in the last thousand years why you shouldn't follow the children of the Living God into narrow mountain places, we'll remind them again."

The Klasma that were with them chuckled at Duncan's words, but under the smiles Ra'ah saw long-healed wounds. He pondered that as he lifted his eyes toward the distant forest where it met the now undeveloped trail heading south. They obviously hadn't improved the road at all that way. Movement caught his eye as he stared. A group of travellers on foot came out of the forest and stopped as they caught sight of the earthworks.

"Someone is over there," he pointed.

Everyone looked south, studying the distant figures that were now at least two dozen strong. They were dressed in the familiar clothes of the Valley, and even from this distance their bows could be seen, one sticking above each shoulder.

"Let's go meet them," David offered, and loped back down the slope toward the road.

They met the group of wary young men in the middle of the field. Ra'ah recognized many of them from not even two weeks before. They were obviously very surprised and more than a little concerned to find people in this part of the valley. Several of them watched the approaching strangers with wariness until they caught sight of the five mixed in among them. But their surprised cry was cut short by a bellow from their midst.

"David, bless my eyes, what a sight you are!" The group opened up to allow an older man with a travel-stained cloak to pass through.

Nebaya's happy shout of surprise echoed Ra'ah's own, but David beat them to speaking.

"Amon! How are you, my friend?" He laughed and ran to meet the older man. "Look how old you've become!"

"Aye." Amon nodded and grabbed the other man in a great hug, but his eyes were looking beyond him to the group and five members in particular. "And I see I'm not the only stray you've found since leaving your soft life on the Mountain."

"Amon, it's good to see you," Ra'ah called. "I certainly didn't expect to see you again so soon."

"Nor I you five," Amon admitted. "Here is a story—and not likely a short one, I'm guessing."

"There will be enough time for that," David said as he waved Amon's group to follow them. "My sister and her friends have been delivered into my care for the rest of their errand. Come, let's get you all settled."

Amon nodded, and motioned reassuringly to the dozen men behind him. They looked between David and the Klasma and the five in wonder and uncertainty, but fell in behind Amon.

"It's good to see you again." He nodded to them as they also fell in beside him. "But I admit I am anxious to see you all here and not down the Valley. How goes the message?"

"Meletsa and Kathik have both heard," Ra'ah assured him. "We were racing back to Kathik when a Maylak brought us to the City."

"Truly?" Amon breathed in awe. "And you were brought into the City itself?"

"The gates only, my friend," David said. "They were not permitted to enter any more than you were."

"I suppose not." Amon nodded as he looked them all over. "But it's still a wonder you yourself are allowed out."

"Grace is portioned to each of us according to our purpose, old friend," David reminded him.

A look of deep longing crossed Amon's face, but he just nodded.

A sudden rush of grey flew into the group and skidded to a stop at Kawani and Ange's feet. In the surprise of seeing Amon and the youth from Cardaya, Ra'ah had all but forgotten about Amon's companion, Pestos. The great hound's tongue hung in a happy grin, and the two women dug their hands into his scruff.

Something that David had said finally caught Ra'ah's attention.

"Wait!" He shook his head. "Amon, you have been to the Mountain and the City? Why didn't you tell us? You had time on the way up from Pethe."

"I took an oath," Amon answered shortly. "And you kids didn't need confirmation; you had already set your eyes to the path."

"Amon is a member of a very small fraternity of people over the years who have found the path to the Mountain," David interjected. "And one of an even smaller group who, having reached the Mountain, accepted a greater Call, and returned to life in the Valley. Like you five, he has been fulfilling his Call."

"And what exactly was that Call?" Nebaya asked sharply.

"That is a long story, and I do not feel the time has come for its telling," Amon said flatly and changed the subject as he nodded to the rising earthworks ahead. "The Klasma have been busy."

David nodded. "The artisans have come out of the City to put their skills to work. Although they are eager for fresh labourers."

"I'm sure I can provide more than a few." Amon shook his head. "It is no small relief to find you all here. We have already established camps on either side of the river a day above Bato. I brought these boys north with me in the hope of setting up a forward camp and making some kind of contact with you. But you have exceeded my greatest imagination."

"You've seen nothing yet," Angelis piped up.

"It's true," David laughed. "You have nothing to worry about on this end. The Living God has provided a refuge for those who obey his warning."

"And this will be enough?" Amon looked over the walls being raised in front of the earthworks.

"It will be," David replied, "Because He has said it will be."

Amon nodded, and they walked in the silence of their own thoughts through the gap into the valley beyond.

The journey back toward the falls was narrated by Angelis, who proceeded to fill Amon in on all that had happened to them after they had parted a week before. Ra'ah found himself marvelling at all that had actually happened in that week. Amon simply nodded and grunted as his eyes took in everything that Ra'ah had seen on the way down to meet them. The only time he interrupted was when she recounted Nebaya and Ra'ah's interaction with Dunhamai.

"Dunhamai?" His voice had an odd edge to it. "She's still guarding her pass?"

"Not for much longer," Ra'ah interjected. "She took a wound, and Nebaya and I had to carry her down off the pass. I suspect she'll be leading refugees toward Kathik by now."

"She won't abandon that post so easily," Amon muttered, but then waved for Ange to continue.

They had reached the site of the future inn, and Amon looked at it appreciatively.

"Who's going to get the task of running that monstrosity, I wonder?" Amon shot a look at David. "Leave it to you people to build a permanent inn in a refugee camp."

David's eyes took on a distant look. For the first time since they had been reunited at the City gate, Ra'ah saw a vast sense of time reflected on his face. He caught David's gaze, and he felt like he was falling into time itself. David broke the contact and shook his head.

"There is nothing simpler and less likely to survive than a plan before it is implemented," David said cryptically. "That was something my father once told me before he died. As for this refugee camp, well, He has other intentions."

"I thought we were supposed to all go to the Mountain," Anatellia challenged him. "That is the message we were sent with."

"And that is the message you should continue with, dear sister," David assured her. "Everyone has been given a task. Don't get caught up in critiquing other people's Calling. We are a people who move under His purpose and His plan, and we certainly don't get to see the entire thing. I among all of you know this the best. For you, this has all happened in a few days. But I lack the time or words to describe the waiting, the endless distraction of days, the longing to see my Calling fulfilled. None of you can understand the temptation, the very desire to cross the temple floor and to pass utterly from this life into the next. But the Spirit of the Living God sustained me, held me, trained me, and honed me into who I am now—a tool for His purposes."

A wave of emotions crossed Anatellia's face, but she just nodded. They continued from the site of the inn and Kawani took up the lead, heading toward the lower pool of the falls.

"Come on," she called out. "I see no reason to keep Angelis waiting any longer."

Ange's cheer was drowned out by the laughter of the Klasma and her other friends. Amon's small troupe of men looked at them in amused confusion but followed along in an overwhelmed daze. Amon simply looked between David and Anatellia as he walked in deep thought.

23

CALLED THROUGH WATER

Kawani led them back through the camp and down a well-worn path to the shores of the first pool. Ra'ah breathed the humid air deeply; there was a strange peace beside the pool that was tangible. Everyone seemed to feel it except Nebaya, who appeared to be scanning the far side, looking for something. Ra'ah caught her eye suddenly and he was surprised to see a deep sadness set into her eyes. She quickly broke the connection, and when she looked back the sadness was gone, or at least buried deep.

"Are you okay?" he whispered.

"Fine." She gave him a small Nebaya smile. "Or fine enough. I'll explain later, I promise."

He watched her for several moments longer, but the sadness was well under her control now. He turned his attention back to Kawani as she and Angelis waded out into the pool. She looked over to David, but he just shook his head and motioned for her to continue.

Kawani turned to address the group on the shore. "If Simon were here, he would explain that this was a very old practice for servants of the Living God, long forgotten. The One called Joshua gave us back this practice through David. Baptism should not be taken lightly; it is a public declaration of our setting aside our lives as they were and swearing to live in the service of the Living God. The Living God will come and make a dwelling place in you."

Ra'ah considered her words, and his mind travelled back two days earlier to the experience of the light, staring into the very face of love. The face that looked so very much like Joshua. Questions and confusion rose in his mind; a lifetime of learning about the Living God left him completely lacking the knowledge to explain the last few weeks, and especially those last few days. But one certainty he found in his thoughts: given all that had happened to them, consenting to be baptized seemed the least of responses he could give.

Angelis stood excitedly beside Kawani, her arms crossed over her chest. Kawani asked her if she would forsake herself and serve the Living God all the rest of her life. Ange all but screamed "Yes!" and the taller woman plunged her into the pool. With a small heave, Kawani pulled her back out of the water. Ra'ah expected a squeal of surprise to come out of her mouth, but when she opened it, a song came out of her unlike anything he had ever heard her sing.

She simply stood in the pool, her hands raised to the sky and her head lifted, singing a song both haunting and beautiful and completely unintelligible to everyone watching on the shore. Something in Ra'ah leapt to life as the song rose up the cliffs. He almost felt like he understood the words, but they remained elusive and foreign. Kawani looked surprised at first, but then her voice joined in and she raised her hands. Together they sang the unknown hymn as the crowd on the shore looked on. An almost tangible presence of peace, like a weight, descended on them all.

He was halfway into the pool before he realized he was moving. He wanted whatever it was that had come over Ange. His soul was hungry in a way he had never felt, urged on by the blanket of the presence in that stone bowl.

Kawani motioned to one of the Klasma on the shore, and the big man Temian strode out to meet Ra'ah in the water. He asked the same question of Ra'ah, and Ra'ah heard his own voice shout "Yes!." The sudden rush of cold water almost made him gasp, and then the strong arms pulled him back up.

He shook. The bright sunlight beat down on his shivering body. He looked around and realized that he must have gotten water in his ears. The roar of the falls was distant and dull. Ange and Kawani's singing was muffled. Over everything was a sound like a great wind.

He stumbled toward the shore, confusion and disappointment flooding past him like leaves on a stream. He took another step, confused by the muffled sounds around him. The roaring of the wind in his head was not played out in the scene before him. He heard Temian's voice—was he talking to him? He turned to look at the big man and realized he must have lost his footing. He was falling backward, but his arms weren't responding.

He felt the water envelop him again, but it felt strangely distant from his senses. He closed his eyes tightly as a great current seemed to tear him away. In muted panic, he realized he was in the main stream. He braced himself to hit the stones of the rapids below the pool, fighting with his arms to move.

Hands grabbed him by the shirt and pulled him up to the surface. He sputtered, and suddenly his arms worked. He opened his eyes, expecting to see the bowl of the lower falls and everyone rushing to help him, but instead he stared into the face of a familiar old woman, backlit by torchlight on a stone roof.

"Karis," he whispered.

"Matron Karis," the old woman corrected sternly. "And there is no time for your foolishness. There is healing to attend to."

He looked around in confusion. He was in a cave lit by torches. The water was gone. He looked down and saw the clothes of an apprentice healer on his body. The woman staring at him was Matron Karis, pride of Bato and one of the Valley's most gifted healers. He looked across the chamber to a raised dais where a man lay unconscious, blood-soaked bandages wrapped around his head and body.

The old woman moved quickly to the wounded man, her speed always deceptive and graceful for her age. She looked back at him impatiently.

"He will be harder to heal if he dies," she scolded.

Ra'ah stumbled over to the wounded man in confusion. He looked down at the face before him, and recognized the patient immediately. He shook his head and closed his eyes tightly. This man was already dead. He had died years ago. What kind of dream was this? He opened his eyes, expecting to see the pool and the falls and his friends, but his only companions in the strange cave were the old woman and the dying man.

"Heal him," the old woman commanded.

"I couldn't!" He shook his head. "I mean. I can't. Neither could you at the time. This man died, and there was nothing we could do."

"That was then." The old woman's voice still had the power to cow him. "You know what killed him then—heal him now."

"I have no more knowledge to heal him now than I did then." Ra'ah's frustration grew. "No one does."

"There is One who does." The old woman's eyes bore into him. "And where we fail, He prevails. But He's looking for hands to use. We are His hands."

Ra'ah shook his head in frustration as he looked down at the dying man. This was one of Matron Karis's favourite declarations. Of course she was referring to the Living God. She was adamant that the Living God could heal, even when the healers had done all they could and it looked like it wasn't enough. She had said the same thing to him concerning this man the first time he had lived through this memory.

"He is already dead," Ra'ah repeated.

"Who are you, that you have such power to declare life and death?" Matron Karis scolded. "You certainly did not learn that from me. And look at him, he breathes still."

Ra'ah looked down at the man on the stone dais and gasped. The man he knelt beside was no longer the man from so many years ago—it was David. He tried to stand up in shock but careened over backwards, his arms flailing. Gone were the cave, the torches. He was in a clearing with blurred images and chaotic noises. Someone screamed—a sound that cut him to his soul—and he landed flat on his back as the air left his lungs like a bellows. Darkness overtook him as the shadow of Matron Karis leaned close to his ear.

"You are His hands, Ra'ah," her voice whispered. "Trust in Him, in everything. Yours are the hands of the Healer."

He did not know how long he floated in the darkness. The peace returned immediately, a peace that passed all his understanding. There was a feeling about him of patient watching, as well. He found himself content to simply float.

After a time, noises started filtering through the darkness. A beautiful voice singing softly around him in the darkness. Muted laughter from a distance. Slowly he started to be aware of his surroundings. The sound of the falls and the pool. There was a rock digging into his back. He opened his eyes to see Ange smiling down at him from the rock she was perched on, singing softly.

"Hey," she giggled. "Welcome back."

"What happened?" he asked.

"You tell me," she laughed. "You came up, took two steps toward shore like a drunk, and then fell back into the pool. Temian had to drag you out of the water, you were so out of it. What happened?"

"I think I had a dream." Ra'ah sat up to look around. "It was so real."

"Do you want to talk about it?" Ange asked eagerly.

He shook his head. "Maybe later. What happened while I was out?"

"Daskow and Anatellia got baptized." Ange ticked off a finger. "They were kinda boring after our baptisms. All the young guys from Cardaya got baptized. They were a lot more lively and fun. One of the Klasma came with a message for David just a few minutes ago, and they took off somewhere."

"What was that song you were singing?" Ra'ah interrupted. "I have never heard you sing it before."

"I never have." She laughed again. "And I don't know. It rose up out of me and I just sang it. I'm not sure I could sing it again if I tried."

"It was beautiful," he admitted.

"It was." He was surprised to see a tear in her eye, but she smiled happily at him.

"Ra'ah, Angelis!" Kawani called from the rim of the bowl and waved them up. "There is someone coming down from the City you should meet."

They stood, walked together up the path, and joined Kawani on the rim. She motioned them to follow, and they proceeded toward the cave.

"Who are we going to meet?" Ange asked curiously.

"An old friend," Kawani said softly.

— 24 —

AN UNEXPECTED FAREWELL

The three of them rounded the final bend of the winding road to the tunnel to see a small crowd of familiar faces gathered at the entrance. David and the Klasma were there, as were Daskow, Nebaya, and Anatellia. They were all talking amongst themselves quietly. An air of solemnity hung over everything that Ra'ah felt in his chest.

"What's going on?" he whispered to Kawani. "You said we were going to meet an old friend?"

She nodded. "We are. He's on his way down now. And he wanted to meet you five."

"Who?" Ra'ah's mind raced. He thought maybe Joshua was coming, but dismissed the idea immediately. Somehow, he knew Joshua wouldn't need to walk from the City to visit them. He was about to ask another question when the doors of the tunnel swung open.

Standing in the now open doorway was a man much like any of the other Klasma. Young and hale yet ageless, he stood there, taking in the small crowd, some of them gazing back with surprise, others with deep affection. He wore a brown travel cloak with little sign of wear, and a satchel slung at his side that bore signs of much use. His eyes rested on David and a great warm smile broke across his face.

"David!" His voice was very deep and strong and carried a hint of humour. "It turns out you were right. If I had listened, it would have saved me this miserable trip."

"Simon, I did tell you that you needed to get out for a walk." David laughed. "I feared I would never see you again this side of the temple."

The barest hint of a shadow crossed the man's features and he nodded. Ra'ah caught something unspoken pass between the two friends and it rippled through the other Klasma. Simon broke eye contact with David then and focused his attention on Daskow. The young tutor bowed his head in deep respect.

"I have come with a tool for the young scholar," Simon continued. "And I didn't want to entrust it to anyone else to deliver."

He motioned for Daskow to come forward as he reached into the satchel and pulled out an ornately bound book. Daskow stepped forward hesitantly, his eyes moving from the man's face to the book and back. Simon simply extended the book to him in impatience.

"Stop acting like I'm some great man out of ancient history," Simon scolded. "It's more exhausting than you could ever know."

"Thank you, sorry, thank you," Daskow sputtered and accepted the book reverently. He turned it to read the cover and went instantly white.

"It's complete," Simon assured him casually. "I copied it from the City library. The binder didn't listen when I told him to keep it simple— or maybe he did, by his standards. Craftsmen in the City tend to become obsessed with beauty versus practicality. Few people value the perfection of simplicity itself."

"I don't understand." Daskow's voice barely carried to Ra'ah's ears. "Why?"

"Why?" Simon was surprised by the question. "So you can break the stone ears of the stubborn, of course. Not everything can be solved with a stick, unfortunately."

"I will treasure it," Daskow assured him.

"Treasure it?" Simon scoffed. "No, you need to use it. That's what I'm talking about with the binding. Make it too nice or ornate and people think it's not meant for serious use. Read it, study it, understand it."

"I will," Daskow said, nodding, and held the book to his chest as he stepped back. "And now I understand."

David swept in and embraced his friend then. Simon's surprise melted into brotherly affection, and he returned the hug.

"Come, let's get a drink and some food, and we can all catch up." David motioned down the road.

"No." Simon shook his head. "I am afraid this will be a short farewell. The weight of longing is already almost unbearable."

"But you've come this far, already!" Kawani called from beside Angelis. "Come on, Simon, we have all missed you."

"Dear Kawani, I'm afraid that I have come to the end of my strength and the grace given me by coming even this far." Simon regarded all of the Klasma. "Isn't it funny that the greatest peril we have all faced is the irresistibility of the Living God? Honestly, I thought I had seen the last of you all when I heard the day had come for your departure from the Mountain. But He gave me one last task. A task with two purposes. The first was easier than the second. The book is delivered. The second task, dear friends, is that of farewells."

"No," Kawani stated flatly, tears suddenly springing to her eyes.

Simon nodded. "Yes, Dear Heart. I will return to the City and the Mountain, and without hesitation cross the floor of the Temple. I am ready, so ready. I have completed my tasks, save this last."

"Let us walk the tunnel back with you," David offered. "And then we can make proper farewells of it."

"That is good," Simon agreed, and then looked beyond the gathering Klasma to the five that drew together to watch. "To you five I say this: look after my family. Do not put them in harm's way unnecessarily. Serve the Living God with everything in you. Until we meet again in places where time has no meaning."

Taken aback, the five just nodded. Simon then looked to the gathered Klasma and turned back up the tunnel. Temian caught the tunnel doors and pulled them to.

Ra'ah looked at his friends and read various versions of the confusion that he felt. Everyone except Daskow, who was staring at Simon's book. He leaned over to read the title.

"Via Eterna?" He searched his memory. "It sounds familiar somehow."

"Via Eterna is the name for the complete works of the holy texts," Daskow explained softly as he ran his hand over the leather. "There has never been a complete collection in the history of the valley. The closest to complete rests in the House of the Living God in Pethe. We don't call the holy texts Via Eterna specifically to honour and recognize that we don't have the complete texts."

"I always understood that phrase to mean something unattainable," Anatellia mused. "What do you suppose is written in there?"

"The fullness of our path to the Living God," Daskow declared. "But it may bring correction where correction is not welcome."

"I don't understand," Ange chimed in.

"What he means is that there are those who have studied the fragments of this book all of their lives," Nebaya said. "And their teachers before them. Where interpretation failed, assumptions have been made. Look at the squabbling between the villages. The different takes on what the holy texts mean. This book could be viewed as a threat to anyone who doesn't want to see their own error."

"This book could be more incendiary than Anatellia's book was," Daskow said. "In here will be the complete telling of the God Who Bled. The pieces we have are all but illegible. This book fills in all of the gaps. Joshua, baptism, the Living God actually making a home in us. Imagine if everything we've experienced in the last few days isn't actually new, but very, very old."

Anatellia shook her head. "Nebaya and Daskow are right. There are some who will be eager to know what is in this book. But there are others that I fear will consider it blasphemous and inauthentic. I have to wonder why Simon brought it to you."

"Because he knows I've been called back to Pethe," Daskow said in a voice that almost didn't carry over the sound of the water nearby. "I have to take this to Pethe and bring correction to the Brotherhood."

"What do you mean?" Nebaya asked sharply. "Called by whom? When?"

Daskow answered her last question first. "When I came up out of the water. I had a kind of vision. I saw myself standing in the courtyard in Pethe in front of the House and the library. There were a great many people with me. Suddenly a cry went up on the far side of the crowd. I saw a great smoke and flame, and the wind suddenly picked up to blind me. I called everyone to follow me to the river and it was only then that I realized they were all bound by the ankles to a great chain. I started to panic, and then a great weight of peace fell on me and I heard this booming voice say 'free them.'

"The crowd suddenly parted and I saw that the chain wound its way up the steps of the House to where it was wrapped around the pillars before the front doors. There, in the centre of the chain, was a great brass lock. Another voice suddenly boomed beside me, 'Take this and break the lock.' I turned and a great Maylak was standing there, holding a bright sword. Without thinking, I grabbed the hilt and ran for the steps.

"Shadowy men moved to stop me but somehow or another I made it past them. With all my effort, I struck down on the lock and chain and it shattered like hard candy struck with a rock. Suddenly I was alone with the Maylak and he just stared at me for several long moments before I heard a voice say 'Move quickly, the time is short.' And then the vision was gone and I knew, beyond doubt, that I needed to get back to Pethe. That I was needed there."

They just looked at him holding the book for some time. Finally Anatellia spoke.

"Bato is three days from here. We need to fulfill our mission there. It's another day and a half to Pethe from there. And we were promised arrest if we returned."

"Except that I was the only one I saw in my vision," Daskow pointed out. "And I feel like I need to get there as quickly as possible."

"Well I don't know how you're going to get there quicker than five days, no matter what we do," Anatellia shot back. "Unless you're going to ride the river like a thrill-seeking fool."

"No!" Daskow went white. "I'm not interested in riding the river. But I have a different route in mind. There is now a ferry across the river above Cardaya."

Anatellia opened her mouth to respond but then snapped it shut. Ra'ah realized she had forgotten about what Amon had told them. She looked at each of them as she thought.

"We'll have two days to consider what we should do," she finally said. "My head wants to say no, but something deeper in me suggests you're right. I don't want us to separate again, but we may have to. We will also have to include my brother and his Klasma in the conversation. I cannot pretend they don't have a say in this."

Daskow nodded and slipped the book under his arm. Ra'ah looked up at the afternoon sun and as if on cue, his stomach rumbled loudly. He looked sideways at the others to see if anyone had noticed over the sound of the Gellah. They were all looking at him. Angelis laughed.

"This is a good time to find a late lunch," Ra'ah announced.

They all laughed then and headed down the road toward the mess hall.

25

BACK ON THE ROAD

The Klasma returned long after the sun had set, bathed in moonlight and a sense of sadness that covered them like a blanket of soft snow. Ra'ah had stepped out of the hall to get a breath of fresh air and a break from the rather packed room. They came down in one great knot, murmuring in quiet conversations. Ra'ah stepped quietly off the road in respect and they greeted him with nods and warm smiles. All except David and Temian, who stopped to stand beside him as the others passed.

"How is the soup tonight, little brother?" Temian asked him quietly. "Or did you get your fill when you went into the water a second time?"

"The stew is excellent," Ra'ah said self-consciously. "And I do not remember drinking any of the stream."

"Truly?" Temian laughed. "You had me worried for a long minute. I thought you'd hit your head."

"My head is fine." He turned it side to side to demonstrate.

"Whatever happened to you, we'd love to hear about it," David cut in. "None of us remember that kind of reaction happening before. Do you remember anything?"

"I remember…" Ra'ah paused; the memory of what he had experienced was fresher than any dream he'd ever had. "I remember everything."

"Are you coming back in?" Temian asked. "You can tell us over a drink and maybe a little more stew."

"It's fairly packed in there," Ra'ah said. "The Cardayans apparently weren't the first ones here. There are about two dozen more that came up in the last week. Add to that your thirty, and it's like a village banquet in there."

"Well, it's up to you." David squeezed his shoulder. "We'll be packed up and on the trail at the very first light."

Ra'ah nodded and the two men opened the door and passed into the loud and brightly-lit hall. He was alone again with his thoughts and the fresh memory of the vision in the cave.

"I am the hands of the Healer," he murmured.

Something deep within him stirred. A response from something greater than himself, now dwelling close to himself.

The next morning found them all gathered in the pre-dawn chill. Amon was busy instructing the young men whom he had brought north, shaking his head firmly when one or the other asked to return south with him. And Ra'ah knew it wasn't because they weren't excited to be here and to get to work. He knew they wanted to be some of the first to tell others what awaited them as they fled north. But Amon was steadfast in only taking three others back with him. The rest would be taken under Duncan's care and assigned jobs setting up the refugee village around them.

The Klasma were all around them, checking packs and each other, softly laughing and talking and acting like they hadn't spent most of the night in the hall. The weight of sadness had lifted off of them, and they were restive, impatient to get going. Kawani came over with his pack, which she had taken from him just minutes before.

"You are a good packer, little brother," she admitted. "You've got nothing to learn from me."

"Lots of experience," he said as he swung it onto his shoulders. "Despite what Angelis might tell you."

Angelis stopped short of passing them and gave him a measured glare.

"My only true complaint has ever been the meat, *little brother*," she said pointedly.

"Why is everyone suddenly calling me that?" Ra'ah asked.

"Because you're like a little brother to us," Kawani stated obviously. "All full of youth's curiosity and innocent wonder."

Ra'ah was filled with a mixture of indignation and frustration at her description. It must have shown on his face because Ange burst out laughing. Ra'ah felt his face flush, and he searched in vain for some kind of escape. He found it in Temian, who had just finished a conversation with David and Anatellia and was within earshot of his sister's observation.

"Keep in mind, young Ra'ah," Temian's voice boomed, "that my sister was friends with your great-grandmother fifty times removed. So young Amon over there could be little brother to her."

Kawani's fist moved impossibly fast and struck the big man in the shoulder. He bellowed and shook his arm as he lifted his other hand in surrender. Kawani looked absolutely fierce.

Ange gave a whistle. "That, Ra'ah, is why you never mention a lady's age."

They passed the earthworks and crossed the open field into the forest as the light of dawn turned the sky a deep blue. With the full moon hidden behind the western mountains, the world was lit in a dim twilight that would have made the trail hard to follow if it wasn't so established.

As the light increased, Ra'ah recognized signs of work on either side. Deadfall had been removed and trees that encroached on the trail had been harvested. At one point, a new bridge of rough-hewn logs had been erected where a steep banked stream cut its way to the river. He could make out the path as it swerved away and down the small gorge then back up to meet them.

"We thought that was peculiar when we passed it," Amon mentioned casually from behind Ra'ah.

"It would raise questions," Ra'ah said. "How far down have they gone?"

"That marks the end of the work," Amon said. "Or the beginning, if you come the other way. But Duncan will have those boys working hard to turn this into a proper road all the way to the Bato Road."

Ra'ah considered that. The Bato Road continued north out of the village to where the valley itself narrowed. It was maintained by the numerous farms and woodsmen's cabins that extended to that point. From there, he knew the road dwindled to a well-worn path. The carts of woodsmen could probably navigate it, except for spots like the bridge they had just passed.

"How far below the Valley Narrows is the crossing?" Ra'ah asked.

"Not far at all," Amon said. "There is a point a mile below the Narrows where the river meanders and gets deep and slow with a gentle slope on either side. We've set up cables there and a good-sized barge. By now they'll have ferried across a good number of wagons and supplies and they'll be waiting for word from us."

"What about all of the people?" Ra'ah asked. "They're more important than supplies at this point."

"What you don't understand is how much supply it will take to move that many people north," Amon explained patiently. "You're used to wandering the valley with your friends, hunting and drinking from streams. You can't travel the same way with families. The elderly and small children can't walk all day like you and I can. You have to feed them. They have to drink. How long does it take to water a hundred people from a stream? Imagine a thousand. You can't let them all go down to the stream to drink. You'll need buckets, water skins and people dedicated to filling them and passing them around. And that is just water. Now just imagine trying to feed the same amount of people."

"Well…" Ra'ah considered. "We could tell people to prepare enough food to travel with. And to fill their own water skins before they start out."

"Those are good ideas," Amon agreed. "And many are already doing that. Many are emptying barns and preparing livestock. We are not fools here in the Valley, although this evacuation is without precedent. And your thinking is more rural than urban. There will be people coming up the road who have never spent a night in the forest under the stars.

People who have never carried a pack full of a week's worth of provisions on their back. And we have to get them north, as well."

"I hadn't really thought of that," Ra'ah admitted. "I kind of assume everyone is like me for the most part."

"Everyone is guilty of that at one time or another," Amon said.

They stopped only briefly for lunch under the shade of the forest. For the first time since they had left, Pestos appeared. He was panting and soaking wet, but went dutifully to each person to see if they would share their lunch.

"Where have you been?" Ange mused as she gave him a piece of her jerky.

"He's been across the river," Amon said. "Better hunting over there, at least until we stop for lunch."

"I may be tempted to jump in the river myself before the day gets much farther along," said Ra'ah.

In fact, the heat of the midday sun reminded Ra'ah more of late summer than the middle. It took Daskow to remind him that the next full moon would be the harvest moon. Ra'ah had a moment of panic when he thought about harvest. How would they harvest before the Sacheth arrived? *They won't*, he realized. Another thought occurred on the heels of that one. The Sacheth would be able to harvest all of that food for themselves.

"Could we harvest earlier?" he asked Daskow.

"No, I don't think so." Daskow shook his head as he pushed Pestos away from the cheese in his hand. "We've got two weeks left, but probably only half of that time to try and harvest. And it won't be anywhere near ready. The fields were all green from the rains last week."

"Couldn't we cut it early?" Ra'ah pondered.

"I'm no farmer, Ra'ah," his friend said. "But I think you would just end up with animal feed."

Ra'ah looked around to see Anatellia watching them from a nearby stump. She smiled when their eyes met, but there was worry in her eyes.

She got up and wandered over to talk with David, and Pestos followed in search of more lunch.

The moon rose full, even as the sun set, and they pushed on deep into the night by its light. David and the Klasma seemed driven by an unseen urgency, and the five weren't inclined to argue. They all but fell into their bedrolls as the moon settled toward the peaks of the western slopes.

Ra'ah watched as the moon passed slowly out of sight. It was possibly the last full moon he would see in the valley. They were half way to the Maylak's deadline. He marvelled at how much their lives had been turned upside down in just two weeks. *Are we more than half done?* he wondered. *How much more lies ahead?* Surely his village of Bato would be the last group they needed to warn, and then it would be a matter of evacuation as Amon had explained.

He felt a moment of uncertainty as his thoughts went to Bato. Had rumour of them already reached the village? Had his parents heard of the five young people stirring up trouble all over the Valley? Did they suspect he was one of the troublemakers? He drifted off to dream of the conversations he would have to have with his father and mother.

26

THE CROSSING CAMP

The morning started much like the morning before, and they were once again on the march. The three young men that Amon had picked to return with him were not of regular stock and showed even less signs of tiredness than the five. Ra'ah regarded them out of the corner of his eye as they sprung onto the path to follow the lead Klasma. Ange walked past him, still rubbing sleep from her eyes, and simply glared.

"It's been too many days since I've had the pleasure of an inn," she muttered. "We can't get to the next one soon enough."

Ra'ah just snorted and fell in beside her. The sky was clear and blue and the forest was cool as they made their way along the broadening path. He looked down the length of mountains across the river and realized they were much closer to the Narrows than he thought. They'd be back in the broader valley by mid-afternoon.

He looked around for the others. Nebaya and Daskow were behind them. Nebaya wore the same expression she'd worn since the night David had brought her in soaking wet. Her eyes were locked uncharacteristically on the path in front of her and the rhythmic thump of her quarterstaff spoke a wealth of warning that she wasn't interested in chat. Not that Daskow was looking for a chat. In fact he was doing what only Daskow could do. Eyes down and forward, focused on the open book in front of him, he walked with a practiced glide that kept whatever he was reading steady. He had once told Ra'ah he was still paying attention to the road and trail when he did this, and Ra'ah still marvelled.

Anatellia was harder to find. But once he remembered to look for David, he found her easily enough. She had not been far from David's side since they had left the morning before. It was like she was trying to settle that he actually was still her brother, asking him question after question and listening intently as he answered. In fact, she had seemed generally unsettled since they had come to the Mountain and joined up with David. It was like she wasn't even sure how to act. Ra'ah frowned at the thought that Anatellia had somehow lost her confidence. He wondered how David had caused that. He wondered if he could help.

The group continued down the path like a pack of wolves on the hunt, moving with the speed of experienced travellers and the grace of youth. There was a silence among them for a very long time, the silence of people comfortable with each other and their surroundings. Several times they came upon deer feeding along the river and startled them so badly they jumped into the river to find the far bank. Then about four hours after sunrise, a shout came up from the front of the group.

All of them stopped as Kai came trotting back from where he had been scouting ahead. He spoke softly to David, and then David called for Amon.

"We've got a large party of woodsmen coming up the river," he explained loudly as the old man moved forward.

"I half expected them," Amon admitted. "It's good that we can stop them here."

A voice hollered greeting from the path ahead, and Amon stepped out to wave the approaching group of men forward. There were about two dozen of them, ranging from men almost as old as Amon all the way down to young teenagers. Ra'ah recognized a few almost immediately. These were Cardaya woodsmen, several generations' worth. They approached quickly when they recognized Amon, but slowed in surprise as the Klasma became visible among the trees.

"Henry!" Amon greeted one of the men in front. "I expected to find you following me."

"I told you I'd collect a few families and be right behind," the man said as he eyed David and Temian, who stepped to either side of Amon. "But I didn't expect you to be coming back with... who are you with?"

"This is David," Amon said. "And this is Temian. We have the five young people who delivered the message to Cardaya several weeks back, and these others are sworn to their protection."

Henry nodded simply. "Hello. We're headed up to the Gellah to start cutting back a road for wagons. Where's the rest of the group you left with, and where did you meet up with these folks?"

"The plan has had some happy adjustments," Amon said with a laugh. "And I will leave Paul with you to catch you all up on it." Amon waved one of his three companions to come forward. He did not seem impressed to hear he was being left behind.

"We will not tarry, ourselves," Amon continued, "but you should start here with your task and work your way north. A group is already at the Gellah, and they are working south."

Henry raised his eyebrows, but only nodded.

"How long do we have before you send wagons to get in our way?" he asked after a pause.

"A couple days," Amon said. "We'll send whatever extra hands we find your way. There is no good reason to delay."

"Two days?" Henry scoffed. "Who do you have coming south? And who is preparing shelter at Gellah? More of these strangers?"

"Paul will explain everything," Amon assured him. "You know me, Henry, so you know better than to distrust my word."

Henry snorted and looked back at the men with him. None of them said anything, though they shared skeptical looks with him. Finally he stepped off the path and motioned the others to do likewise. With a broad sweep of his arm, he presented Amon the trail.

"Thank you, my friend," Amon nodded. "We'll laugh about this later."

Henry snorted again and the group hurried past the staring woodsmen. Ra'ah smiled at them as he passed, and a few of them called to one or the other of the five in greeting. Ra'ah took one last look back to see them gathering around Paul expectantly.

"That would be a fun story to tell," Ange laughed.

"You've got a bigger story to tell when we get to Bato," Ra'ah reminded her.

They were driven by the closeness of the Narrows into the open mouth of the Valley ahead, and they walked through lunch. About an hour past noon, the river flowed out into the broader valley and they passed through the Narrows. It was there that they found another group of woodsmen working on the trail and clearing deadfall. This group had several teams of horses and wagons, and they were just as surprised to see them. Amon left another of his companions to explain and they continued on with as much haste as before.

Soon after that, Ra'ah could make out smoke rising ahead, and within a short time they walked into a bustling clearing full of tents and sheds of all kinds. It looked to Ra'ah like a makeshift market had sprung out of the forest. The trees were cut back all the way to the riverbank, and he could see rope cables spanning the river. The barge they were using as a ferry was midway across the lazy current on its way to their side.

A shout went up and a great group of men and women came into the clearing from all sides. Amon shouted back and there was a cheer. Within a minute, the group was surrounded by a crowd, all asking questions at once and staring at the Klasma with keen interest. A few of the people asked if they were Maylak. There was nervous laughter at that.

"Amon!" The tall figure of Deacan the sheriff waded through the crowd. "We didn't expect you back this soon, and with more hands than you left with. And Living God bless us, it's our five messengers returned. But from the wrong direction, if I'm not mistaken."

"Deacan." Amon returned the greeting. "A lot has changed since I went north to survey the Gellah."

"By my estimate, you've barely had time to get there and back," Deacan noted as he looked everyone over. "And these men and women are not from the Valley any more than they are Maylak."

"These thirty have been given as our protection." Anatellia stepped out of the knot that the group had formed. "The whole story is longer than ought be told from the centre of a mob, even a friendly one. But

I'm afraid that at least some of us need to push on to Bato. After a brief rest and regroup."

Deacan nodded. He motioned toward a grove of trees on the river side of the clearing, and they made their way through the curious crowd. The trees revealed a cold fire pit with rows of log seating around it. Anatellia silently motioned her friends to sit, and the Klasma spread out around them without word or instruction.

"Deacan, I need you to stay and I know it's a lot to ask, but can we have a little privacy?" Anatallia motioned to the following mob.

Deacan stood on a bench to be seen. "Everyone, go back to what you were doing. I promise there will be opportunity for stories and questions later."

The people hesitated, but none of them could stand under the stern stares of the Klasma, and they all drifted away to attend the ferry that had just arrived. As if on cue, Pestos trotted out of the grass along the riverbank and joined Amon as he waited. Satisfied, Anatellia turned to Daskow.

"Have you decided?" she asked simply.

"Yes—I'm going to cross the river here and make for Pethe."

"Good." She nodded. "We agree. Ange will go with you. David will also send whichever Klasma he thinks appropriate."

"What?" Nebaya and Ra'ah said together.

Anatellia just looked between them for a long moment. Ange looked uncomfortable but not surprised. Ra'ah realized Ange had known she was going before Anatellia announced it. He looked for support from Nebaya, but she was locked on her friend with an intensity Ra'ah had never seen.

"The final choice fell to Daskow," Anatellia finally explained. "Ange already expressed her desire to go with him, and I agreed he shouldn't go alone. Ra'ah needs to go with us to Bato."

"We. Make. Decisions. Together." Nebaya clipped each word. "You never gave us a chance to discuss this."

"I didn't," Anatellia admitted. "I need my oldest friend with me, and I was afraid you'd demand to go back to Pethe with Daskow."

Nebaya and Anatellia faced each other in silence. Ra'ah realized he was holding his breath as he watched them. On Anatellia's face was written nothing but determination. But Nebaya seemed to be fighting a battle inside. It wasn't like Anatellia to make an arbitrary decision for the group, but it wasn't totally unprecedented either. And Ra'ah realized he agreed with her on it. He cleared his throat quietly and it broke their standoff. Nebaya turned her attention to him.

"She's right," he admitted quietly. "With Ange going south with Daskow, we need you with us in Bato. And sending you south with Daskow would seem like throwing a torch into the straw pile."

Her eyes flared and she opened her mouth, only to snap it shut again. The anger drained away from her and she nodded.

"Well, that part is true," she admitted quietly. "And if heads need bashing, the Klasma are better suited. But Anna—you should have trusted me."

"Nebaya," Anatellia whispered, "I do trust you."

Nebaya nodded and looked away. David cleared his throat and stepped into their ring.

"I'm sending Kawani, Hanah, and the ten Klasma they choose to go with Daskow and Ange across the river. Of those twelve, four will stay with you both at all times and the other eight will spread out as a perimeter. The enemy is here, in the Valley. Not in force, but with enough force to do harm. You both will listen to Kawani and the others and obey them without question. Your lives depend on this."

Daskow and Ange nodded silently. Now that they were back in the Valley, the reality of what they were up against settled on them with new weight.

"The rest of us will make our way to Bato with all haste," David continued. "Anna and I both feel the need to be there by tomorrow. Ra'ah, do you think your parents would take us in tonight?"

"Uh…" Ra'ah was caught off guard by the question. "Yes? I mean, once they get over the shock of having two dozen people at their door with their son in tow."

"Well, it will only be five or six of us," David assured him. "The rest of us will be setting up a perimeter around Bato.

"A perimeter?" Ra'ah asked incredulously.

"Yes." David nodded patiently. "From here on out, the Klasma will be more militant than you're used to. Our enemy is not civil, so we cannot afford to treat them as such."

"Do you really think it will come to open violence?" Ange asked quietly.

"Without a doubt," David responded gravely. "The Sacheth will not be deterred by the sight of us. And we will have to match their determination to harm you five with our greater determination to protect you. Oh yes, there will be violence. May God have mercy on them."

The Klasma suddenly slammed their staves on the ground three times. Ra'ah was taken aback. All this time he hadn't really taken to heart that these men and women were being sent along to protect each of them. To stand before whatever threat and prevent it from reaching him or his friends. An image of the top of Koreb Pass flashed across his memory. The sound of Nebaya's bow. The black bodies falling where they were shot. The wound on Master Dunhamai's side. All of that a precursor to what was coming.

The five said their goodbyes, and Daskow boarded the ferry with Ange, Amon, and the escort of twelve Klasma. Kawani put an arm around Ange and pulled her close in sisterly affection, and they waved as the ferrymen pulled on the ropes and the barge left the crude pier. With a whistle Amon called Pestos, and the huge hound came out of the bush, careening down the ramp and off the pier in a fluid motion. Ra'ah smiled as the dog skidded into Ange and Kawani and then sat happily at their feet as if he'd been there the entire time.

Ra'ah continued to watch as they slowly crossed the river until Nebaya called to him and he turned and joined the others. With a sigh, he wondered briefly when he'd see the others next but then set his mind to the matter ahead of him. In a few hours he'd be knocking at his parents' door for the first time in a year. They knew he had been avoiding them. They knew why. He wondered what he was going to say to them.

He fell into step with the rest of the group as they left the clearing and headed south. He looked up at the sun and estimated they'd reach Bato an hour or two after dark.

"Thinking about your parents?" Anatellia asked from beside him.

"Thinking about what I'm going to say, yes."

"Tell them the truth," Anatellia offered.

"The truth..." Ra'ah pondered for a second. "Mom, Dad, I've been avoiding you every time we've been back to visit the village because I feel like a disappointment to you both and I don't know how to tell you I'm okay with that."

"Are you?" Anatellia asked. "I mean, are you really?"

"No," Ra'ah admitted. "I recognize that if I was, I wouldn't be avoiding them. And everything over the last week has just made the feeling worse."

"Ra'ah"—Anatellia put an arm around his shoulders—"I cannot for one second imagine we could have done this without you. You are where you are supposed to be."

Ra'ah nodded. He believed that. He was convinced he was where he belonged. But he realized there was truth in what his parents believed as well.

"I just have till we get to Bato to figure out how to tell my parents they were right." He shrugged and smiled at his friend. "But so was I."

"So what are you?" Anatellia looked at him questioningly. "Ra'ah the Baker or Ra'ah the Healer?"

"Yes!" Ra'ah smiled more broadly. "Both of those. Both and more."

"That sounds right." She returned the smile.

He changed the subject. "How about you? What's going on with you?"

"I am coming to accept I am my mother's daughter." She raised her hand as he tried to protest. "But I am not my mother."

"I don't understand."

"Neither do I," she admitted. "But I'm open to learning. The Spirit of the Living God has been given to us, Ra'ah. And He is speaking to me in ways I do not yet understand."

"That I do understand," he said.

"Yes?"

"Yes."

27

GUESTS FOR DINNER

R a'ah knocked firmly on the side door of the bakery. The sound of a chair sliding and soft voices inside filled his stomach with knots. He could feel the footsteps of someone approaching the door through the wooden landing, and they seemed to fall in time with the breathing and shifting of the five others standing in the shadows at the bottom of the short flight of stairs. He shook himself and braced for the opening of the door.

In short order the door did open and light from a lamp flooded out into the night. By its light Ra'ah recognized his father.

"Hi, Dad," he began.

"*Ra'ah!*" the man bellowed, and swept him into a one-armed bear hug.

Ra'ah was rendered temporarily speechless. His father held him close, and then looked down at the others from over his son's shoulder.

"And there is Miss Anatellia and the tall Miss Nebaya. But who are these three others?" He eyed the tall men behind the girls with suspicion as he raised the lamp in his other hand a little higher.

"Good evening, Master Baker." Anatellia bowed her head. "This is my brother, David, and his two friends, Temian and Kai."

"Brother?" Ra'ah's father looked David up and down in the lamplight. "Well, you're not lying to me, but there is much more to this than meets my eyes in this light."

A matronly woman appeared suddenly behind Ra'ah's father in the doorway. She was wearing a flour-dusted apron and carrying what looked to be a rolling pin.

"What's going on here, Father?" she asked as she took in the five young people standing at the steps. Then her eyes jumped to the face peering over her husband's shoulder, and she gave a short happy shout.

"Praise the Living God, Ra'ah!" She clapped her hands. "You've finally come home."

"Hi, Mom." Ra'ah tried unsuccessfully to slip out of his father's hug. "I've brought friends for dinner."

"Of course you did, dear." His mother looked closer at the two women at the bottom of her steps. "I see Nebaya and Anatellia. But the others aren't Daskow or Ange. Did those two decide to settle down together?"

"Mom!" Ra'ah was mortified.

"Honest question, dear," his mother said unapologetically.

"May we come in?" Ra'ah asked feebly.

"Of course," she said. "I'll need six more settings on the table, and help in the kitchen."

"Yes, Mom." Ra'ah patted his dad's arm and slipped out of the hug.

"Thank you, Mistress Baker." Anatellia proceeded up the stairs as Ra'ah's father stepped to the side to let them in.

"Mistress pish posh," the older woman scolded. "You will call me Aster and him Peylos, or Mom and Dad. None of that formal foolishness for friends of my son."

"Bows beside the door," Ra'ah's father said as they filed into the house.

They followed Ra'ah and his mother into the house one at a time under the watchful eye of Peylos. He pointed to David's staff, and David nodded silently and leaned the quarterstaff against the wall with his bow. The two other men followed suit with Temian bringing up the rear. The big man nodded politely to Ra'ah's father, but the other man just raised an eyebrow.

"Your parents grow them big," he noted sagely.

With one last look into the forest and darkness outside his door, the elder baker followed Temian into the house and shut the door.

The baker's dining room was large and spacious, and the six guests soon found their cloaks hung and packs lined against one wall. They were seated at the great table, all except for Ra'ah who was quickly dragged into the kitchen to help his mother. The remaining five sat as Peylos found mugs and a pitcher of water for them. Then he sat and regarded them silently.

"Thank you for taking us in," Nebaya offered after a long silence.

"What, exactly, have we taken in?" Peylos asked pointedly. "There is more here than a homesick Ra'ah."

"We have business in Bato," Anatellia said.

"I am sure you do." Peylos's glare never faltered as it moved from Nebaya to her.

Ra'ah entered the room with a stack of plates and cutlery and handed it to Temian, who took it all too eagerly and started distributing the implements around the table.

"Mom is wondering if you could get another loaf of your braided bread for supper," Ra'ah said to his father.

Peylos ignored the request. "Are you in some kind of trouble?"

Ra'ah looked at his father in silence for several long breaths.

"We both will be if mother doesn't get her bread," he finally said.

The baker snorted, but he got up and disappeared to the front of the building. Ra'ah looked at the others and then turned and went back into the kitchen.

"This is absolutely refreshing compared to meals with Mother," Anatellia whispered to David.

"That's a truth that a thousand years cannot erase," David agreed.

"There is something behind his questions," Anatellia continued.

"Definitely." David nodded. "How do you suggest we go about asking him?"

"Asking him what?" Peylos asked as he stepped back into the room. "And don't bother whispering around here; I've got the ears of a fox."

"What have you heard about us?" Nebaya asked immediately. "There's obviously something going around."

"Yes." Peylos nodded. He didn't answer the question immediately. "Of all of his friends, Nebaya, you are my favourite. Always to the point, and always protective of my son."

He paused and considered them all. Finally he nodded.

"Fine, I'll tell you what I know and what I'm thinking. About a week ago, rumours came up from the south about five young people telling stories and causing trouble all over the Valley. That was followed by people coming up from Kathik claiming that we were being invaded by barbarians from the south. And then a couple of days later a large group of students came up from the city claiming they were securing a route up through the Gellah to the Mountain of the Living God for a whole mass of refugees. They set up a regular tent city to the south of the village between the river and the road. Hundreds of people are already there.

"So three days ago the village elders send an envoy to Kathik with a request for explanation. The envoy finds the city gates closed and gets sent back here with a curt response that it is being dealt with. Now today a bunch of officials ride in and ask for a meeting with the elders. And with them are a couple of men who are most certainly not Valley residents, if you get my meaning. And I see by the looks in all your eyes that you do.

"Now my son suddenly shows up the same day as these people from Kathik. With only two out of four of his friends in tow, and three men who are undoubtedly foreign, like the men I saw earlier, although they are also clearly different from them. Men who carry walking staves tipped with metal, one with a sword carefully hidden on his pack. Five friends, down to three, with bodyguards in tow. And there is nowhere in the valley they could be from, even though this one is your older brother, plain as day. But guessing his age compared to yours has my mind muddled. Their voices speak youth, but their eyes and something in their faces speak of time beyond my counting."

He shook his head and closed his eyes. When he opened them, he locked eyes with Ra'ah in the kitchen door holding a tray of food. Temian jumped up and took the tray, but Ra'ah just held his father's stare.

"So I ask again," his father said quietly, "are you in some kind of trouble?"

"We all are, Dad," Ra'ah said quietly, and returned to the kitchen.

Peylos sat back and waited. Anatellia looked across the table at David for several long seconds, but he ignored her and turned to Kai.

"I need you to find the others and tell them fives instead of threes," he said in a low voice. "Tell them to pull in closer."

Kai nodded and excused himself. He was out the door before another word was spoken.

Peylos nodded. "That speaks a clearer word than anything you could have said to me."

"To be honest, I'm missing Angelis in this moment," Anatellia laughed awkwardly.

"Maybe Nebaya ought to fill me in on this story," Peylos said. "As I said, I've always found her directness the most refreshing. Too much yeast makes the bread flat."

Anatellia turned to look at Nebaya. The tall woman was staring at the door that Kai had just left through, and hadn't heard anything. She suddenly realized everyone was looking at her.

"Hmmm?" she asked. "What was the question?"

"Master Baker wants you to tell our story," Anatellia explained.

"I'm no storyteller," Nebaya protested.

"I think that's his point," David said simply.

"It is my point exactly," Peylos confirmed and spread his arms wide. "Give me the Nebaya short version of all of this."

"Okay." Nebaya shrugged. "My short version."

She took a long drink of water as she sorted her thoughts. Aster stuck her head out of the kitchen and gave her husband a significant look.

"Peylos, dear, did you get me a braided bread?"

"We're sold out," he said, never taking his eyes off of Nebaya. "You'll have to do with biscuits."

"Okay, I'll get Ra'ah to whip some up." She returned to the kitchen.

"Go ahead, Nebaya," Peylos encouraged.

"Here is the short version." She placed both hands on the table. "Two weeks ago we were attacked by a black beast and then visited by a Maylak of the Living God. The Maylak told us that before the next new moon, the Valley would be overrun by an unknown enemy. We were instructed to tell everyone from the villages and the city to flee North to the Mountain of the Living God.

"So we told Cardaya and Pethe first. Ra'ah and I got attacked by more black beasts but those were also killed by Maylak. Anatellia, Angelis, and Daskow went to Kathik where they discovered that Anatellia's mother is responsible for inviting the enemy, who are called the Sacheth, to come to the Valley. They start trouble in the city. Meanwhile Ra'ah and I went to Meletsa to warn them. We rescued a woman named Dunhamai in the pass being attacked by even more beasts. David came to Meletsa and we rode back to Kathik against my better judgement. But we got ambushed by even more black beasts and met up with the other three. Then we were rescued by another Maylak who took us north to the Mountain of the Living God.

"Now things get a little harder to believe." She paused to take another drink.

"*Now* they do?" Peylos repeated incredulously. "Do go on."

"David here, apparently, doesn't come with us north but ends up…" She paused to glance at David. "He ends up completely out of time and apparently has spent the last thousand years in the City on the Mountain waiting for us. With him were Temian, here, Kai who just left, and twenty eight others who are our protection so that we can come back and finish our mission to warn the Valley. I am assuming that the men who came with the city's envoys are Sacheth, and behind them is an army that will be here in less than two weeks to destroy the Valley. That's the short version."

Peylos stared at her and she simply stared back. He then switched his gaze to Anatellia, Temian, and finally David. His face was unreadable.

"A thousand years, huh?" he asked David.

"That is…"—David struggled for words—"a longer story."

"I can only imagine." Peylos shook his head. "Or rather, I can't. If that had come out of anyone else's mouth, I would have called her a liar and left it at that. In fact I wish it had been anyone else who told it. I wish it wasn't my son and his friends in the middle of whatever this is."

"I know it's hard to believe…" Anatallia began.

"Peace!" Peylos held his hand up to stop her. "I pride myself on being a man of evidence and study. I bake bread every day, and every day my bread rises and bakes. If it doesn't, it isn't because faeries got in my ovens. Not because I'm arrogant and say 'There is no such thing,' but rather because I have never found a single faery in my ovens."

They looked at him with various expressions of confusion, everyone except Temian. The big man just nodded.

"So are we enough evidence for you?" the big man asked.

Peylos looked back at Temian and nodded.

"I will be forthright: I do not want any of this to be true," Peylos said. "I would rather dismiss this story as anything else but its face value truth. Maybe food poisoning, bad mushrooms, anything that could account for the fever dream Nebaya's story offers. But I've seen the men who came into town with that silk merchant and her city envoys. They did not sit well with my soul. And I've seen you three with your walking sticks that were never meant for walking. Between what my eyes have seen and what Nebaya has told me, I am forced to consider the truth of it all."

"The truth of what, dear?" Ra'ah's mother stepped into the dining room with a large pot of soup and Ra'ah in tow with a tray of biscuits.

"Faeries in the oven," Peylos stated flatly.

"Ah." Aster shook her head. "Well, enough of such talk for now: supper is served."

Ra'ah set the tray of biscuits on the table and looked around the table at his friends. David and Nebaya were looking between each other and Anatellia. Anatellia had a white-knuckle grip on her mug, and her jaw was set. Only Temian looked relaxed as he scooped up two biscuits from the tray.

"Where's Kai?" he asked as he sat down.

The meal was spent in peaceful silence, with only compliments between bites and everyone enjoying the table that Aster had set before them. Ra'ah spent the time trying to figure out what he had missed as Aster chatted about her garden and the various herbs she grew. She was the perfect hostess, gracious and engaging. Finally, as everyone was pushing away their bowls, she sighed with a smile and gave David a penetrating look.

"So you and Anatellia are obviously related somehow," she noted casually. "I'd say brother, except you're far too old. In my youth I was taken by the idea of entertaining Maylak unawares. You remember those stories old lady Helen used to tell, Peylos? She would tell these stories of disguised Maylak showing up at a poor widow's door begging for food, and when the widow would give away her last meal the Maylak would bless her and suddenly she'd be looked after and never in want again. Fun old stories."

"I've never heard those stories," David said quietly.

"Well, of course not." Aster smiled at him. "Those stories aren't in fashion anymore. Maybe it's because we don't have hardships like the past. We're not used to truly being in need, anymore. So we don't look to the Living God for help like we used to."

Aster changed direction suddenly. "So are you married, David?"

David's eyes flashed quickly to Nebaya and then dropped to his bowl.

"No."

"Ah." Aster smiled. "That's a surprise. A wise woman would have attended to that by now, I would have thought. Where have you been hiding?"

"Mom," Ra'ah cut in as David and, oddly enough, Nebaya, both flushed, "you're making my friends uncomfortable."

"A mother's prerogative, dear." His mother turned her full attention to him. "So when can this mother hope to have grandchildren?"

"Mother!" Ra'ah's face suddenly felt like he was on fire.

"There is an inn matron currently working on that very problem," Anatellia said.

"Oh?" Aster turned her attention on Anatellia. "Which inn?"

"Willard's Ox, at the Crossroads."

"Ah, Abigail." Aster nodded and her eyes flashed. "I'll have a daughter-in-law by spring."

Ra'ah covered his face with his hands and breathed out heavily. There were only ever two subjects with his mother these days.

"Which reminds me…" Aster's tone shifted. "Guess who was asking about you just this morning?"

"Matron Karis?" Ra'ah mumbled through his hands.

"Why yes, good guess!" Aster said. "She still refuses to give up on you."

"She shouldn't," Nebaya chimed in. "Ra'ah has proven to be a good healer in his own right."

"Has he now?" Aster's eyes glittered with a fierce motherly pride.

"If you have achieved all your motherly goals," Peylos cut in, "there are concerns that need to be addressed."

"It could be said that a mother's concerns are chief among concerns," Aster teased as she patted her husband's hand.

"They are the five," Peylos stated flatly.

"Oh, I know," Aster said.

"Of course you do." Peylos sighed in exasperation. "And just *how* do you know?"

"Because unlike you, I listen when people want to talk," she said. "Five young people scaring people with stories of Maylak and invasion and such. Didn't take much imagination to figure out who the five were."

"Well there's a lot more to the story," Peylos said pointedly.

"I'm sure," she nodded. "But first we need tea, and the pie in the kitchen. If you would, Ra'ah."

Ra'ah stood up and left in such a fluid motion it impressed them all.

"I'm sure you told them the sheriffs are looking for them?" Aster asked sweetly.

"No." Peylos gave his wife a look. "I'm pretty sure they already have a good idea they aren't welcome."

"Is the other young man returning?" Aster asked suddenly. "Should we set aside some food?"

"I sent him on an errand," David said. "But I'm sure he would appreciate it."

Aster gathered some cheese and biscuits on a plate and ladled the last of the soup into a bowl. Before she was finished Ra'ah returned with a pie and a stack of plates. He set the pie in front of his father and distributed the rest.

"Now be a dear and bring the teapot I set on the edge of the stove. We'll just have to use our mugs." Aster smiled as she sent Ra'ah off again.

"He's grown into such a good man." She smiled as she glanced at Nebaya but then settled on Anatellia. "He'll make someone a good husband."

"Yes." Anatellia nodded as she held out her plate for pie. "We've all said that."

Aster nodded back. Ra'ah returned and looked at his mother suspiciously. He proceeded to pour the tea. Aster watched as the tea was poured and the pie passed around. Then she cleared her throat.

"I know Father has already interrogated you all, except Ra'ah, of course. I won't ask you to repeat everything. But just tell me, is it true? Is the enemy coming? Are we all truly in danger?"

They looked around the table at each other.

"Yes, Mom, it's true," Ra'ah said.

"Okay." She nodded. "So you know who came into town just before you did?"

"I'm afraid so," Anatellia admitted with dread.

Aster looked at her husband. "Peylos, we should send a message to Elder Cela. They are going to need an introduction."

"No need to go out into the night," Peylos assured her. "I see him every morning for his daily scones."

"I did not know that," Aster said dryly. "His wife would not be impressed."

"Which is why you did not know that."

"Well, then, that is taken care of," Aster continued. "He will help us understand who has come from the city."

"We already have a good idea," Anatellia said. "The silk merchant you mentioned, Peylos—that merchant would be my mother."

Peylos looked between Anatellia and David, and then nodded.

"Your mother?" Aster said in surprise. "My, my, but little Angelis must be in her glory with this story. I am sad she is not here. But now let's settle in. Tell me everything; leave nothing out. There'll be another pot of tea when this one's drained.

They talked long into the night. Between Anatellia and Ra'ah, they managed a reasonably thorough retelling. Even David took a turn, offering a much-abridged version of his part in the story. Peylos stayed silent, tending the hearth fire as his wife became an engaged listener, asking quick questions, tsking and gasping at the exciting parts. They were both silent and still as stone when they each described the Mountain, the City, and Joshua. Finally they reached the end of the story, coming right up to the bakery door in the finale.

As if on cue there was a small rap at the door, which opened to reveal Kai. He blinked in the sudden light and apologized for simply coming in.

"No, think nothing of it." Aster stood up and retrieved the food set aside by the hearth. "Come and sit and eat. You must be hungry."

"Thank you," Kai said as he sat.

"Is everything settled?" David asked.

Kai looked from David to the bakers and back. David simply nodded.

"Everyone has moved in close," he confirmed quietly. "The people from the city are staying at the inn. There is a refugee camp on the southeast side of the village. There is another camp on the southwest side nestled up against the slope."

"Whose camp is that?" David pressed.

"Most certainly a military camp." Kai shook his head. "I took Ethan and Noah and we circled around to see what we could see. They've got sentries on a large perimeter. Well-hidden, and very, very aware."

"Were you detected?" David's tone took on a frustrated note.

Kai shook his head. "Of course not. Not even the owls saw us. But we couldn't get close."

"You said military?" Peylos asked. "How can you be sure?"

"We've trained to be sure," David said. "And if Kai can't sneak right past them and steal a sock, they aren't typical villagers."

"I have quite a collection of socks," Kai said matter-of-factly.

"I wonder how we could prove they're there and they're military," Peylos pondered out loud.

"Unfortunately the only way to prove it would be to kick it," Kai said. "They're buried deep off the road and they'll know anyone is coming before you've confirmed they're there."

"And only a fool kicks a hornet's nest," Peylos nodded.

"Unfortunately we may end up doing just that in the morning," Anatellia said.

Ra'ah felt a knot of fear in his stomach as he listened to the conversation. The idea of soldiers had been an abstract concern all the way up to this point. Now it suddenly jumped out, real and alive and very much a threat. He looked at David, Temian, and Kai and wondered if they were really enough.

"May the Living God have mercy on their souls," Aster muttered, "if they dare bring violence into the Valley."

ᴮAKERIES AND
ᴮACK ᴿOOM ᴾLOTTING

Aster finally took charge of the late evening and dispersed them throughout the house to find whatever sleep they could before the morning came. David and the other two Klasma excused themselves to go check on the others, and Ra'ah wondered if they would take the time to get a quick nap. The women were given Ra'ah's old room, and Ra'ah got a blanket and the hearth.

Ra'ah settled in in front of the dying fire and drifted off to sleep, only to be awoken a short time later by his father lighting the bakery ovens. He opened his eyes, thick with sleep, and found the fire in the hearth had burned to warm coals. He got up with a sigh and quickly folded the blanket.

He entered the bakery to find his father securing a clean apron around his waist. Peylos barely acknowledged his son; instead, he motioned to another apron sitting on the workbench closest to Ra'ah. He smiled as he picked it up and put it on.

"I hope you haven't forgotten everything I taught you," his father said softly.

"Scones." Ra'ah nodded. "I can still do a passable scone and biscuit."

"Oh?" His father nodded. "And where have you been practicing those? You better not have given away our family recipe to the Willards."

Ra'ah smiled. His father always surprised him with his sharp observations delivered in the quiet of the morning. There was something simple and peaceful about this bakery and this man. Homesickness struck him like a sack of flour, and he felt overwhelmed by a desire to just stay here. And then another realization rose from deep within him. The Call had been replaced. What had been a quiet whisper was now a soft voice—still like a whisper, but carried with a force that moved his soul under it.

He started when his father called his name, and realized it was the second time he'd called it. He looked across the table at the older man's concerned face.

"It's all coming to an end, Dad," he said softly. "All of this, the Willard's Ox, the villages and the city. It's all coming to an end."

His father grunted as he started to prepare the bread dough for the morning's patrons. There was a silence between them for so long that Ra'ah wondered if the other man had really heard him.

"For many months I thought you'd come back," his father finally said casually. "I was frustrated with you, of course. But your mother knew better. 'He's being called out,' she'd say. Of course she always thought you'd be the next village healer. Maybe we were both wrong."

"Dad, I'm sorry..." Ra'ah began.

"No need." His father shook his head and waved a floured hand at him. "What I mean to say is, the man I see before me is not the child who wandered off. I see something in you that I do not understand. A maturity that, frankly, you could not have earned in such a short time. I have met a few men and women in my life that carried the Call. But I've never met so many in one place at one time as I did last night. I do not think you are even aware of it."

Ra'ah nodded. The still small voice stirred within him. He nodded again and gathered the tools and ingredients he needed to create the scones. His father pointed silently to several baskets of fruit that were to be added. With a smile, Ra'ah set them up on the table with him.

"I want to tell you what's happened during the last two weeks," Ra'ah said

His dad gave a short nod as he kneaded the dough, and Ra'ah started from the night of the beast and the Maylak.

The first of the scones were just coming out of the oven as Ra'ah finished his retelling. He had left nothing out that he could think of. Their journey to Cardaya, Pethe, and Meletsa seemed so long ago and so easy to believe. He told his father about the great Maylak with the sword, about being in the overwhelming presence of Love itself. He explained as best he could about David and the Klasma. He fell at a loss for words when he tried to describe the Mountain with the City built upon its great arms. He then talked about the refugee camp at the base of the Gellah. Finally, he dove into the baptism and his vision.

"And now here we are," Ra'ah whispered.

"My head says you're fevered," replied his father. "But my heart says you've never told a truer story."

Ra'ah opened his mouth to speak, but his father held up a hand. His head was cocked and his eyes went to the door. Ra'ah's heart jumped in his throat as the door suddenly shook, but the soft cry of dismay from outside was anything but threatening.

"One moment, Cela," Peylos's voice rose in a deep boom. "I forgot my door this morning."

He strode to the front door and threw the latch. The door opened to reveal a small, rather rotund elderly man in robes illuminated by the lamplight. He hurried in and shut the door softly behind him.

"You're going to get me caught," he scolded the baker. "She's got her spies everywhere."

Ra'ah heart jumped a second time. But then his memory flashed to the conversation between his parents the night before. He smiled and took a fresh scone from the pan and offered it to the man. The old man's face lit up as he quickly wrapped a clean handkerchief around the offering.

"Good lad." He smiled as he wafted it under his nose. "Is there coffee to be had?"

"Alas, we have been neglectful," Peylos chuckled. "I slept in this morning, since I had help."

The old man looked Ra'ah up and down. "So I see. I assume his friends are here as well?"

"More or less," Peylos said.

"More or less?" Elder Cela snorted. "What on earth does that mean?"

"How much time do you have?" Peylos asked.

"I have a meeting to attend when the sun hits the courtyard. So you've got that much time."

The baker nodded. "Then we should get started. Ra'ah, we're going to need coffee."

Ra'ah nodded and headed for the door to the main house. Upon opening it, the smell of coffee and bacon hit his nose.

"Mom's up," he announced as he passed through the door.

He stopped short as the faces of David, Nebaya, and Anatellia turned to face him from their breakfast plates. His mother was busying herself preparing a tray of bacon and eggs and a kettle full of coffee. She looked up with a smile as he entered.

"Just in time, dear," she said. "Take this back with you. There is enough for three."

"Thanks, Mom." He took the tray from her and she held the door for him to return.

He walked back into the bakery with the tray. His father looked amused. Elder Cela's expression, by contrast, was one of suspicion as he ate the scone that Ra'ah had presented him.

"Everyone's up," Ra'ah announced.

"Very good!" Peylos clapped his hands. "Ra'ah, please watch my ovens while I introduce Elder Cela to the rest of his day."

"Okay." Ra'ah looked at his father helplessly as the two men walked past him. "But I'm eating your share of the bacon."

He quickly checked the ovens and took a quick inventory of what needed to go in next. Then he poured a mug of coffee. When his mother came in to get the tray, he grabbed a handful of bacon.

"You're not taking their bacon?" he teased.

"Neither Cela or your father need the extra fat," she said with a wink. "And there are berries and oatmeal to go around."

With that she was through the door, and Ra'ah was back to the quiet of the predawn bakery. This was an old familiar feeling that he hadn't realized he missed. He quietly hummed a song he'd picked up from Angelis on their way down from the falls as he removed another tray of scones and a tray of bread, replacing them with the trays they had already prepared before Elder Cela had arrived. He then decided to try his hand at braided bread while he waited. He was so engrossed in what he was doing that he missed the opening and closing of the front door.

"You always preferred flour to blood." It was a voice that made him jump in surprise.

"Matron Karis," he stammered as she lowered the cowl of her cloak.

"Young Ra'ah, but not so young as I remember." Her eyes reminded him of the vision he'd had just three days before.

"Matron…" Ra'ah began, but was silenced by a wave of her hand.

"Don't!" she said simply. "I knew from the very beginning you had a gift, but I also knew I could only start you on the path. I had to bow to the greater plan."

"I don't understand." Ra'ah felt the lie before it was out of his mouth.

"Yes, you do." She nodded as he flushed. "A true healer knows that where we fail, He will prevail. But He's looking for hands to use. We are His hands. You are His hands."

"That is the second time this week I have heard those words," Ra'ah mused.

"Keep watch," she scolded. "Life-changing lessons often come with three witnesses."

"That is a new one." Ra'ah chuckled softly. "What can I do for you this morning, Matron?"

"Point me toward your father and that old fool, Cela," she said. "And I'll take one of your scones. I always fancied yours over your father's."

He picked up a warm scone from the tray and pointed toward the door to the house. She took the scone from him and wafted it under her nose. The faintest of smiles cracked her lips and she entered the house without a word. No sooner had the door closed than the front door opened again and Kai slipped in.

"Good morning," Ra'ah greeted him quietly.

"Good morning, Ra'ah." Kai looked around the room before casually settling his eyes on the scone tray. "Your father's bakery must drive his neighbours crazy every morning."

"He does a good business. What's the news around the village?"

"Our nest of hornets hasn't stirred all night. But we're watching to be sure they don't go around us. Even a small band of soldiers could do incredible harm if they got between the Valley and the Gellah."

"I hadn't thought of that!" Ra'ah admitted.

"Why would you?" Kai asked sincerely. "Thinking of that is why *we're* here now. We all have our Callings and our assigned roles to carry out."

Ra'ah looked at the man standing in his father's bakery in a new light. This man had been born over a millennia ago in a land far away. He had seen things that Ra'ah had never seen, been places that Ra'ah had never heard of. He had lost family and friends to an enemy thought long dead, yet reborn in some new way. In that moment he was entirely a foreign stranger, someone never belonging to the Valley that encompassed all of Ra'ah's life. But here was a man he would happily call a brother. And he was completely focused on the tray of scones.

"How many shall I bundle up?" Ra'ah laughed softly as he gathered a basket.

Kai was long gone and dawn's glow lit the smoked glass windows of the bakery when his father returned to him. He nodded approvingly at the braided breads and then shook his head at the depleted scones until Ra'ah pointed to the ovens where a fresh batch baked.

"They won't last," he assured his son. "Not when people find out who baked them. I didn't think I was that good a teacher, but the proof is in the scone, as I've already heard twice this morning. But go and be with your friends. A plan is forming that you are involved in."

"Don't burn my scones," Ra'ah scolded gently.

The drone of soft conversation in the dining room died off as he entered the room. Elder Cela sat beside Matron Karis at the head of the table. The girls, David, and Temian were arrayed on either side of them.

Anatellia motioned to an empty spot beside her. "Good timing. We've finished giving our testimony and we're just about to work out our strategy."

"Strategy?" Ra'ah asked. "Isn't telling the truth enough?"

"Lady Raphael has greatly muddied the water," Matron Karis muttered. "Things are not as clear as they should be."

"I don't understand," Ra'ah admitted as he sat.

"My mother has brought the leader of the Sacheth here," Anatellia said. "They are here to pitch her trade union lies. And they're here to refute our message, of course."

"But we have the message from the Maylak," Ra'ah sputtered. "We have everything we've seen. We've even seen the Mountain!"

"And yet it always comes down to our word against theirs," Anatellia said.

"I cannot believe people would believe your mother and this Sacheth leader over us…" Ra'ah argued feebly.

"They don't have to believe." Nebaya shook her head. "They just have to cause delay. The moon is waning; our time is growing short."

"We need something to prove these people are our enemy," said Ra'ah.

Anatellia shook her head. "My mother will not make that easy. She won't allow anything to tarnish her plan."

"Even so," Elder Cela broke his silence, "we must be vigilant to find the weaknesses in her arguments. Bringing these foreign men with her may be one of those weaknesses."

"The three of us will go with Elder Cela and Matron Karis to the meeting," Anatellia said. "The Elder will be sure we get equal standing in the conversation. David, who will you send with us?"

"Temian and I," David confirmed. "I can't believe they would dare to threaten any of you openly in the courtyard. And the sheriffs are of no concern. But I am suspicious they might try to move around the village and send a small force north. That must be prevented at all costs. I will leave Kai with that task."

"No one has seen these soldiers you talk of," Elder Cela said.

David nodded. "I'm not surprised. Consider what effect we've had, and you've only seen Temian and me. It doesn't help my mother's plan to have foreign soldiers parading around openly."

"Maybe we should reveal the Klasma?" Nebaya offered. "The nineteen of you would be quite a surprise in our favour."

"And then our enemy would know we are here and in what numbers," Temian spoke up. "Surprise is not an ally we should throw away needlessly."

Elder Cela nodded. "No, that is correct. And you might end up looking like the aggressors. As it stands, you'll be blamed for spreading panic in the valley. There are many here in Bato who will look to the encampment of refugees from Kathik as you are doing."

"How many refugees are there?" Ra'ah asked.

"About three hundred," Matron Karis said. "They're setting up a way station of sorts. Mostly university students, by the look of them."

"That would be Governor Taman's doing," Anatellia reasoned. "He'd recognize the need to not overwhelm Bato itself."

The sound of voices from the bakery brought them all to silence. The voice of Peylos carried through the opening door, followed immediately by a tall, young sheriff with flushed cheeks. He had the aura of impatience about him as he panned the room, but he stopped dead when his eyes fell on David and Temian.

"Michael," Elder Cela said. "I trust there is a good reason for this intrusion?"

The sheriff's eyes were locked with David's for an uncomfortably long time, and then he scanned the others in the room in quick succession, like he was looking for the source of the voice that had spoken to him. He finally saw the Elder and nodded hesitantly.

"Well?" Elder Cela pressed.

"The delegates from Kathik…"

"What of them?"

"The delegates have asked to meet earlier," the sheriff tried again. "I was sent to find you, and, if possible, Matron Karis."

"You found us both," Karis congratulated him.

"Yes."

"Meet us outside," Elder Cela said firmly.

The sheriff nodded and pushed past Peylos, who was still standing in the doorway. The baker shook his head and followed the young man back out into the bakery.

"Rumours rarely need to be fed," Cela sighed. "They inevitably feed themselves. Strategizing time is over."

Ra'ah looked around at the six people settled around the table with him. They didn't have much of a strategy to go with. His thoughts went to the Living God. Their lack of any real plan hadn't been a problem for Him yet. In fact things seemed to just work out in spite of them.

Something settled in the pit of his stomach. It wasn't so much worry, he realized, as a deep sense of watchful expectation.

29

YOUR STORY OR MINE?

D avid and Temian left through the home's side door, and the rest of them filed through the bakery to stand in the brightening dawn light of a mountain morning. A small knot of sheriffs was waiting for them. The one named Michael recognized immediately that two were missing and made to go look for them, until Elder Cela shook his head.

"They will join us shortly," he said in explanation. "Let's get to the courtyard."

Michael nodded, and the sheriffs set off at a brisk pace. Matron Karis shook her head; she and Cela set their own pace, forcing the sheriffs to stop and wait for them every thirty paces. Finally the old woman lost her patience and snapped at the young men.

"Either set pace with us or begone with you," she scolded. "Your impatience is contagious."

Chastened, the men slowed and matched their pace, although Ra'ah saw it chafed them.

He looked around at the village he'd grown up in. Nothing much ever appeared to change. A new fence here, maybe. Or a new porch there. But all of it was familiar. All of it felt like home. For the briefest time he wished he could just go back to when he was the baker's son, the Healer's apprentice. And then another thought rose in him. He was more than that now.

They came up on the back of the crowd so suddenly that Ra'ah almost walked into Elder Cela. They had arrived at the edge of the village courtyard and Ra'ah could hear someone talking loudly from somewhere near its centre. It was a powerful and oddly familiar voice. The sheriffs pushed a path through the crowd and led them toward the community hall that dominated the centre of the courtyard.

The people parted for them, but a whispering arose in their wake. It looked like most of the village had gathered to hear what the Kathik delegation had to say. And by the whispers, Ra'ah realized they already knew about his friends and himself. More than once he caught his name being mentioned. He didn't stop to look at who was talking about him, however, because the authoritative voice was becoming more clear and commanding, drawing him forward.

The crowd parted suddenly and before them was the Elders' table, with the Elders sitting on seats behind it. In front of them, to the right of where Ra'ah and his friends stood, was a group of chairs for the visiting dignitaries, and a tall woman—the source of the familiar voice—was speaking to the four Elders currently present. Ra'ah realized the woman was Anatellia's mother, Lady Raphael, almost immediately as she turned her head to regard them coldly.

"These rumours and stories being spread by irresponsible children must be stopped," she was saying. "That is why I have come from Kathik. This is one of the greatest opportunities in the history of the Amatta Valley, and we should not let superstitious storytelling guide our wisdom."

Elder Cela and Matron Karis moved around the table and took their seats. Ra'ah felt suddenly very vulnerable with Nebaya and Anatellia as they stood alone in front of the table. Anatellia was rigid and tall under her mother's condescending glare. Nebaya stood behind her friend like a wall, returning the older woman's stare with one of her own.

Ra'ah found his eyes wandering to the group of men and women in the seats behind Lady Raphael. They were typical Kathik merchants by the look of them. But then his eyes snapped to two men behind the chairs and his skin crawled.

They were very obviously foreigners to the valley. They were in quiet conversation as they regarded Ra'ah and his friends. The tallest of the two was the living representation of the phrase "built like a brick house." He was dressed in a red tunic and black pants, but the cloth was definitely not Valley-woven. His arms were like tree trunks and his hands rested on his hips. He fingered the hilt of a hunting knife as the second man talked to him. He nodded often, but always his eyes were surveying the crowd.

It was the second man that unsettled him the most. He was smaller than the first man, but he moved like the mountain cats that sometimes made their way into the Valley. He was dressed in silks like a merchant, but a flash of light around his collar suggested a metallic shirt under the silk. There was almost a presence about him, a presence that caused the presence of the Living God to stir within him.

Suddenly he realized that both men were looking right back at him. The big man's eyes held no real surprises—the hostility in them was right on the surface. But the eyes of the man in silks were like pits of night. Ra'ah shuddered and looked away. He preferred the honesty of the big man's gaze. He then realized he'd missed something being said from the Elders' table and he turned his attention back to the drama unfolding there.

"I ask to be allowed to speak to the Elders of Bato," Anatellia said.

"This girl and her vagabond band should be arrested, not entertained," Lady Raphael cut in.

"We are not vagabonds," Anatellia shot back. "We are known in all the Valley. We have done trade with many people here in attendance. I dare say we are better known and respected in the villages than the silk merchants of Kathik might be."

Lady Raphael's face flushed, but her attention remained focused on the man in the centre of the Elder's table as he rose. Ra'ah recognized Elder Sophos and nodded as the man looked him over before regarding the other two women.

"There are only three of you," he noted in his soft voice. "Will your other two friends be joining us?"

"They are on another errand, sir," Anatellia said.

"Too bad." The old man shook his head. "I would very much like to hear young Daskow's version of this story you are bringing. You've blazed quite a trail of rumour across the Valley in the last weeks."

"The rumour is regretted," Anatellia said. "But our message, and the mission it has inspired, are true, and the threat is real."

"They are spreading rumours and misunderstanding," Lady Raphael interjected. "That is why I have brought Lord Gerig with me. If you will just let us speak first to the matters at hand, you will see."

The man in silks had made his way back to the chairs of the Kathik delegation, and nodded to the Elders when Lady Raphael gestured back to him. But he was studying the three of them closely with those dark eyes. Ra'ah wondered suddenly where David and Temian had gotten to.

"This is a curious situation." Sophos nodded as he looked to the other elders. "Who shall be first to tell their story, and who will be stuck responding to the first story?"

"This meeting was called by us," Lady Raphael pressed. "These children are interrupting what was meant to be a conversation between Kathik and Bato eldership."

"A curious point," Cela spoke up. "Especially since you have none of Kathik's governorship in your party."

"They were unable to come north," Lady Raphael lamented. "They are busy cleaning up after the unrest these children have stirred up."

"Indeed." Cela's smile didn't reach his eyes. "My friends, Matron Karis and I had the opportunity to hear Miss Anatellia's story earlier this morning. They also delivered to me these letters from our peers in the other villages. I suggest we first let the young people deliver their message and then we can allow Kathik and their friend, Lord Gerig here, to respond."

"My friends!" Lady Raphael protested.

"No." Elder Sophos raised his hand as he scanned one of the letters Cela had laid on the table. "No, I think Cela is right in this. You didn't go to Cardaya or Meletsa to counter these rumours. You didn't go to Pethe, who among all the villages is closest to Kathik's heart. You came here. You came to block the message here."

Lady Raphael looked back at the man in silk. Ra'ah saw the recognition in her face that she'd lost the argument. The man just shrugged.

"Very well," she conceded, and returned to her seat.

"The short version, if you will." Elder Cela offered the centre to Anatellia.

"Elders and people of Bato!" Anatellia's voice carried well in the courtyard. "Two weeks ago my friends and I were camped on the slopes above Cardaya when we were attacked by a great black beast. It was unlike any animal we had ever seen and it moved like a creature gone mad. But before we could even react, it was shot dead at our fire by a Maylak of the Living God."

A murmur ran through the crowd. Ra'ah looked around to see worried and concerned faces everywhere. And an equal number of skeptical faces. His eyes fell on the Kathik group who stared impatiently at Anatellia. All accept Lord Gerig. The man was staring at Ra'ah with a measuring look, like he was assessing Ra'ah's value. The quiet presence within Ra'ah stirred, and the man's eyes flashed in something akin to hatred. He broke the contact and returned his attention to Anatellia as she continued.

"The Maylak told us that an old enemy was coming to the Valley. We were charged with going to all of the villages and the city and giving this warning. Everyone is to flee north, to the Mountain of the Living God. And we only have until the next new moon."

The murmur of the crowd broke into the chaos of many voices at once. Elder Sophos stood and raised his hands for silence. When that failed to quiet them, he raised his voice to a surprising boom that surprised them to stillness.

"Peace!" he said. "I guess I asked for the short version, and that was certainly short. But now I have more questions than answers."

"If I may?" Lady Raphael rose. "I can shed light on this foolishness."

Elder Sophos waved her to continue and sat back down.

"People of Bato, I regret that I am in no small part responsible for this whole affair," she said.

Anatellia turned to face her mother in shock. Nebaya snorted softly, and Ra'ah felt confusion and no small amount of suspicion arise in himself.

"It is true that a large group of foreigners is coming to our little Valley," she continued. "They are coming at my invitation. For many years, the Sacheth Syndicate has been one of our greatest trade partners. They have been instrumental in bringing wealth and exotic goods to our little valley. At first it was through their trade partners, but as our trade out of the Valley increased, we caught their attention. Lord Gerig and I have been in contact with each other for many months, and when he expressed interest in setting up a Trade Hold, I naturally saw an opportunity for us to mutually prosper. The so-called 'army' that these children are scaring everyone with is actually a caravan of tradesmen, artisans, and labourers coming here to build that hold."

"If that is so, then why do we have a Maylak of the Living God warning us about them?" Elder Cela cut in.

"Unfortunately, I believe that my daughter and her four friends were deceived by the enemies of this economic alliance," Lady Raphael said. "When I heard the rumours coming across the river, I immediately started searching for their source. It did not take long before the arrival of my daughter confirmed her group as that source. I immediately sent word to Lord Gerig for help, and was relieved to discover that he was much closer than his caravans. He came with all haste and if you will allow, he also has an explanation for this so-called Maylak."

The man in silk stood up and nodded to the Elders. Sophos motioned for him to join Lady Raphael. He nodded again. The man's movement continued to make Ra'ah uncomfortable, and once again he wished David and the Klasma were closer.

"Good people, my name is Gerig." The man's voice was like the silk he was wearing. "As Lady Raphael has already said, I am leading a large group of tradesmen and artisans to come set up a hold, a village of sorts, in your beautiful valley. The Sacheth are a great union of people, and as you can imagine, we have more than a few enemies who would like nothing more than to obstruct us and take advantage of you. I believe that one such enemy has snuck into your valley ahead of us and deceived these youth into starting these rumours."

"That's not true," Anatellia insisted.

"I'm not saying he wasn't convincing," Gerig purred. "There is so much outside of your sheltered valley life that could seem wondrous to you."

"You see, my friends," Lady Raphael cut in, "how easy it is for us to be swept up by rumours? My daughter and her friends fell for a very convincing deception. I, myself, was struck by the differences in appearance of Lord Gerig and his men to the people of the Valley. You all saw his servant, Deuver, just a short time ago. Is it too much to think that someone else, someone outside of the Valley, was this mysterious Maylak? Someone with trained animals and the intention to destroy this alliance before it even starts."

Ra'ah suddenly understood what Nebaya had said earlier in the dining room. He knew everything that Anatellia's mother and this Gerig were saying was untrue. He wondered how much Lady Raphael knew was false, and how much she just believed Gerig's lies. But Gerig, Lord of the Sacheth, here was a practiced liar. Now it was word against word, and he had to admit that the lies sounded convincing.

"The Maylak we saw was not some foreigner like this man," Anatellia said. "And what we have seen and experienced since cannot be explained by your lies."

"Keep a civil tongue, young lady," her mother warned. "There could be an argument to excuse you because you were deceived, but not if you continue to stack story upon story. And to what end? You'll lead hundreds of people to abandon their homes and wander off into the northern mountains looking for myth and legend? No, this has to stop here and now. You three need to be taken into custody."

"No, Mother." Anatellia shook her head. "You are wrong. We've seen Maylak. Actual living Maylak. And we've seen the Mountain. We've stood before it and spoken with the Living God himself."

Ra'ah thought he saw the man in silk flinch at that admission, but his attention was drawn back to Anatellia's mother. The woman walked slowly to stand in front of her daughter with a deep look of disgust on her face.

"What has become of you? Truly? I did not raise my daughter to be such a foolish liar. You are no daughter of mine."

"As much as she'd like to disown you herself, she's still your daughter," a familiar voice called out.

Heads turned as David and Temian strode through the crowd to stand with Anatellia and the others. Lady Raphael watched them approach in mild confusion and remained silent.

"What's wrong, Mother?" David asked quietly. "Don't recognize your own son?"

A wave of emotions flashed across her face. Confusion, indignation, and uncertainty warred with a normally perfectly controlled visage. Her lips parted to speak but nothing came out. She shook her head and her eyes narrowed. There was complete silence in the courtyard for several breaths.

"David?" It was a confusion of question and statement.

"Who else?" David asked.

"What happened to you?" She struggled to regain her composure. "You've aged years in days. What is going on here?"

"The Living God happened," David began, but then fell silent as Gerig stepped from behind her.

The two men locked eyes and Ra'ah felt a sudden tension between them. David seemed to be struggling with something deep inside himself. His gaze hardened and his jaw tightened. Gerig's eyes narrowed, and Ra'ah wondered if he was about to leap at David.

"Saucan," David whispered.

The man in silk staggered like he'd been slapped. For the briefest of moments his entire composure seemed to fail, and in that moment Ra'ah saw such hatred in the man that his heart quailed. But just as quickly he had his walls back up, and he shook his head.

"No, my name is Gerig. Lord Gerig of the Sacheth Syndicate."

"Sacheth…" Temian breathed the name.

David turned to lay a restraining hand on Temian's chest.

"I'm sorry," David said. "You reminded me for one brief moment of someone I met a long time ago."

"A friend, no doubt," Gerig nodded.

"Ever he pretended to be," David stated flatly.

"What mischief is this?" Lady Raphael finally composed herself. "You sound like my son David; you bear a resemblance to my son David. But you are not David."

"I am David," he said. "David reborn. The David you knew but a few days ago is gone. I remain."

She shook her head but simply stared at him. David returned her stare. Gerig, momentarily forgotten, continued to study David as if trying to recall his face. Ra'ah watched subtle emotions play off the man's face. Suddenly something seemed to occur to the man, and his gaze flipped to Anatellia before resting on Nebaya. A look settled on his face then that made Ra'ah's guts turn. But as quickly as the look had appeared it was gone, and the man's face once again became unreadable.

"Excuse me," the voice of Elder Sophos called out.

The two groups turned to the Elders' table. Ra'ah almost laughed at the look on their faces. The whole exchange had played out like a show that Angelis might have put on. He realized that their position was still precarious.

"We've gotten a bit off topic," Elder Sophos suggested dryly. "May I ask who you two gentlemen are?"

"Forgive me." David bowed to the table. "I am David, and this is Temian. We have come from north of the Gellah as protection for the five messengers sent by the Living God to warn the Valley."

"Indeed." Sophos's eyebrow shot up. "From north of the Gellah?"

"Yes."

Elder Sophos looked to his colleagues helplessly.

"This is a mess," he finally admitted. "A tangled knot complete with foreigners on both sides that may very well take years to unwind. But by both accounts, we have only weeks. An event is approaching that will change our Valley forever. So the question before us is this: how do we respond?"

"You respond by joining Kathik in embracing the future," Lady Raphael stated pointedly.

"Kathik has always paraded itself as the big brother to the villages," Elder Sophos said. "Ever they have taken it on themselves to tell us how we ought to live and govern. The Lady is a shining example of Kathik arrogance in that matter. By your own admission you have brought these people to us. What lands will they occupy? Where will they build this trade hold of theirs? It seems you've made arbitrary decisions for the Valley that quite frankly weren't yours to make."

"My friends!" Gerig stepped forward. "Truly, this has become a tangled mess. As the spokesman for my people, I will say that we never intended any of this misunderstanding. May I suggest a recess and then a return to civil discourse at a later time?"

"Indeed," Elder Sophos agreed. "Although we'll retain the company of the Lady and her daughter. Maybe we can untangle some things before we meet again."

"Very good." Gerig bowed stiffly and turned on his heel.

David watched him go before he whispered something to Temian and headed back through the crowd. Anatellia headed for the Elders' table with her mother. Nebaya snorted and then looked at the two men left with her.

"I'd like to go check out the refugee camp down by the river," she said.

"Let's wait until Kai and a few others join us," Temian said softly. "None of you should be without escort from now on."

"Surely you're enough of a deterrent?" Nebaya pressed.

Temian's lips thinned in what might have been a frown. After a long moment of thought he simply nodded and turned his gaze to Ra'ah.

"I'm going to return to the bakery," Ra'ah decided. "That ought to be safe enough."

"As safe as anywhere," Temian agreed. "If you see David or Kai, let them know that Nebaya and I are heading for the refugee camp."

"Will do." Ra'ah nodded as the two turned and headed for the east side of the courtyard.

With a sigh and a look around at the clusters of villagers staring at himself and his friends, he turned and headed back down the road toward his father's bakery.

30

ANOTHER APPOINTMENT

David made his way through the back paths and side streets of the village until he passed into the forests below the steep western slope. The well-spaced trees and worn cart paths were a marked difference from the last time he'd walked these forests, he mused. Woodsmen kept this part of outer Bato well-tended. The lumber from these woods was made into all sorts of products for the valley. Bato woodworkers made the best hand tools.

He did not have to go far before he found Kai and the others. As arranged, they had pulled in from their watches, and they waited with unmoving faces for his word. He nodded to them all and noted that bows were strung and quivers uncovered.

He cut to the point. "Where are they?"

"They've broken their camp," Kai said. "A dozen appear to be making their way toward us, and at least twice that took off back toward the city."

"Three dozen?" David said in dismay.

"We should assume there are more," Kai said.

"We *have* to assume there are more. How long do we have before the twelve are here?"

Kai and David turned as a bird call sounded through the trees to the south. The quick, lithe form of Luca appeared through the trees at a lope.

"I'd say we've got just enough time to set an ambush," Kai said.

Luca made no sound as he changed his course to meet them.

"What's your report, Luca?" David asked.

"Twelve men moving slowly along the base of the slope," Luca said. "They're very worried about being seen. But three more just left the village, and they aren't being subtle at all."

"That would be their leader, Gerig," David muttered. "There is something utterly unwholesome about that man. Let's intercept the twelve. I'd rather have them boxed up before I have to deal with him."

"None of these men have a wholesome feel," Luca said dryly.

"How are they armed?" Kai asked.

"Unstrung bows," Luca said. "Knives, hatchets, and short clubs. They're obviously trying not to raise alarm. If they had gotten themselves some local clothing they'd pass for hunters or woodsmen at a distance."

"No doubt they're trying to get north of the village." David shook his head. "Let's disabuse them of that idea."

"How subdued do you want them?" Kai asked softly.

"I am loath to shed blood in this Valley," David admitted.

"They are unlikely to feel the same," Kai said dryly. "Even with our training, I doubt we will be able to keep these encounters to cuts and bruises."

David nodded. "I know. And I know there is little wisdom in letting them choose violence first. But it still grieves me."

"You've been one of us for so long, I forget that our first years were remarkably different," Kai said. "Unless the Sacheth are greatly changed, violence will be the only language we will have."

"But I pray not today." David shook his head. "Come, let's greet our visitors."

Kai gave a call, and like a wave the Klasma arose from their rest and started southward through the trees. Shortly, they came to the mouth of a shallow gully that came off the slope and cut through a narrow clearing. David nodded in satisfaction. Anyone wanting to move unseen would surely come this way. The Klasma spread out to cover the clearing.

They did not have to wait long. From the far end of the defile a line of men moved, slow and steady, toward the spot where David and Kai were hidden. David watched as the twelve men scanned the forest all around them but failed to see the equally skilled Klasma that now had them in a potentially deadly crossfire. Once they were as fully exposed in the clearing as they could be, he called out to them.

"Ho, there, strangers. I suggest you go no further."

The men dropped immediately to either side of the defile, scanning the trees for the threat that they now knew was there. The lead man looked intently toward where David was crouched. David sensed a very short window of opportunity to talk and stood up, his quarterstaff loose in his hand.

"You are surrounded and outnumbered," David said. "We have arrows nocked and your bows are useless."

"Why do you threaten us so?" the leader asked.

"We know who you are," David said. "And we will not permit you to pass."

"I doubt you truly know who we are," the leader said, with a slight sneer. "But why should we fear a bunch of Valley kids with bows?"

"Look at me." David stepped forward into the sunlight. "I am not a child. And I do not want to shed blood in this valley. But if blood must be shed, it will be yours."

"Big words," the leader said. "But I think you'll find our blood harder to spill than yours."

As he spoke his men sprung, moving with a speed that would have surprised anyone other than the Klasma. The hum of bows filled the clearing and four men were struck, even as they were fluidly stringing their bows. The rest dropped to cover again. All except the leader.

With a knife in his hand and a wild, crazed look in his eyes, he rushed David with a scream. His remaining men stared after him. No bows called out. No one hindered him. He raised the knife, and then a blur from David's left appeared. Kai's quarterstaff caught the man in his midsection, and then came down on his skull just as he started to double over. The man crumpled, senseless. The seven remaining men threw unstrung bows and weapons away from themselves.

David looked down at the man who had tried to attack him. Blood matted the back of his skull, and he didn't move. First blood was theirs. He felt strangely at peace with that. He looked toward the other eleven men. The Klasma had aimed well. The four wounded men would never fire a bow again, but they'd walk away. *Well, maybe,* David thought darkly.

"Who among you will speak now, since this one can't any longer?" David called out.

"Oh, I think I can," a voice called out from across the clearing.

David looked up in surprise to see Gerig standing in the shadow of the trees on the far side. He had a smile on his face that did not reach his eyes as he looked about the clearing. He held his hands out, palms up, but there was murder in his eyes. Gerig stepped forward and made his way in leisurely fashion across the clearing.

"David, son of Lady Raphael, you are full of surprises," he laughed coldly. "What am I to do with this development?"

"Go back where you've come from," David suggested.

"What?" Gerig feigned shock. "And miss all of this fun? But maybe you're right. I think we'll return to Kathik to rethink things a bit."

"What if we don't let you?" David asked.

Gerig laughed. His laughter was deep and loud and harsh. He laughed so long that David shifted nervously, wondering if the man might be mad.

"Oh, David," he said as he caught his breath. "Truly, you are going to be fun. In all seriousness, you probably shouldn't let us leave. You should kill every single one of us. Pour our blood out all over this clearing. Bathe the Valley in murderous blood for the first time in its history. Do it. We are much alike, you know."

"We are not alike." David was repulsed.

"Oh, but we are. We're both servants to a greater power. Both possessed of our master's purpose and will. I can feel Him in you, you know. I can feel Him in all of you."

Gerig spun slowly and gazed at the forest around him. David felt the Spirit of the Living God arise in him; peace flowed into his thoughts and sharpened his senses. One more time he looked at the man in front of him and saw the face of Saucan. A thousand years had not erased that face from his memory. Was it possible?

"Is it truly you, Saucan?" David asked.

Gerig turned to him again, his face contorted in hatred.

"My name is Gerig Ebed Saucan," he admitted. "Do you understand what it means to bear that name? No—how could you? But that is the second time you've spoken it. Do you wish to see him?"

"I see him in you," David said.

"How could you, unless you've seen him before?" Gerig mused. "But if you've truly seen him, you would never want to see him again. He is the Scourge of the Weak. He is the Tormentor of the Unworthy. He is the Lord of All."

"He is not lord here," David stated flatly.

Gerig changed the subject. "You are familiar to me. This place is familiar. I have never been here in my life, and yet I know this place and I know you."

He looked at his men in the clearing. David exchanged worried looks with Kai. Whoever or whatever Gerig Ebed Saucan was, he was dangerously unpredictable. David was sure he could just as easily order his men to their deaths as talk about the weather.

"Lay down anything that could be even remotely threatening," Gerig suddenly commanded. "Leave it all on the ground, gather the wounded, and return to the city barracks."

The soldiers on the ground looked nervously from Gerig to David but did what they were commanded. David almost cursed. The soldiers left their packs and weapons on the ground, moving slowly with hands in plain sight. They gathered the four arrow-stricken men and two of them came to remove the troop leader's pack and weapons. The man groaned as they lifted him between them to make their way back to the others.

"You see," Gerig said, smiling, "I do know you. You can't make the hard choices. You can't see what needs to be done. And now I'm taking the opportunity away from you. And that makes me happy, taking things away from you."

"You don't just look like him, you sound like him," David said.

"Well of course I do," Gerig snorted. "I am his vessel. I was set apart at birth. Taught and trained since I could stand. I was chosen from all the initiates. I earned my place. I paid every price, made every oath, took every vow. Only one may bear the name, and that is me."

"This man is crazy," Kai whispered in David's ear. "What are we going to do about them?"

David watched as the soldiers slowly and warily walked back the way they came. He knew there was nothing they could really do. They certainly wouldn't murder unarmed men. They couldn't easily detain them. And that wasn't what they were sent to do, anyway.

"We let them retreat," David said. "But we follow them all of the way back to the city. They cannot be allowed to double back."

"Double back?" Gerig laughed again. "No, that plan has changed. We weren't sure how He would respond to us. We couldn't know about your little band. But it's of little consequence."

"How so?" Kai said in frustration.

"I came to deal with your five friends," Gerig said. "You've made that harder, I'll admit. But I also came to sew a little confusion. And I'm a gifted seamster. We're going to play a game, you and I. And we'll see how many run off north with you before my army gets here. These people don't know Him like you do. They're ripe for what I'm offering. Prosperity, comfort, a promise of peace. What are you and your five friends offering? The northern mountains and a coming winter.

"Frustrating, how blunt I am being. With you I'm direct and straight forward. I see the anger it creates in you. How many of you are there? Ten? Fifty? A hundred? Who cares! Even if you were to slay every last one of us here in this pitiful valley, you could do nothing against what is coming. I am bringing a fist to smash the Mountain itself.

"So gather up who you can. Run north. When we are done here, we'll follow. And He won't help you. He could release His legions of Maylak on us, but he won't. Oh sure, He makes quick work of the hounds. But he will not release the armies of Heaven on flesh. And that will be His downfall. And you'll be left. Left to watch as your friends and everyone you tried to save gets slaughtered before His gates."

"I think not," David said simply. "You are very much like your namesake. You talk too much."

"Do you think?" Gerig's smile suddenly made David's skin crawl. "Well let me assure you, I am also a man of action. I have enjoyed this conversation, dear David. I suspect we will not have another quite this civil. I recognized you, David. But did you forget so easily? I also recognized her."

Confusion flashed through David's mind and struck him like a spark on spilled lamp oil. Suddenly anger flared through him, and then a deep fear and panic. With an anguished cry he called to Kai and the others, and then broke into a sprint back toward the village.

Even as he ran he heard Gerig's deep, maddening laugh carrying through the trees.

31

Costly Mistakes

R a'ah had barely walked into the front door of the bakery before his mother had him turned around with baking for the Elders. She handed him two large baskets and hefted a large one herself as they set back out down the same road he'd already walked twice that morning.

"To be honest," she said as they walked, "I didn't expect you back this early. I was going to get your father to help me."

"Well, the meeting was a bit of a mess," Ra'ah said.

"How so?"

"They are turning it into a 'we say, they say,'" he explained. "No one is denying something is coming. It's the nature of the something that is being argued."

"So often it seems to come down to obedience over comfort," his mother said. "And we've all gotten a bit too comfortable."

Ra'ah nodded. He missed conversations with his mother. She always seemed to understand him better than his dad did.

"We've known for a while that something was coming, though," his mother added.

"What do you mean?" He looked at her in surprise.

"There has been a stirring in many hearts for some time. A growing sense of unease and watchfulness. For some, like dear Amon, it's become a lifelong calling."

"Wait…" Ra'ah stopped dead. "You know Amon?"

"Well, of course I do." His mother looked back at him. "I wasn't always the baker's wife. And your father wasn't always a baker, for that matter. Before you were born we travelled all over the Valley. But after I got pregnant with you we settled down here."

"Dad travelled the Valley?" he asked incredulously as he began walking again. "Then why was he so mad when I left?"

"Oh, honey, sometimes when we get older, we forget what it's like to be young and searching," she said. "Your father wasn't mad so much as worried you might miss your calling trying to find it."

"I don't understand," he admitted.

"I think you do," she countered. "You're just not seeing it fully. But it's written all over you. The Living God has called you out. You just need to stop fighting it."

Ra'ah thought about the last week. Yes, she was right. Although he didn't understand what that calling was, exactly, she was right.

"Oh look, here are Anatellia and the Elders." His mother pointed ahead.

Ra'ah looked forward and saw that Anatellia, Matron Karis, and Elder Cela were indeed walking toward them. They were deep in conversation and hadn't seen Ra'ah and his mother yet. Ra'ah called out and they looked up. Anatellia smiled and then appeared troubled.

"Where is Temian and Nebaya?" she asked when they got closer.

"Nebaya wanted to check out the refugee camp," Ra'ah explained. "She convinced Temian to take her."

"Alone?" Anatellia seemed peeved.

Ra'ah shrugged. "Temian wanted to wait, but you know Nebaya."

"Why don't we try to meet them?" Elder Cela suggested. "I'd like to talk to the organizers of the camp myself."

They all agreed, and made their way toward the southeastern side of the village.

Temian and Nebaya made good time through the village, and made their way around the vegetable farms that covered the land between it and the river. According to Elder Cela the refugee camp was about a mile below Bato, beyond the encircling farms.

They hadn't spoken much since they'd left. Each was enjoying the beautiful morning with the sun and the birds for company. Nebaya jumped a creek and turned to watch Temian try the leap. But instead of following her, he frowned and stooped by the water's edge.

"What is it?" she called curiously.

"Nothing good," he muttered as he stood up and scanned the trees and fields around them. "We need to go back."

"What is it?" she repeated as she came back to the creek bank.

Looking down where he had stooped, she saw the deep impression of a heavy boot in the muddy bank. She looked up at the man and nodded. He didn't have to explain further. She knew every type of boot, shoe, sandal and slipper print in the valley. She could identify the size of the person and even what village they were from. However, this print she didn't recognize. She'd never seen a print like it. But whoever made it was at least Temian's size.

An icy fist of fear wrapped around her heart as she looked to Temian for direction. He placed a finger to his lips as he took his bow from his shoulder. He nocked an arrow and motioned with a sharp nod back toward the village. She leapt quieter than a deer back over the creek. Together they hurried back along the treeline that ran the length of the path they had been following.

They moved quickly along the trees, watching the field beside them and through the trees ahead and to their left. They had to cover three quarters of a mile to get to the creek, and they recovered half a mile before Temian signalled a stop. They stooped in a hollow and he bent protectively over her.

"Do you think they saw us?" she whispered.

Worried creased the big man's face. He shook his head hesitantly.

"That's just it," he whispered in her ear. "We haven't seen them. That footprint was a rookie mistake."

"Maybe they aren't as good as you thought?" she offered

He shook his head. "No, Nebaya. Not their rookie mistake—mine."

"I don't understand."

"A single footprint in a muddy creek bank. They might as well have left a note saying 'We're here. We're watching you.'" He was frustrated now.

"A deliberate footprint…" She felt a rekindling of fear.

"We may have fallen into a trap," Temian stated—something suddenly obvious to both of them.

"If so, how do we get out of it?" she asked.

"We need to get back to the village." He pointed northwest. "Through this wood."

"Isn't that a great place to ambush us?" she whispered pointedly.

"Yes. They know that. They would assume that we know that too. It would be absolutely foolish for me to take you that way, and we all know it."

"So you're hoping they don't think you a fool?" she asked incredulously.

"Yep." He nodded. "Let's go."

They made their way deeper into the forest. Nebaya recalled that the road lay to their left, probably only two to three hundred yards away from this point. This part of the wood had been cut back years before and then allowed to grow to give privacy to the dozens of small farms and gardens on their right. The path was a diagonal run of about a quarter mile. Once they got to the cleared edge of the village they should be safe. Gerig and his henchmen wouldn't risk attacking them in the open with witnesses.

Their flight felt like it took forever. Nebaya, used to hunting and tracking in denser forest than this, all but flew across the ground. Temian kept pace with her, his eyes everywhere. He ran like one of the stags on the upper slopes, impossibly quiet for his size. And the entire way they encountered no other living thing larger than the startled animals they passed.

They came out of the unkept forest into a park-like birch glade. Nebaya felt a sudden relief as she made out structures of the village ahead. She turned her head to tell Temian when she saw the soldier enter the glade on their right. She cried out in surprise and Temian immediately drove his body toward the man.

She skidded to a stop and cursed the fact she hadn't brought her bow. The soldier saw Temian coming and fled back into the thicker timber. Something in the man's look caused Temian to look back behind them and his face went white as he skidded to the ground.

"Nebaya!" he bellowed as he fumbled for his bow.

Nebaya turned to see the largest man she'd ever encountered in her life standing at the edge of the forest they had just left. In his left hand was a bow. His right hand released.

Time seemed to blur. She was too slow. Something crossed into her peripheral vision from the right. A body imposed itself between her and the giant. A familiar body of a man.

The arrow appeared suddenly out of the cloak and she felt a spray on her face. She knew that man. She felt a pain in her chest, like her heart had exploded. But it wasn't from the arrow. It was so much worse.

A scream ripped through her. In the scream was a name.

"David! No!"

32

THE HIGHEST PRICE

D avid's heart pounded in his ears as he ran. Gerig's last words were like a knife through his heart. The whole thing had been a feint, a trap to remove his attention from their main assignment. And he had walked right into it. He heard Kai's footfalls nearby keeping pace with him. They had to find the others. They had to find her.

Dear Living God, he cried into the vaults of his own mind, *help me find her!*

As if in response, the image of a birch glade came to his mind. He didn't have to ask where it was. He had never been there. His mind raced. She probably wanted to go to the refugee camp. She wouldn't sit still. How foolish he was! Of course she wouldn't sit still. She would convince Temian to take her. South and east of the village, that's where he'd find them. But there was excruciating urgency in his heart. He might already be too late.

He changed his course to pass just south of the village. There were people on the paths here and he shouted for them to make way. He ignored the shouts of challenge and surprise as he passed. They reached the main road and flew over it, ignoring everyone and everything but the goal ahead. He didn't question. He trusted the Living God. He trusted His guidance.

A familiar voice cried out just ahead through the trees. *Birch trees,* his mind noted. He adjusted his course, never slowing. Kai called to him in warning but he ignored it. If he failed now, he was done. He would never forgive himself.

The glade suddenly appeared through the trees. David took in everything in a split second. His two friends. The man with the bow, already drawn back. Temian screamed to Nebaya in warning. There was no time, he was too late. But not entirely too late, he suddenly realized. With all of his will and strength he surged ahead, aiming his entire purpose and being for the only option left.

Time seemed to slow. David heard a short staccato of two bow strings. He saw the arrow leave the big man's bow and felt the giddy satisfaction of not failing. He staggered as the arrow found its new home. The world seemed to burst around him in a fury of excruciating pain and sound.

Ra'ah and the group had made it to the edge of the village when a scream rose from the forest ahead. It was the most heart-rending, anguished sound Ra'ah had ever heard, and his blood ran cold. A name was carried in the scream, and Ra'ah staggered at a memory just days old.

"Dear Living God," Anatellia breathed, "that was Nebaya!"

Ra'ah dropped the baskets he was carrying and broke into a sprint through the forest toward the direction the scream had come from. He heard Anatellia's panicked breathing just behind him, but he didn't wait for her to catch up.

They did not have far to go and he burst into the birch glade. Ra'ah looked around in confusion. The memory of his vision seemed overlapped with the scene before him. Half a dozen Klasma were scattered around the glade. Kai was barking orders through angry tears. The body of the big man he had seen earlier in the morning lay sprawled on the forest floor some distance away, the feather of an arrow sticking up out of his chest and bow still clenched in his fist.

But there, in the centre of his vision, was a sight that tore his heart apart. Nebaya sat hunched over the prone body of David. Her hair covered her face, but she was weeping bitterly. Ra'ah saw where the arrow had struck. He knew what it meant. Anatellia skidded up beside him and took in the scene, but upon seeing her best friend and her brother she screamed and ran over, falling on her knees beside them. Ra'ah felt frozen in place, confusion and grief racking him.

Matron Karis and his mother came into the clearing soon after. Ra'ah wondered where Elder Cela had gone. He shook his head and then caught Matron Karis's eye. She would have seen the arrow as well. Would have known better than him what it meant.

Something unexpected rose in Ra'ah. A presence so full of peace that it almost made him swoon. He staggered.

"Are you hurt, Ra'ah?" Temian looked over at him through grief-filled eyes.

"No." Ra'ah shook his head.

He walked over to his two friends and knelt beside David with them. The arrow had pierced his chest right over his left breast. He would have been dead before he hit the ground. Ra'ah looked up at Nebaya. Her face was flecked with blood where her tears had not washed it away. David had stepped in front of her, Ra'ah realized. He looked across the body to Anatellia. She was looking at him through tear-filled eyes.

"This can't be the end of it," she sobbed. "There has got to be something we can do."

Ra'ah looked helplessly down at David's body. There was one thing he could do, but it was useless.

"Someone help me roll him," he said.

Anatellia reached over the body and pulled as Ra'ah felt around for the shaft of the arrow. Once he had it, he drew his knife and sawed at the shaft. With a twist he broke it and removed the arrowhead. It was a cruel, barbed thing made to do more harm when it was removed. He motioned for Anatellia to lower her brother and then he gripped the feathered shaft and pulled it slowly out. Nebaya whimpered as it came free.

Ra'ah set aside the two pieces of arrow and then looked around helplessly. A crowd was gathering in the glade as people came in response to Nebaya's scream. Elder Cela was talking with Kai and a small group of sheriffs. He looked for his mother and found her and Matron Karis standing behind him. There was an intense look on Karis's face. She came over and knelt down beside him.

"We always feel so helpless in the face of death," she whispered.

"Yes." Ra'ah nodded through fresh tears.

"If it was in your power, how would you heal him?" Karis mused almost to herself.

Ra'ah looked at her in shock. This was his friend. This was Anatellia's brother. This wasn't time for one of her theory discussions.

"He said he loved me," Nebaya whispered. "Those were his last words to me."

They looked at her with broken hearts. Anatellia put her hand over her friend's. Nebaya just held David's head and sobbed afresh.

Ra'ah suddenly understood. It was like someone had gone back through his memories, from the first time Nebaya had introduced David to him in the common room of the Dancing Dove to their reunion at the foot of the Mountain. The memories lined up to create a picture. The picture of a man who had never forgotten his first love, who seemed determined to win her love, and who inevitably died to protect her. Ra'ah found himself weeping uncontrollably.

After a time Kai approached them. His grief was heavy but contained under years of training. He looked around the glade before clearing his throat.

"We should go," Kai said. "Elder Cela has arranged a private cottage for you all. We need to get you out of the open.

Ra'ah nodded. He tried to stand but felt a hand push him back down. He looked around in confusion. There was no one near to do that. He tried again to the same result.

Ra'ah. He felt the voice shake him like a leaf.

"Lord?" He whispered.

Ra'ah, the voice repeated, *have you so quickly forgotten Me?*

"I haven't forgotten you," he insisted.

Anatellia gave Ra'ah a confused look.

Can this man live?

"Oh Living God, he lives with You now," Ra'ah whispered.

Ra'ah, can this man be healed?

He shook his head in confusion. He half entertained that in his grief his mind was playing tricks on him, imagining voices in his head. He felt a brief flash of fear that he might be going crazy in this moment.

Can this man be healed?

"Oh Living God," Ra'ah spoke out in frustration. "Only you truly know, but this man is dead. There is no healing and no healer I have ever heard of that could fix this."

Everyone was staring at him now. He felt their eyes on him. He looked at Anatellia and then at Nebaya. She was staring at him with wild eyes. Hopeful eyes.

"There is One," Matron Karis whispered beside him. "And where we fail, He prevails. But He's looking for hands to use."

The memory of the vision from his baptism flooded through his mind. He shook his head, but the images were persistent. What he was being asked to do was impossible.

"I can't." He shook his head. "It isn't possible."

"You can't?" Karis snorted softly. "Of course you can't. Neither can I. We muddle around with scrapes and bruises. We treat fevers and infections. We have no power over life or death, Ra'ah. But there is One who does. And He looks for hands to use. Right now, you are His hands."

Ra'ah wanted to say He should pick someone else. He wanted to deny that he could be those hands. The living God should pick a different pair. But in his own mind he came face to face with the reality that the Living God had chosen him. He pictured the face of Joshua in his mind.

"Fine—here are my hands."

Nothing happened. He once again considered that he might be going mad. What was the question again? Could David be healed? It would take a knowledge beyond anything he had and power beyond what his feeble hands could produce. The whole idea was fantasy, really. He imagined himself putting a hand on the man's chest and commanding the flesh to be whole. If he did that, then everyone would know he'd gone crazy.

Something rose in him, picking up his consciousness and sweeping it forward in a wave of giddy surrender to the foolishness of his own imagination. He laid his palm over the bloody wound on David's chest.

"By the power of the Living God, according to His word and desire, wounded flesh be restored. Heart be made whole. Lungs be drained and made whole."

Ra'ah suddenly gasped. His hand felt like it was on fire. The glade became so still he could hear the fabric swish of the Klasma shifting around him. A familiar presence fell on the entire assembly of people. The Living God had come.

Ra'ah felt the dead man's flesh move and he almost jerked his hand back. He looked half expectantly into the face of his friend, but it remained ashen and cold. Confusion struck him in that moment. What else needed to be done?

Call him back, Ra'ah.

No sense stopping half way, Ra'ah decided. *"David, come back!"*

The silence returned. Nothing happened. Ra'ah closed his eyes and sighed. Suddenly he felt the very ground fall away from under him. He opened his eyes and gasped.

He was standing in the middle of a great building filled with light. The floor looked like polished granite or opaque glass. In the wall in front of him were hung two great open doors, and through them he could see a great City spreading out and descending into a valley far below. The light in the room was coming from behind him, and his shadow stretched in front of him and out the door. The realization of where he was struck him with a certainty. He was standing in the Temple of the Living God.

"Ra'ah," someone said from behind him.

He turned and beheld Joshua. But not like he had been when they had met on the valley floor below. Here he was radiant, hard to look at. At first Ra'ah thought the light came from him. But the light seemed to be coming from behind him, as well. No matter how hard he tried after, he could never describe the moment or the Man who was God before him. He fell to his knees.

"Am I dead?"

"You have never been more alive, child," Joshua laughed.

"Why did you bring me here?" Ra'ah asked before he thought better of it.

"You've been sent on an errand."

"David," Ra'ah said, and nodded past Joshua. "He's beyond the Temple, isn't he?"

"Yes."

"But how can I get him?" Ra'ah asked in confusion. "No one crosses the Temple floor and comes back."

"No one has, until someone does," Joshua smiled. "But that is why I am here, child. I'll be your guide. We'll collect David and I'll bring you back."

"In that case… lead the way?"

Joshua laughed and waved his hand toward the light. Ra'ah walked with Him across the floor and into the light that blinded him to everything else. Try as he might, he could see nothing but that light. The floor and ceiling were gone. The walls were gone. Only he and Joshua seemed to remain.

Suddenly out of the light two figures appeared as dimmer shadows of light ahead. As they drew closer, Ra'ah fancied that he recognized one of them as David.

"David," Ra'ah called. His voice sounded oddly coarse and rough.

The two figures turned toward him. One of them certainly was David. The other one, Ra'ah realized, was Simon, the man they had met at the Gellah. Their faces radiated the light all around them. They gave off peace and contentment that flooded through Ra'ah.

"Ra'ah?" David looked at him in surprise. "What are you doing here?"

"I've come to bring you home."

"But I am home," David laughed.

"Not yet." Ra'ah shook his head. "You're not done yet. We need you. Nebaya needs you."

Confusion clouded David's perfect face. Ra'ah almost regretted saying what he had said. But he knew it was true. David reached up to rub his chest where the arrow had pierced him. He shook his head.

"No, she doesn't," he said. "And I'm finally home. Look around you, Ra'ah: this is where we were meant to be. Stay here with us. This is your home, too."

Ra'ah looked around him in confusion. At first all he could see was light. Light was everywhere and everything. Then, as if his eyes started to focus, he started to see. The world beyond started to take shape and for one brief moment he realized the trap of eternity.

A strong arm wrapped around his shoulders and he looked into the eyes of Joshua. But not Joshua. He was a being of tearful, heart-rending beauty and unfathomable power. Ra'ah broke into tears. He knew he couldn't stay. He knew he had to stay focused. He wrenched his eyes back to David.

"I cannot stay," he said through his tears. "I came here for you. You know you can't stay here, either. Not yet, David. It's not yet time."

David looked around himself. He looked at Simon, who shook his head. He looked at Joshua, his eyes pleading. But something in Joshua's face washed the confusion away. He looked at Ra'ah again and just nodded.

The clearing was still deathly quiet. Ra'ah opened his eyes and looked up at Anatellia and Nebaya. Nebaya still had the wild, almost hopeful look on her face. He had no idea how long he'd sat there, but his tears felt dry on his face. He smiled gently at her.

And then the body of their friend inhaled a ragged breath. The women looked down at David in stunned shock. He breathed again more easily, and his eyes fluttered open. He looked up into Nebaya's eyes and smiled.

"I do love you, wild girl," he whispered.

"David!" New tears sprang into her eyes. "By the Living God, my David!"

She bent over his face and kissed him. Anatellia looked at Ra'ah in shock. The entire clearing was filled with murmuring and prayers. The word "miracle" was on every lip. Matron Karis put her hand on his shoulder and squeezed. He looked at her and saw tears.

Ra'ah. The voice had not left. The voice of Joshua—this strange Joshua who seemed greater than Joshua but yet the same.

"Lord, I am here."

One more, Ra'ah.

He looked over at the body of the dead Sacheth in shock. Surely He did not mean that one? *Surely not, O Living God. That one is the enemy of everything they are trying to do. He killed David. Not that one, Living God.*

One more, Ra'ah.

He stood up on shaky legs. The voice filled him. Deafened him to his own thoughts. People were gathering around them. Hands touching him. But he didn't really notice. The body of the big soldier drew him like a lodestone draws iron filings. There was no doubt in him left. There was no question greater than the voice of the One and the evidence of the last few minutes.

He knelt down and grabbed the feathered shaft of the arrow sticking from the man's chest. With a deft twist he broke the shaft. Then he braced himself and pushed against the man. The body was far too heavy. He looked around for help and saw looks of shock and disbelief from the Klasma around him.

"Help me."

"Leave it," Kai snapped. "Let it be buried with him."

"No." Ra'ah shook his head. "It needs to come out."

"Why?" Kai was getting angry now. "He's dead. Leave him dead. He is our enemy. He murdered our leader, our friend. Leave him to rot."

"*No!*" Ra'ah felt something rise in him. "It is not for any of us to decide—who lives and who dies. That power lies with only One. All those years you've spent in that City. On that mountain. How have you come all of this way, Kai of the River Peoples, and not found compassion and forgiveness?"

Kai turned white and fell to his knees like he'd been struck. Tears filled his eyes and he simply stared at Ra'ah in shock and a little fear.

"I will help you, Ra'ah," Temian offered softly from behind him.

Ra'ah thanked him, and together they rolled the man over enough for Ra'ah to wrap a piece of the fallen man's cloak around the arrowhead. Carefully he pulled the shaft free, and then they lowered the big man back down.

Hesitantly he laid his hand over the man's chest and prayed as he had over David. His hand burned and he felt the Spirit of the Living God flow through and around him into the dead man. He hadn't noticed that sensation with David, but he felt like Joshua was right there this time, flowing around him in the form of the Spirit. Ra'ah closed his eyes and marvelled in the feeling. For one moment he remembered the light and the feeling of being beyond the temple.

Call him back.

"*Come back!*" Ra'ah shouted at the man.

Ra'ah expected the same thing as when he called David back. He closed his eyes and waited. Nothing happened. Slightly frustrated, he called again. Again, nothing happened. The wind picked up and threw leaves around him. *Feels like a fall wind,* he thought to himself. But the day was hot. The wind was wrong.

His eyes flew open. He was standing on a barren, desolate plain. All around him were pits and fissures in the ground. There was nothing as far as the eye could see, no tree, no plant, no other feature. He felt a presence beside him and turned, expecting to see Joshua. But instead he saw the bright shining figure of a Maylak. Surprised, he nodded to the tall being.

"I will take you to the very border, but you must go no further." The Maylak extended his arm in invitation.

Ra'ah nodded silently and followed the being over the barren landscape. They skirted the pits and fissures until they came to a sudden precipice. The Maylak held up a hand in warning.

"I can go no further," he said solemnly. "Neither should you. The man you seek will hear you from here or he won't. If he does, the Living God will pluck him from where he has found himself. If he does not, he is lost."

"What is this place?" Ra'ah asked.

"This is the very edge of the Abyss," the Maylak explained. "Those creatures that reject relationship with the Living God go here. This is where they spend all of their remaining ages."

"I don't see anything but rolling darkness." Ra'ah peered over the edge.

"The Living God has removed Himself from that place," the Maylak explained. "Nothing that is God's goes there. That is the inheritance of those that reject Him. They are allowed to exist free of Him."

"Allowed?" Ra'ah asked incredulously.

"That is the nature of Choice. The Living God honours your Choice."

Ra'ah shivered. Somewhere in that rolling blackness was what remained of the dead man in the glade. Lady Raphael had said his name was Deuver. Ra'ah wanted to be gone from here. He felt the cold and loneliness of this place.

"Deuver of the Sacheth!" he shouted into the Abyss. *"The Living God calls you back!"*

There was no response. And then carried on the wind a sound could be heard. Like a pitiful wail it started and then rose to a scream. A tormented cry for help from some great distance.

"Your mission is complete," the Maylak said matter-of-factly. "You should go."

"But…" Ra'ah started to say, but a great force pulled him away.

He blinked in the sudden afternoon sun. The body of the big soldier still lay beside him, cold and dead. He looked at the man and waited. After several long breaths nothing happened, He rocked back on his feet to stand up. He had tried. It had failed.

The man on the ground suddenly jerked upright and screamed. It wasn't the brave scream of a warrior. It was a primal scream of fear and terror. It was a child's fevered scream from the throat and lungs of a grown man. Ra'ah fell backward in surprise. The big man screamed and screamed and then saw Ra'ah. With a cry of relief and joy he lunged forward and grabbed Ra'ah in a great embrace. He buried his face in Ra'ah's shoulder and wept.

33

A Mission Complete

Ra'ah sat in the large chair and stared into the fire burning happily in the hearth. They had hurriedly moved him here after removing him from the embrace of Deuver, the former captain of the Sacheth elite guard and righthand man to Gerig Ebed Saucan. The man had been a weeping, babbling mess. No one but Ra'ah really understood why, and even Ra'ah could only guess much of it.

The big man had immediately fallen prostrate at David's feet and begged forgiveness. David had simply looked at the man in wonder and said "yes" over and over again. David's experience with being dead left him out of place as well.

By that time a great crowd had appeared in and around the glade and the story of the attack was nothing compared to the story of the two miracles that Ra'ah the Healer had performed. At that point it had quickly become clear they needed to get Ra'ah out of there, and Matron Karis took charge of leading him with fierce glares through the crowd and back to the cottage that Elder Cela had arranged.

And now he and Karis sat in silence and stared at the fire, while outside crowds milled, looking for a glimpse of him. He looked up at her then and saw she was regarding him with half-closed eyes.

"It's going to be hard now," she said.

"How so?" he asked, even though he had an idea what she meant.

"People are going to come to you now, looking for a miracle for their children, their spouses," she explained. "You've just suffered a loss, yourself. You will need to guard yourself from demands that He does not put on you."

She pointed upward and he smiled. She had a way of going right to the diagnosis. He thought about her words. What she said rang true, but he was still reeling from the events in the glade. He wondered why him. The Living God could have done this through anyone. He knew that Matron Karis had longed to see Him move in just this way—why not her?

"He chooses who He chooses," she continued like she was reading his thoughts. "Maybe in you he found the right combination of willing hands and belief. I wonder even now, after seeing what He did through you, if I would have had the faith to say 'yes' and mean it. He needed willing hands, and yours were there. I am very proud to call you my apprentice, but now maybe I need to be yours. Your willingness and faith humble me, Ra'ah."

Ra'ah blushed at her words, but was saved from having to respond when the door opened and David, Nebaya, and Anatellia walked into the sitting room. There was a light in David's eyes that reminded Ra'ah once again of the world beyond the temple. He also noted that Nebaya was staying very close to him, and she moved like a weight had been removed from her shoulders. Anatellia was her normal self, and looked him up and down as they found seats.

"You're a celebrity," she said with a hint of new respect. "We've got a list of petitioners looking to meet with the new miracle healer. It looks like Ange is going to have competition everywhere we go for people's attention."

Ra'ah groaned.

"Hey, thank you, by the way." David pulled down his shirt collar to show the ragged scar of his healed arrow wound. "Now I have a scar to impress the lady."

Ra'ah raised his eyebrow at that as he leaned over to examine the wound. It looked pink and freshly healed. He wondered why the scar had even been left, but he was sure there was a reason. With the Living God, there was always a reason. He glanced at Nebaya, but she was looking at David. He smiled and sat back.

"How is Deuver?" he asked.

"He is…" David shook his head and searched for the words. "He is a man pulled from horrors we cannot understand. He refuses to talk about them. He only talks about this kid who called him back from it and the Living God he met on the way back. I have never met a more broken and sincere man, and you have to understand that that is saying something. But you had better get used to having him around, because he's sworn an oath to serve you all the days of your life."

"You are kidding," Ra'ah said incredulously.

"Not one bit," Anatellia cut in. "You've got a servant for life."

"I don't want a servant for life," he protested.

"Then you shouldn't pull people from the Abyss," she said pointedly.

"I didn't," Ra'ah said. "I didn't do any of this."

"No, but you of all people possible were there and willing to be used. If you hadn't offered your hands, David and Deuver would likely still be dead. And before you say something like 'He would have found someone else' you should consider that He hasn't up to this point. God is doing something new, but you've set an example that the rest of us will look to."

"What if He never asks me to do that again?" Ra'ah mused.

"The gifts and the Callings of the Living God are without repentance," Matron Karis whispered. "I think you will find it almost impossible to put that gift away. You are His hands. You all are."

Ra'ah attempted to change the subject. "So what other news is there?"

"Gerig and his soldiers have returned to the city," David said, sensing Ra'ah's discomfort. "My mother is also returning, although much more slowly. She found her welcome had thoroughly run out when news of my assassination was on everyone's lips. The Elders have met with us and your new friend Deuver, and he spilled all the tea on the Sacheth. Bato will be packing up and heading north within days."

"Gerig will regret the mistake he made," Nebaya spoke up. "He gave away his one advantage."

"He knew what he was risking," David said softly. "But his hatred was greater than all of his plotting."

"Well, I doubt he's done plotting," Anatellia observed. "We've completed the task we were given. The message has been given to all the villages and the city. But in the undertaking we've been thrust into a bigger plan and calling. We've got to see this through.

"We will." David nodded. "The Klasma aren't done, either. We won't rest until the last refugee flees north. And I am certain Gerig will not rest, either."

Gerig Ebed Saucan stood on a small rise and looked at the city before him with barely veiled hatred. The decoy had worked just as he planned. David had done exactly what he was supposed to. He hadn't heard from Deuver or his lieutenant, but he was sure that his First would get the job done. The man had never failed him yet.

They had returned to the walled city as quickly as they could, watching ever behind them for pursuit. That had been a small surprise to Gerig, how well trained the enemy was. He didn't recognize or understand what land they were from, but the stench of the real Enemy was all over them. His communion with his Lord had been greatly hindered since they had come to this accursed valley, but he would soon fix that. He would desecrate this entire valley for his Lord. He would make it an offering and augury to all of his Lord's enemies, even the Enemy himself.

He looked back one last time to see a familiar figure staggering through the trees. With mild disappointment he called out to the lieutenant. The man looked up with a mixture of fear and relief. Gerig noted it for a later time.

"Where is Commander Deuver?" Gerig asked.

"Dead, my lord Gerig," the man panted. "Shot down even as he shot dead their commander."

"That was not his target," Gerig hissed.

"No, my lord." The man shook. "But their commander came to the girl's rescue at the last moment."

"And why didn't you finish the mission?" Gerig's anger grew.

"I could not, my lord. The commander used me as a decoy and I was to lead her guard out of position. As it was, they almost had me, too."

"The mission was worth more to me than your life," Gerig said. "Your life is forfeit to me now. Join the others."

The man bowed his head and joined his comrades. As a group they left the rise toward the city gates. The people gave them a wide berth and didn't interact with them at all. The foreigners who had appeared almost a week ago were a bad omen, and Gerig was more than happy not to dispel that idea.

Angelis looked in wonder at the changes Cardaya had gone through since they had visited weeks before. Many of the buildings had been abandoned or repurposed. A rather large industry of cart-making had sprung up, and they had passed many families with their belongings piled onto those carts, headed for the ferry.

She looked over at Amon, surrounded by a large group of young men and women. He was busy giving final instructions to them. They would go out and tell everyone who was waiting that the time had come. There was an open road and a place to go. Ange felt the thrill of excitement at the thought.

Daskow came out of the cottage they had been provided for the night and looked around. He hadn't been sleeping as well as he usually did. Often during the night she'd wake up to find him reading the book he'd been given. She reminded herself to scold him when he was more awake.

"Where are Kawani and the others?" he asked.

"They're waiting around the road to Pethe, sleepy head," she said.

"Then let's go," he said. "Since by the remains of breakfast you've already eaten both yours and half of mine."

"Just your bacon," she teased as she waved a piece at him.

He chased her down the road toward the south end of the village.

This marks the end of Book 2 of the Amatta Valley Chronicles
The conclusion is coming in Book 3: A Decree Resounds

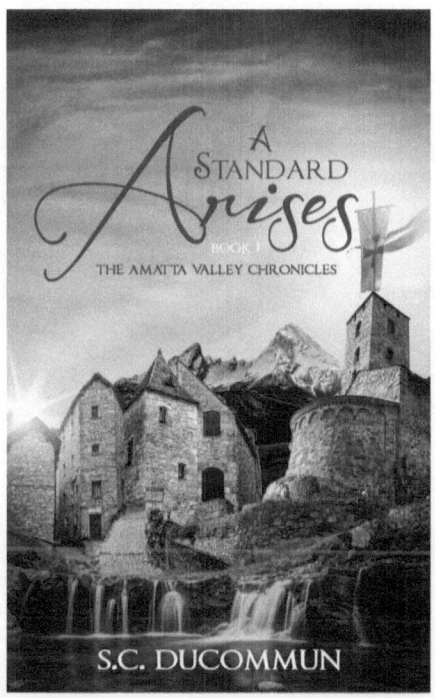

T he Amatta Valley is a peaceful—even idyllic—land populated by the servants of the Living God. This is where Ra'ah and his four friends have spent their lives, travelling between the four villages and the great city of Kathik. Never in their wildest dreams did they think all of this could end.

But in a single night of terror and sudden revelation, they are thrust from relative obscurity to become harbingers of the Valley's very destruction. And now they have to convince everybody that their message is truly from the Living God—that all must flee to the mythical Mountain of the Living God or be swept up in that coming devastation.

Facing both the threat of an unknown enemy and the mounting incredulity of a people comfortable with where they are and what they believe, the five have only four weeks to complete their mission.

www.ingramcontent.com/pod-product-compliance
Lightning Source LLC
Chambersburg PA
CBHW031941010726
47493CB00007B/2026